THE DOODLEBUG WAR

A TALE OF FANATICS AND ROMANTICS

ANDREW UPDEGROVE

By the same author:

The Alexandria Project, a Tale of Treachery and Technology

The Lafayette Campaign, a Tale of Deception and Elections

Available in paperback and eBook at Amazon and in paperback
on order through your favorite local book store

Prologue

IT WAS, AT LAST, TIME. His forces were ready, and his plans were well made. It was proper that America's obsession with money and technology would provide the means for its own destruction. Its vulnerability was so obvious a child could see it.

But the billionaire capitalists of the West would not see. Or perhaps they did and did not care. It made no difference—they worshiped profits above all else. The politicians they controlled with their campaign contributions knew better than to pass laws their masters would not like.

He rose and walked to the entrance of the cave. The village in the valley far below lay peaceful and starlit, embraced by the snow-clad mountains. Not a single light or other sign of life could be seen.

Just as America and Europe would soon appear to the doomed fools circling Earth in their absurd space station.

1

Frank Eats Dirt

T HE PHONE WAS not ringing. Neither was the faint *ching!* of an incoming email interrupting the silence of his day. Even his Facebook page was devoid of likes and visits. After three weeks of waiting, there was no way to get around it: *Frank Adversego, Cyber Eye,* was an abject failure.

He stared with regret at the website he'd built for his new venture. It really did look pretty cool—retro, with just the right Raymond Chandler vibe. And if forced to admit it, he thought he looked sharp in a fedora and trench coat, even if he had pixelated his face into a pink, mosaic blur.

But a pretty web page did not a business make. He'd yet to land a single paying client. Perhaps it had something to do with the fact that he hadn't a clue how to advertise, and would rather subject himself to whole-body acupuncture than engage in face-to-face networking.

But that was where things stood. There seemed to be no alternative to what appealed to him least of all: calling his old boss, George Marchand, to ask for work from the CIA. He scowled as he punched the buttons on his phone.

"Hey, Frank, good to hear from you. How's the new business coming along?"

"Great! Having the time of my life! I can't believe I waited so long to go into business for myself."

"Nice to hear, Frank. Couldn't be happier for you. Of course, we're sorry we can't count on you anymore over here at the Agency. The challenges keep getting tougher—"

"Oh, well, there's no need to look at it that way! I'm sure I can take on a little more work from time to time if it would help you out. You know, fill in the gaps between the really big, interesting projects. Sometimes they go cold for a little while."

"Really? Well, that's good to know."

Frank waited. There was only silence at the other end of the phone. "Uh, George, you got anything right now?"

"Hmm. Maybe. But I don't know if we have anything small enough to fit in between your really big, interesting projects."

Silence again.

"Okay, George. Have it your way. Do you want me to beg?"

Marchand laughed. "Of course not. I just couldn't resist jerking your chain a little. Actually, I've been keeping my eye out for something to send your way and just came across a project that's right up your alley. And at the same pay grade as before, too. You want to hear what I have in mind?"

Frank uttered silent thanks to the patron saint of small businessmen. "Yes, George. I'd like that very much."

"Great. Got time to get together tomorrow?"

"Today, tomorrow, you name it. The truth is, I'm not exactly overbooked."

"How about 10:00 tomorrow morning then. Do you still have the security app on your phone from your last project?"

"I guess."

"Good. You know that doughnut shop in DuPont Circle?"

"Sure, but what's wrong with our usual coffee place?"

"That's enough for over the phone. See you there tomorrow."

* * *

Frank was finishing his second doughnut when he spied Marchand approaching. He had the same authoritative, quick step as ever, but he looked a little stiff. And why not? It must be twenty-three years since they first met. Frank wondered whether he was secretly working for the CIA even then.

His old boss spotted Frank and waved him outside.

"Good to see you, George. Doughnut?"

"No thanks. You better go easy on those, too, if you want to keep that weight off."

"Yeah, well, you picked the meeting place. What gives?"

"Let's talk while we walk. We're going to a new facility we just opened up the street."

"Here? Pretty high-priced real estate for a government agency."

"No kidding. But data analysis is a hot skill now. We're competing with shops like Google that coddle the kids fresh out of school like they were royalty. You need to offer frills like food courts and massage chairs to get the top talent these days. And if you don't have a trendy location, forget it."

"What kind of work is the Agency doing there?"

"This is our new 'big data' center. Every type of information we gather from all over the world will funnel through here now, so we can organize and then analyze it for trends and emerging threats."

"You mean, you've got tens of thousands of servers in the middle of Washington?"

"No—they're in a new data center outside the Beltway. But it's all managed from downtown. Here. Clip this on your shirt pocket."

Frank followed Marchand into the sumptuous, travertine-walled lobby of a new office building. They fell in step with the other commuters streaming past the security guard and toward the elevators beyond. Marchand led Frank past them and around a corner, where they found one more elevator. Next to it was a small nameplate that read "Cloud Data, Inc." He slid a card into a slot on the nameplate, and the doors slid open.

"Private elevator?" Frank asked Marchand.

"Of course."

To Frank's surprise, they stopped on the next floor. Decanted into a narrow, windowless room, he found himself facing a wooden-faced guard sitting behind what looked to Frank like bulletproof glass. Marchand sat down in the first of a row of shallow stalls equipped with computer screens and set his phone in front of him. When prompted by an instruction on the screen, he typed in a number from his phone. Another line of text appeared on the screen, and he typed in an answer. Marchand sat still for a bit longer, and then a card popped out of a slit below the screen, as if he had just paid for his stay at an automated parking lot.

"Your turn," George said, nodding toward the booth. "Three-factor authentication."

Frank followed suit. Three-factor authentication meant he would need to pass three tests before being permitted to proceed further, the first involving something he had with him—clearly, the number from his own phone app. The second would be something only the person being tested would know—that would have been the response George typed in to the second line of text. The last would look for something known that was physically unique to Frank. He had expected only two-factor authentication, so he hadn't been watching for a third procedure.

He sat down and, when prompted, typed in the new six-digit number that had just cycled into view in the security app on his phone. He responded that his best friend from high school was named Jono. Then he waited to see what would happen next. A few seconds later, a penlight-sized light began glowing in the middle of the screen before swiftly moving up and stabilizing at his eye level, and he realized the retina in one of his eyes was being scanned.

Apparently, he was who the CIA thought he was, because a moment later, his card popped out below the screen. He picked it up and noticed it had a computer chip embedded in it, presumably the same type found in the new EMV-enabled credit cards. He wondered by what means, and when, the CIA had succeeded in mapping his retina, as well as how much other information the Agency had ferreted out about his childhood without his knowledge.

He stood up and joined George in front of one door in a line of unmarked doors. "These cards are only good for sixty seconds," Marchand said, "so step right through your door when the green light goes on."

Marchand slid his card into a slot next to the door, and when the small light above it turned from red to green, he opened the door and stepped inside.

Frank followed suit with his own door and found himself in a phone-booth-sized enclosure. The moment he closed the door behind him, he felt himself whooshing upward. Almost as soon as he finished accelerating, the process reversed itself, bringing him to an unexpectedly early halt. The door opened automatically, and he rejoined George in another narrow room, feeling as if he had just traveled halfway across the world via Harry Potter's Floo Network.

"Interesting commute."

"Yeah," George responded. "We may be downtown, but this has to be as secure as headquarters. Drop your card in that box over there."

Frank noticed a wall rack filled with laptops and pointed to them. "Souvenirs?"

"No such luck. Guest computers. You'll have to put any electronics you've brought with you in one of those lockers over there until you leave. This place is an SCIV."

"SCIV?"

"Sorry. It's a 'sensitive compartmentalized information facility.' That means that all the information here stays here. None of the computer systems on-site are connected to the Internet, so there's no remote access. If you want to work with any of the data here, you'll have to do so on this floor, using one of those laptops. Notice anything odd about them?"

Frank slid one out of its cubby and turned it around. "All the USB ports are plugged up."

"That's right. That way nobody can take home any information on a thumb drive. Not that they could, anyway. When you enter and leave through that door there, you'll be stepping through a metal detector sensitive enough to pick up the filings in your teeth. Don't worry about that, though. Your dental records have already been entered into the system, the same as the magnetic resonance of the loaner laptops."

"Why am I not surprised?"

"You always were a quick study. Any other questions?"

"So can I take notes on a pad of paper?"

"Yes, but you won't be able to take them with you. Like I said, nothing leaves here but you. We can't vacuum out what's in your brain, but that's as much as you can take out with you."

Frank wondered whether they actually could vacuum out his brain, given all the other information the Agency seemed ready, willing, and able to acquire. But it was bad news about the note taking. He hadn't had to work anywhere on-site since he left the Library of Congress. Stating that he wasn't a people person would be as much of an understatement as observing that Freddy Krueger would make a poor babysitter.

They stepped out into what Frank realized was an entire floor of the building, unbroken by walls from side to side and end to end. This was quite a switch from the anonymous cube farms he'd labored in for most of his career. There were no cubicles here at all; the whole space was populated by random islands of tables, couches, game tables, and exercise equipment—no, those were treadmill desks. Frank figured just the extreme sports posters on the walls would give a traditional spook apoplexy.

He fell in step behind George, zigzagging his way through the expensive furniture draped with twenty-somethings wearing T-shirts and jeans, cradling their institutional laptops. Ahead was a glassed-in conference room tucked into a corner of the floor. Inside, Frank saw two people seated at opposite ends of a conference table; one was yet another anonymous youngster power-typing away on an ultra-thin notebook computer. The other, his rimless glasses perched precariously on the end of his nose, was poking away with his index fingers on the keyboard of a thick laptop with an oversized screen. A slack tie hung around the unbuttoned collar of his rumpled shirt, and a tonsure of disheveled hair crept around the back of his head like a wispy, white caterpillar.

Marchand tapped on the door and let himself in. "Morning, Hermann. I don't think you've met Frank before, have you? Frank, this is Hermann Koontz. He runs the show here."

Frank shook hands with Hermann as Marchand jerked a thumb at the scene outside the conference room. "Getting used to the new digs?"

Koontz pushed his spectacles up on top of his head and scowled. "What do you expect? I feel like I'm running a frigging college rec center."

Unnoticed by Frank, the young man at the other end of the table was sizing Frank up with interest, noting he was middle-aged and unassuming with thinning hair and severely challenged when it came to fashion sense. He watched Frank stand awkwardly to the side with arms crossed, his body language indicating a strong desire to fade into the background—if that could somehow be arranged—as Marchand and Koontz chatted. Not exactly what he expected the guy who had saved the world from nuclear annihilation to look like, although it did appear that he kept himself in shape.

Slattery stood up and approached him. "Hi. I'm Tim Slattery, Mr. Koontz's assistant ethics officer."

Marchand overheard him and turned around. "Ah, yes, I heard we were adding one of those to every team." He turned back to Koontz. "So—shall we get started?"

Koontz picked up a remote control as they settled in around the table. Immediately the lights of the room dimmed, the glass walls turned opaque, and a hidden projector transformed one of the walls into a screen displaying multiple charts and tables.

"All right. So the information I'm going to walk you through is culled from data we gather from every public and private source you can think of, and many you shouldn't know exist. Telephone intercepts, email, social media, satellite photos, the works. Petabytes of new data every day, and exabytes in all. Then we analyze it using the latest neural network and machine-learning tools."

He turned to Frank. "How much do you know about big data?"

"I'm pretty current at a conceptual level. But no hands-on experience, so no harm in dumbing it down a bit."

"Fair enough. So it wasn't that long ago that we could pick up pretty high-level communications between terrorists from the field. We can almost never get that anymore, because the big fish know better than to use anything electronic. Now what we get is mostly low-level chatter, and when we do pick up something that sounds like it could be big, it's tough to know how seriously to take it. For all we know, the stuff that seems most interesting was sent down the line just to throw us off. So we try to wring every bit of meaning we can out of the chatter, integrated with every other type of data we're collecting. For that purpose, the more chatter, the better.

"So let's talk about what we're abstracting from what we're picking up and how we're getting to those conclusions." Koontz picked up a laser pointer and highlighted a row of a dozen small charts at the base of a pyramid of similar presentations. Each time he paused on one, it dramatically increased in size before shrinking back again when he moved on.

"This set of charts shows the types of data we evaluate to build up a threat assessment. Down here at the bottom are the various original sources, each graded for credibility based on a variety of factors: historical reliability, how far up or down the chain the source individual is, and so on. We've already kicked out the ones we think aren't credible. We associate the score we've given that source to the data we derived from him or her and move the results up to the next level. Let's jump up a couple of tiers now.

"Up here, we start trying to extract a picture of the actual attack—where, how, when, and so on. To do that, we pull in all sorts of additional data: what types of bombs have most recently been in use and what types of situations they've been used in. That gives us another way to test the likelihood that each piece of data is accurate, as well as to fill in blanks with good guesses where we don't have any data at all, based on context and the information we do have.

"For example, if we think we know which country an attack will be in but not what the specific target will be, we can contrast a profile of that place with those of others where attacks have already occurred in the same area, nation, or region—does it have a military base? A big open market? A police training academy? Let's skip up a few more levels.

"Up here at the very top is the description of the expected attack and the credibility of each individual datum associated with that attack. We might be pretty sure of the target, for example, but not the date. Are you with me so far?"

"Yes, it's very impressive."

"Good. So now, here's a dashboard with bar graphs relating to all the potential attacks we're tracking right now on a global basis. These charts display a high-level picture of what we think all the terrorist groups around the world are up to." He was wielding and clicking his laser pointer now as if he were Errol Flynn fencing with an evil opponent displayed on the screen. "And by changing the color—like this—we can show how close each attack is to execution—and now which terrorist groups are involved in which attacks—and now which ones involve more than one terrorist group—and now the severity of the anticipated attacks. Pretty useful stuff when you want to brief the politicos on where we stand or put out a warning bulletin to the field."

"I'll bet," Frank said. "How about that column over on the right—the one that's so much higher than the rest? What threat is that one tracking?"

"Right. That's the one we'll talk about today. George, have you been briefed on this one yet?"

"Barely. Assume I don't know more than Frank, and you won't be too far off."

Koontz's head bobbed in a silent humph. "Well, this won't take long, because we don't know much either. Let's do a pyramid view of this one."

The screen cleared to reveal what looked at best like the beginnings of the foundation of a triangle of charts. Only a few graphs filled the second layer with nothing in the half-dozen tiers that should have been above that.

"As I said, we don't have a whole lot to work with yet. We haven't even been able to populate the first level with all the types of sources we need to do much in the second tier.

"So when you ask what's being threatened, Frank, we really have no idea. For example, what's the target? Maybe the power grid? Communications? Finance? All of the above? So far, we don't have a clue. Except for one point that has been locked down, all we know—or think we know, anyway—is that it's something big and some or all of it's going to occur on U.S. soil. That's why George suggested we ask you to help us out. He says you've got a knack for thinking outside the box and might spot something our in-house guys miss."

"Well, I don't know about that, but thanks. How exactly do I fit in?"

"You'll be on one of several interdisciplinary groups—we refer to them as Tiger Teams—that we're assembling to address every type of attack we think might occur. Besides you, it will have Agency, military, and technical members, each of whom will bring a unique perspective and capability to the effort."

"What will that involve?"

"Mostly just attending weekly meetings, reviewing the information and analyses you're given, and speaking up if you have something to say. You won't have any specific research or other tasks to perform, but you will be expected to stay on top of everything that comes your way, and let us know if you see anything we've missed or you think we aren't paying appropriate attention to that we should. So some weeks you'll be busy, and sometimes you might not have much to do for a few days."

"That sounds fine. One more question before we continue?"

"Sure."

"You said you do have one aspect of the attack locked down. What's that?"

"That's where we're headed next." Koontz clicked his remote, and suddenly every wall lit up with a satellite view of a fractal maze of impenetrable mountains.

"This is a section of the Pakistan-Afghanistan border. We believe that somewhere down there is Mullah Muhammad Foobar. That's the guy pulling the strings on this attack." A large red ring appeared on the center of the image covering one wall.

Ah—so that was it. They wanted his help in finally capturing the Big Guy—the terrorist leader with the most territory, the most followers, and the most atrocities to his credit. Terrorist acts that even the media hesitated to describe in full. Frank felt uneasy at the thought of directly opposing him, even though he was seated in a secret CIA conference room thousands of miles away from the terrorist.

"More specifically, we think he's somewhere within this area—about forty miles across. How much do you know about Foobar?"

"Well, I guess you'd say I've got a basic newspaper level of knowledge. He's the latest guy to claim leadership in the fight of radical Islam against the West. He came out of nowhere a couple of years back and managed to come out on top over the various factions competing to take over."

"That's accurate, as far as it goes. But he's not just the 'latest guy' to claim leadership and try to restore Sharia law to the Middle East. He's also trying to take the world back fourteen hundred years. A lot of his appeal comes from his success in tying his cause to the glories of the original Arab conquest in the first millennium. He reinforces that story line in every way possible. He makes each of his generals assume the name of one of the great Arab leaders that fought their way across most of the known world—westward across North Africa and up into Spain and destroying the last of the Byzantine Empire to the north. He says he won't rest until he's reestablished Arab dominion over the whole shebang."

"That's a pretty big ambition."

"You think? So check this out." The images on the screen gave way to a video showing a gesticulating, bearded man in a robe standing on a balcony above a dusty square thronged with an enormous crowd. "This is Foobar's spokesman. No one from the West has ever seen Foobar himself. But we think we know where he is, so let's take a closer look at the sandbox we think he's playing in."

The video stopped, and they were once again gazing down at the endless labyrinth of sinuous mountain ranges. With a wrenching change of perspective, the view zoomed into the area inside the red circle as if they were falling out of the sky. Frank instinctively clutched the arms of his chair as he plunged downward toward the snow-topped mountains at ever-increasing speed.

Koontz chuckled. "I guess I should have warned you. Kinda feels like you're being sucked into a black hole when I do that, doesn't it?

"Anyway, as you can see, there are no roads down there. It's so rugged that nothing gets in or out except on foot or on the back of a donkey. This particular village is at such a high altitude that the passes into it are close to the operational limits of a helicopter, although a CV-22 Osprey could push through and land.

Otherwise, it would take days for a team to reach him if he was holed up in a place like that—plenty of time for the locals to tip him off that someone unexpected is on the way so he can clear out, just like bin Laden and Omar did back in 2002. Needless to say, that's why he's hiding where he is."

"But wouldn't it be as hard for him to get out as for us to get in?" Frank asked.

"Speed-wise, yes. But he'd have plenty of ways to get out, and it would be hard for us to cover all of them. Let's check that out from this location, as an example." Koontz flashed his controller, and a simple web of blue lines sprang up on the screen. "These are footpaths running out from this village through valley bottoms and over mountains."

The view zoomed out again in abrupt steps. Each time it did, the web of lines expanded and multiplied, with each blue tendril branching and re-branching. Whenever the image briefly stabilized, it looked like a map of the neural networks of a brain composed of mountains.

"Every one of these trails is not only an escape route for Foobar but also a conduit the terrorists can use to get information in to him and back out again. Any questions so far?"

"No, but I guess if you were pretty sure which proclamations came from Foobar, you could use the time it took between when you thought one was sent and where you intercepted to calculate the distance it had traveled. Put all those calculations together like GPS signal data, and you'd get an area you were pretty certain he was in, assuming he hadn't been moving around, anyway. Is that why you think this is where he is?"

"Good observation. Yes, that's one of the ways."

"Interesting. What's your confidence level with the data you're picking up about the attack we're talking about?"

"Not great when it comes to specifics, because we don't have enough data to work with, and all kinds of attacks get mentioned from time to time. It's like starting with a dozen different jigsaw puzzles, all poured on the floor, and then trying to reassemble the picture you care about without knowing what that puzzle is supposed to look like when it's completed. So far, we've only got about twenty percent of the picture we want to talk to you about. But we already know enough to tell we don't like what we see."

Frank noticed that Koontz's assistant ethics officer was listening with rapt attention. He wondered whether this was the first big briefing the kid had ever been in on.

"So what's the picture, Hermann?" George asked.

"We've only got the edges; nothing in the center at all. All we know, like I said earlier, is that it's going to be in the U.S. And also that it's going to be really big."

"How big is really big?"

Koontz clicked his remote one last time, and the glass walls of the conference room gradually became transparent again. Frank blinked a few times to readjust as the mountain wilderness they were sitting in faded back into something that looked like an open study area at a student union.

Hermann took off his spectacles and rubbed his face. "In what—for once—we believe are the exact words of the Mullah himself, 'it will make the scene at ground zero on 9/11 look like a child's birthday party.'"

* * *

2

There's No Place Like Home

FRANK STARED WITH distaste at the chaos that surrounded him. The disorder didn't bother him; his living room was usually a shambles of disheveled shelves and discarded articles of clothing that never quite made their way back into a closet. It was the cause of the mess that was disconcerting. His landlord was converting the building to condominiums, and three weeks from now, he would need to temporarily vacate the cramped, dark apartment he'd occupied since his divorce many years before. When he received the notice, he'd vowed to use his forced retreat as an opportunity to dispose of as much as possible of the accumulated detritus of decades of bachelor life. Now that the task was at hand, he was finding it to be a real pain in the ass.

The door buzzer sounded, catching him by surprise. He looked at his watch and smiled. Of course! He'd invited his daughter, Marla, to come around and pick through the wreckage before he consigned it to the nearest landfill. The buzzer had been just a warning; she had a key to let herself in.

She was duly impressed when she entered. "So, did you just dump everything on the floor, or have you actually packed or gotten rid of anything?"

"Some of both, thank you very much. Where do you want to start?"

"I don't know. Do you have a map?"

"Fine! You're on your own. I'll be in the kitchen, working."

"Oh, don't be such a grouch. And don't disappear on me so quick."

He watched as she meandered around the room, crouching to look into one box or another. As usual, he wondered how he had ended up with such a self-possessed, attractive, outgoing daughter. Clearly, her mother deserved the credit for all of that.

"Are those pictures over there?"

"Yes, I found them in the bottom of a closet. Haven't bothered with them since forever."

"Come on—sit down and look at them with me, will you?"

He hesitated. There was a reason he hadn't looked at them in all these years. But he cleared the couch of boxes and papers anyway, and they sat down, the box of pictures between them.

"Gee, I've never seen most of these before. Look how young you and Mom are in this one!"

Frank glanced at the picture she handed him and then quickly gave it back. Clare, his ex-wife, was radiant, holding a newborn Marla in her arms. And there he was, standing awkwardly at her side, wearing a scruffy T-shirt and a scruffier beard. He was not proud of that period in his life.

"Yeah, well, that's how you look when you're not as old as you get later on. Look, I really do have a lot of work to do. There's a bunch of empty boxes in the bedroom. Throw whatever you want into one of the empty boxes you'll find in the bedroom, and put your name on the front, because I'm going to get rid of just about everything else."

She was about to object, but the look on his face made her decide otherwise.

He stood up. "Coffee?"

"Sure. But only if you're making it anyway."

"The answer is yes."

He tried to shift his thoughts elsewhere as he filled the coffee maker. That wasn't difficult, because he'd made little progress since his meeting with Koontz. He was quick to obsess over details at the best of times, and he'd passed that low threshold days ago. Putting the can of coffee away, he retrieved a notepad from its hiding place inside a box of crackers. In that pad were the notes he'd scribbled down each time he returned from a visit to the CIA facility. Given the Agency's penchant for discovering anything and everything it wished about him, a simple pad of paper in a cracker box seemed far more secure than a laptop connected to the Internet.

Hunched over his tiny kitchen table with his chin resting on one hand, he reviewed his notes relating to the CIA's master report on Foobar and the Caliphate. Something about that report bothered him: some crucial flaw in the underlying reasoning. But he couldn't yet figure out what it was. An hour later, he was no better off.

"Ahem." Marla was standing in the kitchen doorway.

"Yes?"

"How's the coffee doing?"

"Ouch!" He stood up and stared at the coffee maker. It had turned itself off long ago. "Ah, I'd say it's a little cold."

"Really."

"Yeah, I guess I kind of got wrapped up in what I was doing."

"Imagine that. Anyway, I'm all done. How about we go out for a bite to eat before I take off?"

He looked back at the pad of paper, lying open on the table. That wasn't good. "You know I'd love to, but I've really got to finish up what I'm working on."

"Rain check?"

"Of course. I'll give you a call."

She gave him a hug, and turned to wave goodbye from the door to his apartment.

He felt guilty as he stood at his window, watching her walk away. But he wanted to ferret out the gremlin lurking in the report that was teasing him before it gave up on the effort. As soon as Marla turned the corner, he put on a jacket, trotted down the stairs, stuffed his hands in his pockets, and set off in the opposite direction.

Walking briskly with no particular destination in mind, he returned to the incomplete picture Koontz's team had pieced together using the brute force of the CIA's massively parallel super computers. What was it that seemed wrong?

It took more than an hour of rapid walking, but at last, he began to get an inkling of what was troubling him: some of the pieces in the puzzle seemed to have been subtly forced into place. He suspected those pieces were not the direct product of actual data from the field but were based on assumptions the report's authors had failed to identify as such. That could explain why some of the conclusions the authors had reached struck him as being dubious.

On his return, he noticed a framed picture on his bedroom dresser where none had been before. He picked it up and saw himself standing next to Clare. It was their wedding day. Marla must have found the picture in one of the boxes she'd rummaged through. He was surprised it still existed; he was sure he'd thrown everything like this away when Clare had left him.

He sat down on the bed, elbows on knees, holding the picture in both hands and examining two faces he felt he no longer really knew. Clare's, of course, was smiling and beautiful. He was surprised to see that his was open and beaming as well. Uncomfortable and ironic was the look he would have expected, remembering what he had been like at that age.

He set the picture back on the dresser and then paused. If he hadn't thrown this wedding picture away, perhaps he hadn't thrown away the letter she had left, either.

Should he look for it? If he found it, would he want to read it again? His mind had cycled endlessly in an infinite loop of self-justification after she left, obsessively constructing an irrefutable case that put all the blame for the failure of their marriage on her. It was years before memories began to surface that ran counter to that self-serving story line.

He turned the picture face down on the dresser, and there it was: an envelope taped to the back. So there was his sense of irony after all. He must have attached these two relics to each other back to back, like bookends holding nothing in between, to suggest there had never been anything real between him and Clare either. He broke the tape, unfolded the letter, and eased himself back on to the bed:

Dear Frank,

By the time you read this, I'll be in Philadelphia with Marla. I've been accepted into a graduate program at the University of Pennsylvania, and my parents say I can live with them until I graduate. Philly isn't that far from Washington and the bus fare is cheap, so we should be able to work out a way for Marla to spend as much time with you as with me. She won't be ready for school until I have my master's degree, so perhaps by then we'll have worked something out between the two of us and we can all be together again.

Frank, I'm so sorry that it's come to this. You have so much talent—I can't understand why you can't apply it and make something of yourself. I've tried everything I can think of to help you snap out of it and get your feet back on the ground, but nothing has worked. So now I've got to think for myself about the future. I'm tired of worrying about where the rent will come from, and I'm tired of seeing you moping around the house with nothing to do and nowhere to go when you're between jobs. Most of all, I'm tired of feeling like there's nothing left between the two of us. It's like you don't have any room inside for anyone but yourself anymore.

I think that I could have stuck it out, if only you'd been more open with me. When we first met, we were sure we were made for each other— we had fun, we laughed, we had good times, we talked about things for hours on end. I wish that things hadn't gone the way they did while we were in college, and I know that was my fault. But when we finally got together again, it was just the way it had been in the beginning. It was wonderful while you were working on your paper, and then even for a couple of years after you won your MacArthur.

But then you closed up on me. I still don't know why. Maybe it was all the tension from trying to settle down to work on your doctorate or all the jobs that didn't work out when you gave up on the PhD. But you didn't leave me any way in to try and help you or even to connect with the person I had married. There was just a wall, with me stuck on the wrong side. And Frank, I've been so lonely.

I don't want Marla to live this way. I don't want her to wonder why she can't have the things her friends have as she gets older. And I want her to have, if not two parents who are happy and natural around her, at least one that is. I want her to grow up thinking that family life is happy and loving, the way my childhood was, and not aloof and silent, except for arguments at the dinner table over the money we don't have to buy the things that we need.

Maybe I should have told you what I was thinking about sooner. I only applied to one school—Penn—because I didn't want to have to get daycare for Marla while I held down a job and went to school at the same time. It was more of a daydream than a plan when I sent the application in. But when I got the financial aid letter a few days ago saying I had a full scholarship, I felt like I didn't have a choice. Frank, I need to do this for myself, too. I want to have a life with direction and stability, where I can see a future for Marla and me that I can believe in and where I can depend on my own abilities and resources to make it come true, rather than always being dependent on you.

I guess I'm being a coward leaving this way, but you've gotten so angry sometimes lately. I didn't want to go that way, and I didn't want Marla to have that memory in her mind.

Frank, I hope you can forgive me for this. I still love you, and I still want to figure out a way to make things work. I don't think that can happen right now, but maybe with time, if you get a new perspective on your life, we could sit down and talk about it. Meanwhile, promise me you'll take good care of yourself, okay?

Love always,

Clare

Love always. That had sent him into a rage. "I'm gone. Love always."

It took years for his anger to abate to the point where he might have been able to talk about working things out. By then, Clare had finished her master's program, and was well on her way to completing her own doctorate. And, he assumed, she must have someone new in her life. He, on the other hand, had continued his self-inflicted, solitary downward spiral. It wasn't until Marla was in elementary school that he finally pulled himself together to the extent of forcing himself to beg his old MIT boss, George Marchand, for a job, and then to hang on to it, if not flourish. He'd taken a vow to save up to put Marla through college and to keep up the appearance of having a stable life for her benefit. At least he'd lived up to that vow.

He slowly re-folded the letter and slid it carefully back into the envelope taped to the back of the wedding picture lying face down on the dresser. Then he walked back to the living room and sat down on the couch next to the box of pictures Marla had been rummaging through. Besides the family pictures taken before Clare had left when Marla was just two, it held dozens and dozens of pictures of Marla, each one with a note handwritten by Clare on the back, telling him what was happening when it was taken. Many letters, too, telling him about Marla's birthday parties and other special occasions, until finally they stopped. He had to admit, Clare had tried for a very long time to stay attached at some level that could have provided a bridge to reconciliation. But he had never acknowledged receiving a single letter.

Instead, he'd communicated only to the extent necessary to manage the logistics of shuttling Marla back and forth and making shared decisions relating to her care, and then only through email. They hadn't spoken once since the morning his father-in-law helped Clare carry her belongings and all the paraphernalia of childcare down to his waiting car. Frank wondered whether Clare's father was already parked down the street that day, just waiting for Frank to leave for his latest short-term job.

By the time the divorce papers arrived five years later, Frank's anger had burned itself out. At first he'd been too angry, and then too proud, and finally too ashamed, to reach out to Clare. He simply signed and returned what was sent to him without hiring a lawyer.

Why had he been so unrelenting in his animosity? It had been twenty-five years since he had first read the letter Clare had left him the day of her departure, and it wasn't anything like he recalled. It wasn't spiteful, the way he remembered it. It wasn't final, either—again, not the way he remembered it from that single at first incredulous, and then enraged, reading. Clare had left a door wide open to get back together. And he had slammed it shut.

* * *

3

We Be in Trouble

NATE MITTY RUBBED his forehead with one hand as he flipped through the implacably grim numbers of WeBCloud's financials. For three years, he had exercised every creative and, when necessary, conniving fiber of his being to wring the last dollar possible out of the company's cost of goods and operations. And still WeBCloud was unprofitable. Massively so.

He flipped the spreadsheet over and gazed at the chart underneath, wondering why he bothered. He was so familiar with the company's constant losses that he could see that slumping red line inching across that page in his sleep, and often did. Its inexorable decline depicted the rapid depletion of the company's cash reserves. All that kept it from reaching zero every twelve to eighteen months was another enormous cash infusion from the venture capitalists and wealthy technology entrepreneurs the company had persuaded to invest in WeBCloud's continuing rapid growth. But it had been a long time since the company's last capital raise, and he was getting nervous. Without another big slug of cash, the game would be up.

Like its competitors, WeBCloud was trying to persuade the world that it made more sense to pay someone else to host your software and information than to do so yourself. For decades, businesses, governments, and universities had paid millions of dollars to buy servers, house them in air-conditioned rooms in their own facilities, and hire hordes of expensive computer workers to manage them, owning all the headaches that went along with maintaining and updating sophisticated and quickly evolving technology. And all of the responsibility for breaches by hackers, too, when those inevitably occurred. Why not get out of that miserable cycle, and hire someone to do the job for you? Why not just get rid of all those servers and staff and move your software and data out of your offices into the computing "cloud" maintained a thousand miles away by a service provider like Orinoco or WeBCloud?

All well and good for the customer. But it cost a ton of money to build the enormous data centers needed to host all that software and data, each one filled with thousands of computer servers and overseen by teams of top-notch engineers. WeBCloud's strategy was a lot like Amazon's had always been—fearlessly pouring more money into its infrastructure than its competitors were bold enough to invest in theirs and, at the same time, offering services to potential customers below actual cost. It wasn't a game plan for the weak or the timid.

He punched four numbers in on his phone. "Hey, Lou. You got a minute?"

"Right now?"

"Yes."

"Sure. Be right down."

Nate swiveled around in his desk chair and stared out the window at the glossy buildings of WeBCloud's brand new, extravagant campus. Building it had sent the red line that haunted his sleep down even faster, more than erasing all the concessions he'd beaten out of the company's cut-rate server manufacturers in Taiwan. He'd opposed the decision, of course. But the company's charismatic and economically clueless founder was insistent, and as usual, the board of directors ended up agreeing with him, anxious to maintain the kind of façade that would make new investors want to get on the bus.

Some board, Mitty grumbled. After the directors cajoled WeBCloud's founder into giving up day-to-day control of the company and becoming WeBCloud's chairman, they'd recruited Mitty to become CEO, assuring him they wanted someone who would bring fiscal discipline to the startup. But once he was on board, it quickly became obvious that the board's commitment to financial responsibility was more aspirational than determined. Instead, they kept playing the unicorn game, pumping up the illusionary WeBCloud bubble as big as they could in hopes of going public or selling before it popped.

Lou Marcello, the company's CFO, waved to Mitty's administrative assistant and paused at Mitty's open door; clearly his boss was lost in thought. He also looked more harried than usual; his shaved head was tilted forward, chin resting on one hand. Marcello recalled that Mitty had been an athletic-looking, hard-charging executive, full of piss and vinegar and flushed with success when the board had lured him away from the company he'd led through a fantastically successful initial public offering. Now he looked worn out and slightly stoop-shouldered.

"Hey."

Mitty swiveled around to find Marcello sitting down in a chair on the other side of his desk. "Hey, Lou. So what's the latest from Danforth?"

Stuart Danforth was WeBCloud's senior account manager at Silicon Valley Securities, the boutique investment bank that was helping the company try to raise one and a half billion dollars, its largest round of investment to date.

"Hard to tell. But reading between the lines, I'd say he's not sure he can fill this round."

"What's penciled in so far?"

"All but two of our old investors said they'd take their pro rata share of the round. That comes to about five hundred and eighty-five million dollars. But if we don't raise at least that much from new investors, they'll kill us on the price they're willing to pay this time for our stock."

"So what about new money? What's Stuart got there?"

"That's where he starts hedging."

"You mean nothing? He hasn't given you the name yet of a single new investor?"

"Not a committed one. He's meeting with all the funds and private investors you'd expect, or claims he is. He says that after Cloud9 and SocialYou settled for down rounds a month ago, nobody wants to invest in a unicorn without a steep discount from the last financing round."

And no wonder. There were over one hundred "unicorns" now—privately held startup companies with valuations over a billion dollars each—and all of them combined didn't have fifty billion dollars in revenues. Some didn't have any, for that matter, and only a few were profitable. It had been a long time since a unicorn had been sold at a handsome profit for its investors, and almost no startup companies had been able to go public lately, either, making investors properly cautious. Unless it was showing stellar performance, it was tough for a company to raise new money unless it sold its stock for less than it had before—a so-called down round. And lately, WeBCloud's performance had been anything but stellar with its new customer growth slowing dramatically and its acquisition cost per customer rising.

"Yeah, well, life's tough all over. If he wants to make the really big bucks when we sell the company, he'd better get us an up round now. You tell him I can't answer the phone these days without finding an investment banker on the other end who wants to help us sell WeBCloud."

"Don't worry. He knows the score."

"Let's just make sure." Nate opened the drawer in his desk and rummaged around before tossing something to his CFO. Lou made the catch and looked at the name on the barrel of the pen. It read *Goldman Sachs*. He looked back at Nate, puzzled. "The next time you meet with Stuart, just happen to leave that pen behind. Now go find us some money."

"Whatever you say. Maybe StackMagic's IPO will take off like a rocket tomorrow. If it does, we'll be oversubscribed by the end of the day."

"Yeah, maybe. Here's hoping."

Mitty swiveled back to stare at his expensive campus. He'd been counting on WeBCloud being acquired by now, and it hadn't happened. If they couldn't close this financing round, the whole house of cards would collapse. For three years now, WeBCloud's strategy had been to acquire as much market share as it could while steadily discounting its services more and more steeply. Eventually one of its biggest competitors would have to buy the arrogant startup just to get rid of it. Then the big company could start raising prices and finally make some real money on cloud computing. Or at least that had been Mitty's plan.

So far, it hadn't happened, and he couldn't understand why. All of WeBCloud's major competitors were enormous companies. It made no sense for an established technology company to stand by while WeBCloud turned a huge new profit opportunity into a bottomless loss pit for everybody.

He was massaging his forehead again. Maybe they were more determined poker players than he'd counted on. Perhaps they had even privately agreed among themselves to tough it out until WeBCloud's quasi-Ponzi scheme tumbled in on itself and then pick up its customers for free.

That would have to be a violation of the antitrust laws, wouldn't it? But who was he to talk? He'd persuaded all of the same cloud service providers to join a new trade association he'd formed to lobby Congress not to regulate the industry closely, despite the fact the new data centers would constitute critical infrastructure. Bitter competitors they might be, but when it came to government regulation, they were more than willing to work together to keep their cost of doing business as low as possible. And especially so if their upstart competitor was willing to do most of the work and pay most of the bills to get Congress to play ball.

Mitty had recruited an up-and-coming trade association executive named Benno Patricoff to lead that charge. Over the last two years, he'd also poured millions of WeBCloud's cash into an effort to beg or bribe Congress into passing data center security legislation that would ensure WeBCloud would pull through no matter what. Congress had better hurry up.

* * *

Marla paused at the door of her father's apartment before leaving. "You've been spending a lot of time thinking about Mom lately, haven't you?"

"Whoa—where did that come from?"

"Just a couple of comments you've made."

"I think you're hearing things. You know your mother and I haven't spoken since you were a child. That's my fault, not hers, by the way. I was a fool, and she did what she needed to do."

"Oh, Dad, you're such a hopeless romantic."

"Me! Romantic! I'm the least romantic person I know."

"You're teasing me, right?"

"No. I honestly don't know what you're talking about."

"How much time did you spend thinking about Josette?"

"None. None whatsoever!"

"Ahem. Dad?"

"In that case I consider that a highly inappropriate question for a daughter to pose to her father."

"Okay. How about Simone?"

"Well, some, of course. We were seeing each other, after all."

"You were more than seeing each other. I saw how you held her chair for her and took her coat."

"I do the same for you—that's just being a gentleman."

"The expression on your face wasn't the same as when you hold a chair for me."

"Young lady, this conversation is ov—*OOOF!*"

She laughed as he jumped backward from the poke she'd just taken at his stomach. "Okay. Have it your way. Let's just say the two of you looked awfully cute together."

She ducked through the door before he could retaliate, leaving him frowning. Romantic? Romantic was proclaiming undying love and leaving a single rose on someone's pillow.

Wasn't it?

Still frowning, and with lips pursed too, he opened his computer and typed "define: romantic" in the search bar. The second definition read: *of, characterized by, or suggestive of an idealized view of reality; "a romantic attitude toward the past"*

"*OOOF!*" he said again, this time to himself.

* * *

4

Frank Gets a Boy Friday

"SO WHAT CAN I tell you that isn't in the report?" Koontz tapped his mechanical pencil on the table.

"It's not really extra information I need. It's a little help following how you came to some of the preliminary conclusions. Mostly, I want to understand why you believe Foobar's planning a cyberattack instead of something else."

Koontz pushed back from the table. "First off, we don't. But we do believe it's more likely than any of the other possibilities."

"Okay. So why is that?"

"Look, just so you're clear on this, until we can confidently eliminate a possibility, we've got to work up a defense against it, just in case. So let's say we are overweighting this one. So what?"

"Well, maybe we'll miss something that would lead you to the real attack."

"No way. Like I said the first time we met, yours isn't the only Tiger Team. There are as many teams as there are identifiable attack vectors. One's been instructed to assume Foobar is planning a biological or chemical terror attack. Another assumes he's planning to launch hundreds of physical attacks against civilian targets spread out all over Europe and the U.S. The next team is covering nuclear threats, like an attack on a power plant, or using radioactive material to stage a 'dirty bomb' attack, or even somehow getting hold of a working atomic bomb. Unless and until we have conclusive proof identifying what the attack, or attacks, will be, we have to assume that anything is possible."

"Okay, I get that. But I still want to understand the evidence-based starting point for the threat I'm working on. What makes you think this guy's followers have any sophistication in waging cyber war at all? The report you gave me has references to specific data supporting all kinds of conclusions—it's a really impressively documented analysis. It took me a while to notice that I couldn't find even one reference to data indicating that Foobar's people had the skills to pull off any kind of cyberattack, much less a catastrophic one."

Koontz tapped his pen on the table harder now. "I'm finding that hard to believe. But let's say you're right. Foobar apparently believes he can take down America—and Europe besides. Assuming he's not delusional, how is he going to manage that? He's only been able to recruit about eighteen thousand soldiers, not millions. We're pretty sure that no one, not even North Korea—so far, anyway—has sold him any sophisticated weapons. So when it comes to traditional weaponry, all he's got to work with is what his followers have captured in the field. That includes a few planes they don't know how to fly and no ships at all. So he can hardly expect to successfully invade Europe, much less the U.S. You with me?"

"No argument so far.'"

"Good. So what does that leave? Foobar's only got four possible options to pull off something on a grand scale—biological and chemical, nuclear, physical, and cyber. All of them seem unlikely but for different reasons."

"How so?"

"Nobody's going to sell chemical weapon precursor materials to Foobar, and biologic doesn't sound right, either, because we don't think his people have the ability to make their own materials and agents."

"You're changing the rules now," Frank objected. "You haven't pointed out any evidence that they have cyber skills, either."

"Hold on a minute—most of the best hackers have been self-taught, right?"

"Okay, I'll grant you that."

"Right. Now how about this: ever heard of a do-it-yourself anthrax expert? No? I thought not. We track every single person who's capable of creating bioweapons, and not one of them has gone missing. If Foobar's ragtag band of fanatics can't make their own biologics, where are they going to get them? We've already destroyed almost all of Syria's chemical and bioweapons, and it turned out there weren't any Iraqi chemical or bioterror weapons left when Saddam fell.

"Same goes for nukes. All of the tactical and strategic nukes from the former

Soviet states have either been repatriated to Russia or removed and destroyed by us. And we don't think the Pakistanis, Indians, Chinese, or North Koreans are going to share any of theirs. So that leaves just a cyberattack or a coordinated series of bombings. Of the two, he can do a lot more damage with a cyberattack than a physical attack, if he chooses the target wisely. What doesn't make sense about that?"

"Don't get me wrong, I agree with that part of your analysis. I've never understood why rogue states and terrorists haven't hit us harder with cyberattacks in the past."

"So what's the problem?"

"What I said before—there's nothing in the report at all, as far as I can see, that says that Foobar is recruiting true believers with the right skills, or hiring a bunch of Black Hats from Eastern Europe to write malware for him, or trying to train any of the people he's already got. Before 9/11, bin Laden sent teams of foot soldiers over here to learn how to pilot civilian airliners. But nothing in the report indicates Foobar's mounting an equivalent cyberattack preparation effort here."

Koontz shifted in his chair. "I think that's a bit of an overstatement. He's been doing everything he can using social media to recruit young people from all over the world to become jihadists. It's fair to assume that a lot of them would have computer training. And you wouldn't expect him to tip his hand by advertising for experts to launch his biggest attack, would you?"

"Granted. But your average twenty-something isn't a cybersecurity specialist. If he's going to try and learn, he's going to have to be all over the dark Internet learning the ropes, and the Agency should be able to detect that. Has it?"

"I have no idea."

"Well, there's all kinds of Agency data cited in the report relating to the other threats. If there's nothing on cyber-training, doesn't that suggest they couldn't find anything?"

"Now you're the one making assumptions."

"No, I'm just asking questions. How many expert hackers has he recruited?"

"I have no way of knowing. But if he doesn't have folks that can take us down, we've got nothing to worry about in that threat space. And that would be good news."

"Really? Isn't there another possibility?"

"What's that?"

"Traditional attacks using explosives. al-Qaeda's been bombing civilian targets all over the world for more than a decade, and a lot of their best people are working for Foobar now. They've got plenty of experience with traditional explosives."

Koontz leaned forward and smiled. "Come on, Frank. You must know better than that. Look at the attacks al-Qaeda, ISIS, and Foobar have pulled off so far. They've been terrible as far as loss of life is concerned, but with the exception of the 9/11 attacks on the Twin Towers and the Pentagon, the physical damage in the U.S. has been less than trivial. Why do you suppose that would be?"

"There could be lots of reasons," Frank said. "The most obvious one is that all the U.S. attacks so far have been committed by 'lone wolves,' and it's easier for them to buy guns and then just go blast away."

"Maybe," Koontz responded. "Or it could be that they don't have access to enough explosives to pull off something dramatic. And it would take a hell of a lot more than a truck bomb—or even a dozen truck bombs—to seriously interrupt the Internet in even one country, let alone the U.S. plus all of Europe."

"Well, why not more truck bombs then? Why not a hundred? Or a thousand?"

"Because you have to load them with something that explodes! The Middle East is awash in Iraqi and Syrian munitions captured by terrorists, so they can blow things up over there any time they want to. But that material is there, and we're here. A thousand truck bombs would take two thousand tons of explosives. Where is Foobar going to get that kind of ordnance from? He can't order the stuff from Amazon like disposable diapers."

"How about fertilizer, then? That's what Timothy McVeigh used to destroy the Federal Building in Oklahoma City."

"Right. And that's why not just anybody can buy it anymore. Weaponizable fertilizer is strictly controlled now. It's inconceivable to me that anyone could stockpile the amount of material you're talking about. Pulling off a single act of terror that kills and maims a lot of people is one thing. You can do that with a bomb made out of a pressure cooker and a few pounds of the kind of gunpowder people buy to reload their own shotgun shells. The Tsarnaev brothers proved that at the Boston Marathon. But the most damage you could do with a bomb like that would be to take out a single power transformer. Whatever you took down wouldn't amount to much and would be back up in hours, if not minutes."

Frank frowned, annoyed with himself for letting Koontz think he'd won the point. And in fact it was hard to argue with Koontz's answers. But he still wasn't satisfied.

"Okay, so I get everything you're saying. But I guess we can agree that if Foobar is planning on launching a cyberattack, he's going to have to be pretty damn smart about how he does it, and so far, it doesn't look like he's got a lot of talent to work with. So that makes me want to know more about where our points of greatest weakness are. I didn't see anything about that in the report, either."

"That's because it's already well documented elsewhere as part of the federal Critical Infrastructure Program."

"What's that?"

"It's been around for decades, so there was no need to clog up the report with that information. Basically, it's a working list of whatever is critical to maintain defense, commerce, and society—highways, the power grid, et cetera—and the requirements for how you have to protect it. We can give you as much background as you want on that.

"As a matter of fact"—he turned toward Slattery—"Tim is just coming off his ethics officer placement now. New management hires rotate through a series of positions for two years before they settle in to a long-term role. Special projects is one rotation, and I could second him to you for a while to feed you anything you want, within reason. How about that?" Koontz looked at his watch without taking the trouble to be tactful about it.

Until now, Frank had pretty much lumped Slattery into the same category as the conference room furniture. Now he examined the young man more closely. He noted that Tim was likely a bit taller than he was, dark-haired, with a thin, angular face made more serious looking by black-rimmed glasses.

Slattery's face wasn't giving a lot away, and Frank wasn't exactly in the market for a sidekick. Still, the idea of having a full-time research assistant who could plumb the depths of the CIA's databases was tempting.

"That would be great."

"I can also give you access to one of our big data engineers. If there are specific data sets you want to analyze, he or she can do that for you. Is there anything else you want to talk about today?"

"No, that should do it."

Koontz stood up. "Good. In that case, let Tim know what you want, and I'll get back to business."

Clearly, Koontz was fobbing Frank off to a glorified intern to facilitate his escape. Well, the heck with him. If Koontz couldn't see the flaws in his own team's work, Frank would be happy to expose them for him.

Slattery piped up as Koontz left the room. "Can you be a bit more specific about what you'd like me to research for you, Mr. Adversego? I'd be happy to get whatever you'd like."

"Call me Frank. What I want to understand is what cyber critical infrastructure targets should be at the top of Foobar's list. Obviously, if he could crash a big part of the power grid, everything relying on it would come to an immediate halt, so that's clearly a potential target. Taking down the entire air traffic control system wouldn't be as bad, but it would drastically cut down the number of planes that could be in the air at any one time."

Frank leaned back and looked toward the ceiling. "So one factor would be what we depend on most. After that, I'd say which systems would be easiest to take down. And then I guess there's the recovery time—which systems would take the longest for us to get up and running again. Combine those three factors, and that should tell us what threats to look for hardest in the available data. Maybe there are some other considerations to take into account as well—you should spend some time thinking about that, too—and don't limit yourself to what you find in government documents. Some of them are probably out of date."

Slattery nodded with obvious enthusiasm; he seemed almost painfully eager to please. "Got it. I'll start by sending you the critical infrastructure materials Mr. Koontz mentioned right away. I'll also review them and make a list of what infrastructure looks the weakest to me, and then we can compare notes."

"Sounds good."

But Slattery wasn't done yet. "After that, I'll get the big data engineer Mr. Koontz assigns to us to take a deep dive into our databases and see if there's any evidence that someone's been probing or surveilling the systems you decide are most at risk."

Frank paused before answering. He was pleased Slattery was showing initiative and annoyed that now he would have to share his own thinking with someone on an ongoing basis. "Okay, sounds reasonable. Have you worked in this area before?"

"Well, not exactly. I've got an MBA and a BA in philosophy, focusing on ethics. But I'm fluent in Arabic."

"That doesn't sound like the usual background for a career in the CIA."

"No, probably not. But after the congressional report on Abu Ghraib, the Hill has been keeping the Agency on a lot shorter leash. Every department has to have an ethics officer now, with assistants, who reports directly to an oversight committee outside Langley. That way there's always someone around who can speak up immediately if someone suggests something that's over the line and squash it before it goes any further. That's the long-term role here that appeals to me."

Great, Frank thought. *In other words, he didn't have any useful experience at all and had probably been kept on the sidelines and in the dark as much as possible ever since he arrived. But the ability to read Arabic could come in handy.* He stood up. "Well, I hope they give assistant ethics officers their own food tasters in the Langley cafeteria. That way they'll feel safer and won't have to eat alone all the time. Anyway, you can email me any time if you have any questions."

* * *

Frank woke up thinking about what he had fallen asleep obsessing over the night before. He continued to do so, just as he had every morning lately, no matter how hard he tried not to, while robotically brushing his teeth and suiting up for his morning run. To his surprise and dismay, all of his feelings from long ago had come flooding back as soon as he'd unfolded Clare's farewell letter, as if he were Rip Van Winkle, waking up to discover that all the people who were still alive to him were now dead.

He also found himself dwelling on all the companionship he'd missed over the long, solitary years. True, he'd had other relationships since he and Clare had separated. He hadn't handled most of those well toward the end, either. But in every case, he'd eventually gotten past the emotional bruises. With Clare, it had been different. There had always been this churning cauldron of issues and feelings he had never been able to resolve. That and the conviction there was something unique and wonderful about her and the bond between them he'd never experienced with anyone else again. What particularly haunted him now was a question for which he had no answer: what had driven him to so adamantly refuse to have any contact with her ever again?

He got up and opened the hall closet door. He still hadn't sorted through one box, one he'd opened and then set aside after he realized what it contained. Now he picked it up, set it on his kitchen table, and began to empty it. Finally, he found what he both hoped and feared it would hold. There it was, next to his first scientific calculator and a selection of T-shirts from fraternity rush week: a thick, sealed, ten-by-thirteen-inch manila envelope.

He stared at the envelope for a long time before pouring himself a cup of coffee and walking into his disordered living room. He stood by the window, ruminating over the past and watching neighbors he did not know, entering and leaving his building. Then he set his unfinished coffee aside and put on his jacket. It was undeniably time for a long run.

When he reached the door to his apartment, he paused, one hand on the doorknob, staring at nothing, before turning around again. When he left a few moments later, Clare's picture was standing upright on his dresser.

* * *

"Do you want to take a call from Benno?"

This had better be good news, Mitty thought. "Sure, put him through."

"Morning, Benno. Is it safe?"

"Let's just say I've got good news for both of us. The House-Senate conference committee just released the final draft of the bill, and the full, unchanged text of our standard is still in it. It's expected to clear both houses without any opposition. My wife is probably spending my bonus already."

Mitty heaved a sigh of relief. "Good work, Benno. I can't help you out with Ellen. But if the president signs our bill into law, I'll make sure you get your bonus on time."

And he'd pay it gladly, too. Three hundred thousand dollars was a big bonus for a trade association executive, but it paled in comparison to the rest of the money WeBCloud had poured into launching and underwriting the Data Center Security Alliance. Starting up DCSA had seemed like a risky bet two years before. He remembered waiting for Benno Patricoff back then at an expensive K Street restaurant in Washington, D.C. Patricoff was late, and Nate didn't like late. Especially from someone who owed his job to him. And he wanted some time alone with Patricoff before Paul Roach, DCSA's lobbyist, joined them.

Finally, he spied Patricoff weaving his way between tables on his way across the room.

"Hey. Sorry to keep you waiting. I was still getting materials out for the board meeting."

"I know. I just saw them show up in my email. Don't be surprised if you hear from the board about that tomorrow. We should always receive board materials at least a week before a meeting."

There was no use offering excuses, Patricoff knew, even though he had good ones. Mitty only cared about results.

"You're right, of course. But I think I've got all the important things lined up."

"Think?"

"Okay, I know. I'm sure we're in good shape."

"Let's see. Take me through your prep work."

"Right. So I've walked through everything with each of the directors that matter…"

"By phone only—no email?"

"No email. And they're all on board."

For the first time that day, the tension in Mitty's shoulders began to ease. If all of WeBCloud's largest competitors had signed on, he knew he could move forward with his plan. "And the standard? You went through it in detail with them?"

"Yes. I used the working group charter. It lays out everything that the standard will cover—what physical protections a data center must put in place, what levels and types of cybersecurity defenses it has to design into its systems, how often a data center's security defenses have to be tested by third parties, and what scores they have to reach in order to stay in business. I've also spoken to all of the technical committee reps one or more times over the past week. I went through the charter with each of them line by line. They're fine with it only addressing perimeter security and cybersecurity. And, as expected, they'd like to make it as inexpensive to implement as possible."

"Did they buy into the specific features I gave you? Every one?"

"Every one."

Mitty had barely touched his drink so far, but now he took a real slug and sat back in his chair. "Okay. Good job."

Benno relaxed as well when he heard those words. He'd only worked with Mitty for a couple of weeks, but it was already clear to him that compliments would be few and hard-earned. He decided to take advantage of the moment. "Thanks. I was pleased with how things turned out as well. Were you able to get the Compensation Committee to agree to get together after the board meeting?"

"Yes, and I've already spoken to each of them individually."

Good, thought Patricoff. Mitty might be tough, but at least he played by the same rules he set for his subordinates. He decided to take a chance and ask the obvious next question. "With good results, I hope?"

"Yes. You get the standard done and adopted by the DCSA members and directors by the end of this year and you'll get a bonus of two hundred thousand dollars. If you get Congress to incorporate it into a data center law next year, you get a thirty thousand dollar bonus on the second anniversary of your contract."

"That sounds good. What metrics would I need to hit to earn a partial bonus?"

"There are no other metrics. This is all or nothing, just as I said before. That's why the bonus is so big."

Darn it, thought Patricoff. That was the deal Mitty said he'd ask the comp committee to agree to, but Patricoff had been hoping the other directors might talk Mitty into something more reasonable. "Okay. You can't blame a bloke for trying, though." He pointed with his chin across the dining room at a tall, broad-shouldered, impeccably dressed man approaching them. "Is that Paul Roach?"

"Yes. Let me introduce you." The two men rose. "Paul, good to see you again. Meet Benno Patricoff, our new DCSA executive director."

Roach beamed, extending his hand to Patricoff. "Glad we could get together tonight. I'm looking forward to working with you."

"And the same. I've spent a fair amount of time working the Hill in my past jobs, but Nate tells me you're the grand master. I'm looking forward to your advice on how to improve my game."

"I'm sure you're selling yourself short. But if I've got any tricks up my sleeve you don't already know, I'll be happy to share them."

They spent most of the next hour getting to know each other. It wasn't until the waiter was serving coffee that Mitty turned the conversation to serious business.

"So, Paul, what have you got planned so far?"

"For starters, we've figured out all the people Benno needs to meet on a regular basis on the Hill, including on the key agencies and committees, and set up first meetings with each."

Benno was impressed. "Wow. That's fast work. Nate tells me he only signed you up on Monday."

"Of course. That's why he chose us."

That and a few other factors, Mitty thought, *just as there was more to the standard than anyone knew but him.*

"When you get to your office tomorrow," Roach continued, "you'll find a briefing book waiting for you. It covers every elected member of every relevant House and Senate committee and subcommittee and each of their staff people that have an interest in cybersecurity. Same for the key staff on the involved committees, plus the National Institute of Standards and Technology and the Federal Trade Commission and Department of Justice. As you know, the FTC and DOJ are the regulators that enforce the antitrust laws. Down the line, we'll probably want you to speak with the U.S. trade representatives for Europe and the Asia-Pacific regions, and maybe the regulators in California and a few other states. But we don't want to hit you with everything at once."

"Glad to hear it. When should I plan on working lobbying into my schedule?"

"Tomorrow," Mitty interjected.

"Really? Why? We haven't even started work on the standard yet."

"Because we want the agencies to be supportive and for Congress to be waiting for it when it's done. Otherwise, they might adopt standards from someone else, or worse yet, write the regulations themselves."

"Right," Roach added. "We're not the only game in town, and every time there's a big cybersecurity breach in the news, everybody asks Congress what they're going to do about it. We need to convince them DCSA is the organization that's most capable of developing a robust security standard to protect cloud computing data centers. That way when DCSA's standard is available, Congress will turn it into a regulation that every data center will have to comply with. If your working group keeps expense containment at the top of the priority list all the time, that will minimize costs for all the cloud services providers, and for their customers, too."

"I can see why that would be good for business. But why would Congress want to take something that vendors cooked up and turn it into law?"

"Because they don't have a choice."

"How so? That sounds too good to be true."

"Not so. Back in 1995, Congress passed something called the Technology Transfer and Advancement Act, which put government out of the standards development business. Basically, what it says is that if there's a private sector standard that can do the job, the government has to use it rather than develop its own standard or regulation for the same purpose."

"I never knew that. How did a law like that get passed?"

"Do you remember the phrase 'six-hundred-dollar toilet seat'?"

Patricoff laughed. "No. Should I?"

"For someone your age, probably not. But back in the 1980s, it came out that the Pentagon was actually paying that much for a crapper seat. And similarly ridiculous amounts for other items—like seven thousand dollars for a coffee pot. Part of the problem was that the Pentagon kept coming up with detailed design requirements for everything it bought—even for chocolate chip cookies, if you can believe that—instead of just buying products that were already on the market. Congress hit the roof, and one of the results was the Technology Transfer and Advancement Act."

"That's pretty sweet. So the vendors get to write the rules for what the government buys from them, rather than the other way around?"

"When it comes to standards and purchasing requirements, that's right. The government relies heavily on private sector standards organizations—like DCSA— to write all kinds of health, safety, product, and performance standards, not to mention building codes and a whole lot else."

"Including critical infrastructure?"

"Even for nuclear power plants."

"Wow. Is this a great country or what?"

"Yeah. But don't get complacent—getting your standard referenced into law isn't easy. There's at least a dozen other organizations out there already working on standards for different aspects of cloud computing. Luckily, none of them owns the security area yet, so we've still got time to stake out our turf—if we act fast and execute well on the Hill."

"So what happens next?" Benno asked.

"You'll find that your briefing book lays out our strategy for the next twelve months. It's set up with milestones that map against known Congressional committee activities—we'll update that on a regular basis, of course, as legislators introduce new bills. It also has all the talking points you should get down by heart ASAP. I'd suggest you block out a full day a week for the next three weeks to get together with us. That way we can explain why the talking points are what they are and who you'll be meeting with. We can do some pre-meeting coaching sessions, too."

"I guess I can do that; I'm not too booked on other matters yet."

"Good, because we've got you set up for ten meetings on the Hill over the next month. The first one's next week."

"Next week?"

"Yes, but don't worry. The first ones are mostly introductions. As you know, it's all about establishing relationships in this town. That takes time, so the sooner we get started the better. Here—let me take that."

Roach's last statement was directed to the waiter who had just arrived with the check.

"Thanks," Mitty said. "Say, can you stick around for a little while, Paul? There's a couple other things I'd like to kick around with you."

"Sure thing."

Patricoff took the cue and said his goodbyes.

Mitty leaned forward when Patricoff was out of earshot. "So tell me. Do you know anything about a group called the Responsible Technology Foundation?"

"Some. It's a small, non-profit advocacy outfit that focuses on technology-related causes. It was started a few years ago by someone straight out of grad school named Sara Ravitz. Not quite a Luddite, but she tends to see horrible risks behind every new advance in technology. The RTF doesn't have a lot of money, but she gets good attention anyway because her dad's a former secretary of the treasury. He's back on Wall Street but stays in touch down here. That's about it."

"Well, I want you to find out a whole lot more. For some reason she's starting to get a burr under her saddle about physical security for data centers and wants to see regulations passed that would require that data centers be buried at least fifty feet underground. A lot of our competitors have already built super-secure data centers in mine shafts and caverns, and that costs a bundle. There's no way we can continue to sustain our growth if that approach becomes required. Patricoff's job is to make sure any regulation that gets adopted will allow us to keep physical security compliance costs to a minimum. And I need you to make sure that Ravitz's efforts don't get any traction."

"Got it. We'll get on it right away."

* * *

5

Rain Date

THE CRITICAL INFRASTRUCTURE materials Tim Slattery compiled were more than comprehensive, and Frank had no choice but to stake out a corner of the CIA facility for his grumpy, middle-aged self to wade through them on one of the Agency's digitally constipated laptops.

Slattery's materials were not only extensive but meticulously indexed and digested as well. And when he presented them to Frank, he had seemed unduly nervous. Frank couldn't figure out why his assistant was being so thorough and conscientious about a task that was rather menial. It didn't make sense that he should be so eager to please someone who was, after all, simply passing through the department. He probably wouldn't even be asked to rate his performance when the project was finally complete. Very peculiar.

Frank finally waded through the last of the materials. To be sure, he'd found some intriguing information he hadn't known before. But overall, the government reports had simply confirmed his preexisting belief that the country offered a veritable buffet of varied and vulnerable targets. The biggest challenge facing any terrorist would be deciding which ones to hit. That made Frank's task even tougher. He'd have to put himself inside the head of an extremist from another culture halfway around the world and decide which of the many appealing options available to him he should pick.

He ruminated on that for a while, making a few adjustments to his ranking of most likely targets gleaned from the federal Critical Infrastructure roster. Then he added several targets of his own, knowing many industries had lobbied hard to keep their businesses off the government list. No surprise there. Nobody wanted to be more regulated than they already were.

He fooled and fussed over his list for a while before leaning back, satisfied with the result. For the first time on this project, he felt like he'd accomplished something. Then he turned to Slattery's analysis to see how well Tim had done.

Half an hour later, he pushed back from his laptop again. But he wasn't satisfied this time. There was no avoiding the conclusion: the kid with the ethics degree had been more astute than he had. Not that their lists and supporting rationales were all that different. But where they did vary, Slattery's determinations were usually more solid than his own. That stung. He started scanning his source materials again to see where he'd gone astray.

That soon became obvious. Each time he'd slipped up it was because he'd disregarded information that failed to fit in with the conclusions he'd already jumped to—the very same thing he'd faulted the CIA for when it decided on Foobar's probable targets. Slattery had clearly kept a more open mind and absorbed all the information before drawing his conclusions. There was a lesson to be learned there, and Frank didn't like the way he had learned it.

* * *

Home once again, the chirp of his phone announcing the arrival of a text provided a welcome distraction. He glanced at it, stood up, grabbed his jacket, and headed downstairs to meet Marla in the drab lobby.

"So where do you want to go?" he asked.

"Want to stick around your neighborhood for a change? We haven't eaten at Renaldo's in ages."

"Why not?"

A couple of blocks later, Marla was being hugged and fussed over by the same hostess who'd greeted them at the small family restaurant since Marla was three. "So big! And it's been so long! You should come back and see me more often!"

"You're right. It's really great to see you."

"Look—the same table you always wanted is free."

They followed her to a familiar spot by the front window, where a little girl could watch the world go by. The red and white checked tablecloth and candle in a Chianti bottle were just the way she remembered them.

Frank took his place behind her to hold her chair. "Just like old times."

"Yes, that was very cute when I was a little girl. But you really don't have to do that anymore."

"Why not? It's nice for some things not to change."

"Some things, yes."

"What's that supposed to mean?"

"Well, for starters, instead of just moving out of your apartment while they rehab it, you could leave this dingy neighborhood and buy something nice. You can afford to, you know."

"Well, I like this neighborhood. And the owner offered a good deal to any tenant that bought their unit once it was upgraded."

"Well, if you think a fresh coat of paint and a few new appliances turn a claustrophobic apartment on a seedy street into a good deal, maybe. But I don't."

"Well, maybe that's why I didn't ask for your opinion. Anyway, the paperwork's all signed."

"More's the pity." She picked up her menu and then almost immediately put it down again.

"Have you decided where you're going to stay when they kick you out?"

"Not for sure. I've still got the camper, so I can live in that."

"What—in the middle of that storage lot outside the Beltway?"

"No, I don't think I could get away with that. I thought I'd hit the road for a while. Get out of town and do a little touring."

"I thought you told me you have a new project you're working on?"

"Yes, but it's the usual deal. I can work wherever I can get an Internet connection, and with my satellite dish, that means anywhere."

"What's the project about?"

"No can tell."

"Really? I've been pretty helpful in the past, haven't I?"

"You sure have. But I really can't talk about this one."

"Well, you just be that way then. But you can't change the subject that easily. I think you should come stay with me while they rehabilitate your dump."

Frank made a noncommittal grunt and picked up his menu.

Marla sniffed and followed suit. "I'm sorry," she said at last. "I didn't mean to give you such a hard time. Let me hit the restart button, okay?"

"Okay, so what's new?"

"Nothing, really. I've started interviewing for a job after graduation. I guess that's new."

"Really? Are you interviewing for any in Washington?"

"Yes. But hey—before I forget—how's Simone?"

"Ah, okay I guess. She's in France, you know. She got her old position back at the university."

"I know. I was sorry—for you, I mean. Are you going to go visit her?"

Frank picked up the menu again. "Oh, I don't think so."

"Why not? It seemed like the two of you were really enjoying each other's company."

"Well, I'm not very good with long-distance relationships."

"Go on! You sound like a college freshman!"

"Well, whatever. I've never liked long telephone conversations. Or actually, telephone conversations, period. Can we change the subject?"

"Okay, all right. Let me guess—you're going to order the chicken marsala, right?"

"Naturally. And you're getting the ravioli, of course."

"Of course. Oh good! Here comes the fresh-baked bread."

Later in the meal, when Frank returned from the rest room, he found Marla sitting with her hands folded in her lap and a smile on her face that was half-goofy and half-strained.

"What?" he asked, sitting.

"What do you mean, 'What?'"

"What's with the funny look on your face?"

"I don't know what you mean. But there is something I want to talk to you about."

"Uh-oh. Now what?"

"Not uh-oh. This is something good. There's somebody I want you to meet."

"Hmm. Am I right in assuming it's someone of the male persuasion?"

"Well, duh. Yes. And I think he's pretty special."

"You mean this one might be a keeper?"

"Yes, Dad. I really do. And I want you to meet him."

Frank drummed his fingers on his thigh. He always knew this day might come—even hoped it would, for Marla's sake. But she had taken him by surprise. And he was all too aware that not all stories that began like this had happy endings.

"And does this special someone have a name?"

"Of course, he does."

"And that would be?"

"His name is Tim Slattery. Oh, Dad, I hope so much that you'll like him. And don't worry—he works for some sort of fancy data analysis firm, so you and he should have a lot to talk about."

* * *

Frank stared blankly at the stack of papers he'd extracted from the last drawer of his desk and then dropped them into a garbage bag that already held most of the rest of the desk's contents. Later it would occur to him that he had likely disposed of all of his back tax returns.

So Marla was evidently hoping to make Tim Slattery his son-in-law. He had no clue whether that would be a good or a bad thing for Marla in the long run, but it sure as hell would be awkward for him in the near term. Of course, Slattery couldn't tell Marla whom he really worked for or that he and her father were working together on a project, which was the way it would have to stay. And obviously, Tim hadn't figured out whether and how to tell Frank that he was dating his daughter, either. At least that explained why the kid was always trying so hard to please.

And then there was the critical infrastructure report. Frank was still beating himself up for missing things that Slattery hadn't. Beyond that, there was the disturbing information he'd read in the materials themselves.

The concept of critical infrastructure was hardly a new one, as the report's authors had noted in a long introduction. Indeed, the practice of destroying an enemy's crops and draft animals was as old as war itself. The types of infrastructure and means of destruction had simply become more numerous and sophisticated over time. During the Second World War, Hitler's U-boats had attempted to starve Great Britain into surrender and almost succeeded. The Allies, in turn, sought to knock out not only Germany's munitions works but also its bridges so that trains couldn't deliver troops or supplies to the front lines. Indeed, all other things being equal, so long as your critical infrastructure stayed more intact than your enemy's, you were more likely to win.

Then, for a few decades, intercontinental ballistic missiles topped with nuclear weapons made the concept of critical infrastructure seem quaint. Unless you stopped almost all the incoming missiles, everything, critical or otherwise, would be vaporized wherever they struck. Everywhere else, the radiation would be so extreme and society so disrupted that everything would break down. Anyone who survived the initial strike might well envy those who hadn't during the few days or weeks before the "survivors" succumbed as well.

With the Cold War over and terrorism on the rise, though, concerns over critical infrastructure were very much back in vogue. There were more bad guys to worry about than ever, with new groups of terrorists emerging on almost a monthly basis all over the world. The attacks on 9/11 had brought the reality of terrorism to the homeland, making it clear that sophisticated, well-funded organizations like al-Qaeda and ISIS could make terrorism a fact of life wherever they chose to strike. And strike they had, in multiple countries around the globe. Now, with the rise of Foobar and the Caliphate, the attacks threatened to increase in frequency, geographic range, and destructiveness.

What particularly disturbed him was the fact that all types of critical infrastructure were becoming completely dependent on the Internet at the same time that terrorist attacks were proliferating. Now that transportation, banking, government, the delivery of food and fuel, and every other essential service were controlled by Internet-linked computer systems, everything would go down if the Internet did.

Frank had always been shocked that so little effort had been spent engineering robust defenses against cyberattack into critical systems in the U.S., given how much more appealing a target the Internet was in the developed world than its physical infrastructure. In traditional weapons-based—so-called kinetic—warfare, the United States could direct overwhelming force against an enemy either to prevent or respond to an attack. And even if that wasn't the case, America's geographical isolation and naval supremacy made it largely invulnerable to anything other than a missile attack.

But the tables turned dramatically when the targets were computers connected by the Internet. Foobar had a classic asymmetric warfare advantage in this kind of conflict: his followers barely used sophisticated computers or telecommunications for anything, while the U.S. and the rest of the Western world used them to manage everything. Indeed, a terrorist like Foobar could, if he wished, attack anonymously—as had Osama bin Laden—perhaps with the result that the U.S. would never know for sure who had launched the attack that brought it to its knees.

But still. If that was really what Foobar was up to, why wasn't there any evidence?

* * *

6

Tiger Team, Tiger Team, Burning Bright

FRANK EYED THE other members of the Cyberattack Tiger Team as they entered the conference room at Fort Meade. Everyone was now seated around the table, except for Derek R. Henderson, the team's chair. He was an Army colonel attached to United States Cyber Command, usually referred to simply as USCYBERCOM, a military command overseen by the National Security Agency and charged with centralizing and coordinating all defensive and offensive military cyberspace resources and operations.

Frank had already read the bios of all the other team members in the briefing book and decided he was the least qualified and consequential person in the room. Worse, he expected the rest of the team would surely have reached the same conclusion. Certainly, Virgil Cooper, the National Center for Counter Terrorism operations officer seated near the head of the table, must be thinking that. According to the briefing book, prior to joining the NCCT, Cooper had been a Navy officer commanding one of the Navy's elite SEAL units. If Foobar's attack could be intercepted at sea, he would lead the operation. If not, he'd be able to put appropriate land-based forces in the picture as quickly as possible. Cooper looked every inch the buzz-cut, square-jawed part, as did the serious-looking Navy lieutenant sitting at his elbow. Frank imagined the crow's feet at the corners of Cooper's eyes were the legacy of years of squinting through binoculars in all manner of tense, covert situations.

Opposite Cooper sat Hermann Koontz, resembling the commander's anti-matter complement. Next to Koontz was one of his Whiz Kids, who was, of course, deeply immersed in his iPhone. Koontz was lost in thought, as oblivious to Cooper's careful grooming and crisp uniform as Frank imagined the commander was offended by the old engineer's rumpled clothes, dumpy physique, and unkempt hair.

Next to Koontz's assistant sat a tall man in his early sixties who had given Frank a self-conscious smile and nod of the head when he arrived. He had placed his briefing binder and a daybook with lined pages on the table when he sat down. He had aligned them neatly in front of him with a mechanical pencil placed parallel to and equidistant between the two. He had used that pencil to write the day's date at the top (centered) of the left-hand page of the open daybook before closing it again, waiting for the meeting to begin. Frank concluded he must be Bill Fermi, the computer scientist from NIST, and guessed that a slide rule could still be found somewhere in the back of his desk, a relic of his engineering past too sacred to discard despite being consigned decades ago to the dustbin of computational history.

The last senior Tiger Team member seated at the table was a man in his forties, engaged in conversation with a woman perhaps a decade his junior. That would be Barry Shuttleworth, the Department of Homeland Security Response Manager, and his aide. According to the briefing book, his role would be to coordinate an appropriate relief response if the Tiger Teams failed to thwart an attack before it was launched. Shuttleworth's demeanor was distracted and his appearance bureaucratic. Frank wondered whether Beltway apparatchiks went to sleep with their ties still knotted neatly around their necks.

Frank glanced at his watch. He wished he'd brought Slattery along to help him look more important than he was feeling.

Ten minutes after the hour, the door opened to admit the chair of the Tiger Team and his entourage.

"Sorry to be late, everyone. Damn traffic was worse than usual." He took his seat at the head of the table, flanked by a military officer on one side and a civilian on the other.

"Let me start by welcoming you all to the Cyberattack Tiger Team. I can't stress too greatly the importance of the work we'll be performing here. I'll need one hundred and ten percent effort from everyone around this table, and I assure you that you'll get the same from me and my staff. If there's any reason why any of you can't make that kind of commitment, now's the time to speak up."

He swept his gaze around the table, making brief eye contact with each of them. "Good. I see that you've all got your briefing books with you and trust you've already studied them thoroughly. Let's go around the table once so we can put names to faces. Mr. Fermi, please introduce yourself."

"Sure. Bill Fermi. I'm with NIST, where I've spent most of my career. For the last fifteen years, I've focused on cybersecurity. My particular specialty is designing resiliency into Internet and Web infrastructure." He turned to Koontz's Whiz Kid, who reluctantly set his iPhone aside.

"Hi. I'm Gene Ensign. I'm one of Hermann's data analysts." He began to reach for his iPhone again before abruptly withdrawing his hand. Frank was reasonably sure Koontz had kicked him under the table.

"Hermann Koontz, CIA, senior director, Big Data analysis. I've been with the Agency since 1975."

The chairman turned to the staffer to his right. "Lieutenant?"

"Good to meet you all. I'm Barbara Travers, lieutenant, U.S. Army. My job is to analyze and integrate data regarding domestic attacks and threats and feed it up the chain. I pull information from the Department of Homeland Security and over one hundred other government sources and flag the data we really need to pay attention to. I'll serve as our principal liaison with the Bioattack and Kinetic Tiger Teams." She turned to her boss.

"Thank you, Lieutenant. I'm Colonel Derek Henderson, U.S. Army. I took my current position at USCYBERCOM two years ago after a stint with the NATO brass in Casteau, Belgium. Before that, I did five tours in Iraq and Afghanistan. I don't know as much about cybersecurity as I hope each of you do, but I do know how to make things happen. I've been charged by the secretary of defense with making sure this team hits the ground running, and that's what we're going to do." He turned to the young man to his left.

"Pleased to meet you all. My name's Graham Lutz, on loan to USCYBERCOM from the State Department. I'm a Middle East specialist and will act as a subject matter resource for the team. When things are happening in the field you should know about, I'll provide updates. If any of you at any time has questions about the political, cultural, or religious context of what you're dealing with, don't hesitate to contact me, and I'll try and help you out. I'll also be the liaison to the Nuclear Tiger Team."

The commander was next. "Virgil Cooper, operations officer, National Counter Terrorism Center, formerly Navy commander, U.S. Navy, Sea, Air, and

Land Special Operations Force—better known as SEALS—supporting the Agency for the duration of this project." His aide followed.

"Stan Barnett, lieutenant, U.S. Navy, supporting Mr. Cooper."

Shuttleworth nodded to those around the table. "Barry Shuttleworth, deputy assistant undersecretary for Response Management, Department of Homeland Security. Lynn?"

"Hi, I'm Lynn Walters, a DHS external liaison manager. I'm looking forward to working with each of you."

That left only Frank, who had given up on coming up with a way to describe himself in a way that was both honest as well as more inspiring than "unemployed cybersecurity geek."

"Frank Adversego. Ah, I guess you could say I've been heavily involved in cybersecurity for the last few years. I've worked with the Agency in the past, and they brought me into this project."

Henderson nodded and picked up the projector remote. "Thank you, everyone. Now let's take a look at the agenda for the rest of our day."

The first slide in what Frank feared would be a chloroformic series of the same appeared on the screen. It featured the usual self-explanatory topic list, which would inevitably be expanded into a five-minute explanation of the obvious. It read:

- The big picture
  - ○ International
  - ○ Domestic
- What we know
- What we don't know
- Next steps

To Frank's relief, after a short pause, Henderson slid the remote across the table to Lutz, the Middle East expert.

"I expect there's quite a range of knowledge in the room, so let me apologize in advance for boring anyone who's already an expert on the Caliphate. As we all get up to speed, I'll be able to shorten things up in future meetings."

He switched to a slide showing a map of the eastern Mediterranean and Middle East.

"Here's what things looked like a year ago. The areas marked in red were under Foobar's control; those in pink were contested territory, with coalition forces and Foobar's troops gaining and losing ground, sometimes on a weekly or even a daily basis. As you can see, Foobar controlled minor parts of Syria and Iraq, but that was it. And not big blocks, either—more like a patchwork of disconnected villages.

"Here's how things look today." He clicked to the next slide, which showed the same map now drenched in red. "Foobar's made dramatic gains despite the fact that more countries have joined the anti-Caliphate coalition. The Caliphate now controls most of Syria, where the government holds almost nothing outside of Damascus. If Foobar continues his sweep from Aleppo down into Lebanon, it won't take long before Damascus will have to surrender, too.

"Foobar's also consolidated his hold on almost all of Iraq and is massing his troops on the Syrian border with Jordan. The big surprise last week was the revelation that the Kurds had caved and signed a non-aggression pact with the Caliphate. As you know, the Kurds hate the Turks. We suspect Foobar's agreed to give them all the traditional Kurdish territory in Turkey as well as Iraq in exchange for their standing aside if he decides to take Turkey on. That means he could cross through Kurdish-controlled territory to attack Turkey without having to worry about getting cut off by the Kurds from behind. Yesterday, Turkey put the rest of the NATO countries on notice that if Foobar crosses the border, it will invoke Article V of the Treaty of the North Atlantic. That's the provision that allows one treaty member to require the others to regard an attack on one nation as an attack against the entire alliance and join in the defense of the notifying member. Any questions?"

Koontz leaned forward. "Why would Foobar want to risk that? Haven't we been beating him up pretty badly lately?"

"Yes, but it's not actually much of a risk. The coalition is already hitting him about as hard as it can from the air, and that hasn't slowed him down, since his forces are widely dispersed and billeted in civilian villages as well. On our side, nobody's been willing to commit troops to the ground, and that's not likely to change. The U.S., Germany, France, and the United Kingdom are already in the coalition, and, leaving Turkey aside, the rest of the NATO nations put together wouldn't be able to contribute a whole lot militarily. So he may be thinking he doesn't have a lot to lose by taking the next step. And in the short term—by which I mean six months—he'd be right. Even if NATO decided to commit some ground troops, it can't mobilize a force big enough to matter any faster than that."

Koontz wasn't satisfied. "Still, why try and take on Turkey at all? They've got a real army and air force and a hell of a lot more heavy and sophisticated weapons than Foobar has."

"True, but Foobar's recruiting efforts have been lagging lately. The West has clamped down hard on immigration, and we've been shutting down his social media sites a lot more quickly. Not as many young radicals are making it through now, and the Caliphate does continue to take casualties. So in a war of attrition, he has to lose eventually. But if all of NATO declares war against the Caliphate, Foobar would be sure to claim that the entire Crusader West is once again uniting to stamp out Islam. That would certainly bring in more recruits no matter how hard we try to stop them from getting through. Clearly, he thinks he'll gain more than he loses. And he's probably right."

"That's not really what we're here to discuss," Henderson interrupted. "Thank you, Stuart. We've got a tight schedule, so I'm going to ask Lieutenant Travers to give us the domestic and European threat overview."

Travers took over the remote and clicked through to a map of America. It took a moment for Frank to notice there were four black dots widely scattered across the country.

"These are the only attacks Foobar has claimed credit for in the United States to date. So far as we can tell, they were all conducted by self-radicalized, solo Internet recruits. In other words, we don't believe that any of these attacks was managed and directed, as compared to just inspired, by the Caliphate." She clicked the remote, and a map of Europe appeared next to that of the U.S. This one was pockmarked with dozens of dots.

"Unfortunately, that's not the case in Europe. The Caliphate has claimed credit for all the attacks you see here, and most of the perpetrators had traveled to Caliphate-controlled territory for training before Turkey tightened up its border. So as you can see, there have been a lot more attacks, and directed ones at that, in Europe than in the U.S. But it looks like that's going to change." She clicked the remote again, and now more than sixty dots of various colors were scattered across the map of the United States.

"Every dot you see here represents a break-in we believe was engineered by the Caliphate. Most, but not all, are explosives related. The red dots are all out west, and each one represents a mining operation. Most are copper mines in fairly isolated locations. The price of copper has been in the basement for a couple of years now, so each of these mines was mothballed. Since they aren't closed for good, they still have lots of blasting caps and radio controls on-site but only skeleton maintenance staff. It didn't take more than bolt cutters and a truck to empty out those storehouses." She updated the map again, and only the orange dots remained.

"As you can see, these dots are spread out all over the country. They represent large farms and agricultural supply depots. The target in these locations was ammonium nitrate fertilizer, which can be weaponized into the kind of bomb Timothy McVeigh used on the Federal Courthouse in Oklahoma City."

Frank shot Koontz a knowing look.

"Wait a minute," Koontz interrupted. "If this is going on all over the country, how come it hasn't been in the news?"

"It has but just in the local media, because the people behind the thefts were clever. At the mines, they only took equipment and not tons of explosives—although they could have. And at the farm depots, they took lots of unrelated goods as well as fertilizer and never more than fifty bags of that from any one location. So each of these break-ins looked like a small-time, local job. But that fertilizer comes in fifty-pound bags. If somebody steals fifty bags fifty times, you're talking about a lot of boom. So far, the national media hasn't connected the dots, so to speak, and the administration doesn't want to shine a light on what's going on until it's figured out what it can do to protect the country against an attack."

The chair followed up with a question of his own. "Exactly how much 'boom' are we talking about here?"

"A lot. Enough to make twenty bombs the size McVeigh used. And ten miles away from Oklahoma City, that blast registered over 3.0 on the Richter Scale."

"So now let's talk about the green dots," Travers continued. "There are only two of those, and they're biohazard labs. We're not talking about illegal entries here, though, as it would be tough to break into a Biosafety Level IV lab without word leaking out to the media. What happened in each of these locations is that an audit discovered that some 'weaponized' samples, together with descriptions of how they were created, were never received at their intended destinations— someone was able to change the recipient addresses from legitimate labs to other locations before they were delivered. Unfortunately, there are two Level IV labs in the parts of Syria Foobar controls that we think are intact, so he's got everything he needs to propagate those materials.

"The black dots mark the last type of incident I want to talk about. Each one indicates a power grid or telecom field maintenance office. If you look carefully, you can see that there are about a dozen of these. In each case, laptops and records were stolen. We can't be sure that these incidents are related to the others, but it's awfully unusual for so many of this type of facility to be targeted in a short time frame. Questions?"

Frank surprised himself by speaking up. "Has any evidence surfaced that anyone hacked any computers at any of the break-in locations, either before or after the thefts?"

"Not so far as we can tell."

"Thanks." Well. That was interesting. It was also interesting to learn the CIA believed the Caliphate was being financed from abroad, although it did not yet know by whom.

Frank considered what he'd heard as he drove home from Fort Meade. It seemed that the more he learned, the more Foobar's capabilities and strategy seemed to focus on traditional rather than cyber weapons. But he'd learned his lesson about making up his mind too soon. If Foobar was in fact planning some sort of cyberattack, maybe one of America's other enemies was helping him out?

But who? Despite the hostility North Korea and Iraq continued to vent against America and the more nuanced rumblings of Russia and China, the worst damage from a cyberattack that any enemy of the United States had succeeded in causing to date had not been serious. A government agency website had been taken down for a day or two and personnel records from poorly secured government servers had been stolen. That was pretty small potatoes compared to a real war.

No, he was still going to put his money on explosives. But if he was right, he still had to figure out how and where Foobar would strike.

* * *

That evening, Frank opened the door to his apartment and walked to the head of the stairs, but there was no Marla walking up to greet him. That was odd; she'd pressed the buzzer downstairs as usual to announce her arrival. Then he heard the elevator doors open behind him and turned to see her step into the hallway, struggling with an extremely large, gift-wrapped box.

"Happy Birthday!"

"Now what have you done? Here, let me help you with that."

"Bought you a birthday present, of course. Thanks!" She surrendered the box with relief.

"What in the world did you get me? I'm trying to get rid of things, not get more."

"Oh, don't be such an old poop. This is my greatest gift for you ever! I can't wait to see your face when you open it."

His door had closed and locked behind him, so he tried to balance the package precariously on one raised knee while he struggled to retrieve his keys from his pocket.

"Here. I've got my key. You just hang on tight to that package."

She opened the door and he followed her into his living room, wondering what in heaven's name could be inside the box; it was more unwieldy than heavy, but its center of gravity seemed to shift from one side to the other as he carried it.

"Okay. What do you think it is?"

"I have no idea. I really don't. What is it?"

"You'll have to open it to find out. Go ahead. No, wait a minute." She pulled her phone out of her pocket. "I've got to get a picture of this."

With more trepidation than curiosity, he tore away the paper and began pulling up the tape that held the box shut. When he opened it, he saw another large box, this one made out of semi-opaque plastic. "You ... bought me a storage bin?"

She laughed. "Not just a storage bin. That just goes along with the real present. Take the top off."

He did as instructed and found that the bin was filled with more boxes.

"So you bought me a bunch of packing materials for my move. That's my big present?"

She laughed again. "Of course not. Open that one over there first. I want to see how long it takes you to figure this out."

He opened the box as instructed and found a small heat lamp. He stared blankly at Marla.

"Okay, now open that one."

This time he picked it up to examine it first. On the side, it read, "Pet bedding."

"Oh no. Oh no, you didn't—"

"Okay! Now open that big one!" She raised her phone up to her eye.

"Marla, you can't really have done this."

"Open it!"

He took the last box out of the bin. As feared, it had air holes in the top. And something inside was moving. "Marla, I can't have a pet. They take too much time and trouble. I'd probably forget to feed it—"

"Will you PLEASE open that box?"

Now with unambiguously pure and unadulterated trepidation, he raised the lid and stared down into the eyes of an animal that was staring back up at him. He heard Marla's camera make a sound like a prison cell door's bolt sliding into place.

"You bought me a turtle?!?"

"No! A tortoise! Isn't he great! I found him at a rescue shelter, and his name is Thor!"

"Thor?"

"Yes! I figured he'd be the perfect companion for you. You looked so sad the other day when we were talking about Simone."

"I did not!"

"Yes, you did!"

"I did not, but anyway, are you suggesting a turtle—okay, a *tortoise*—would be an appropriate stand-in for a sophisticated French political scientist?"

"Well, no. But you won't have to walk a tortoise or even talk to it. And don't take this in a bad way, but he kind of reminds me of you."

"I'm having a very hard time thinking what a good way to take that would be."

If that was a question, she decided it was a good one to ignore. "Really, he should be perfect for you. You can feed him just about any kind of vegetables you happen to have in the refrig—okay, let me start that one over. You can buy whatever kind of vegetables you want to feed Thor. When you don't want company, you can just forget about him and leave him in his bin in a closet with his light on and he'll be perfectly fine. But if you want company, you can take him out and let him be in the room with you. Isn't that just great?"

It was not just great. Or even a pale shadow of something way over to the wrong side of great and not even within sight of good, but Marla looked so pleased with her surprise gift he didn't have the heart to point that out. So he summoned up a weak smile, said something about it being a very considerate gift, and gingerly picked Thor up to get a better look at him. The tortoise promptly urinated in his lap.

Marla put her hand up to her mouth. "Oh! I forgot to warn you about that! They said a tortoise might do that until he gets used to you. But after that, it will be just great!" She ran into the kitchen to get a roll of paper towels and then pretended to look at her phone. "Oh! I've got to get out of here! Sorry I can't stay any longer, but now you and Thor can start getting acquainted." She gave him a kiss on the top of his head and beat a hasty retreat.

Frank mopped his crotch with a handful of paper towels and looked down at Thor, now back in his bin and inside his shell as well. How did things like this happen to him?

He retreated to his bedroom to change, and on his return, he noticed one more item in the bottom of the big gift box. He was relieved to see it was a paperback book titled *So Now You've Got a Tortoise!* He opened it up and learned to his horror that Thor would likely outlive him. Why couldn't Marla have given him something more short-lived, like a hamster or an octopus?

He dumped some of the bedding into the bin, clamped the heat lamp on the side, and then walked into the kitchen to find something to put water in. But he'd already thrown out or stored just about everything concave he'd ever owned. He finally settled on a peanut butter jar top, filled that, and set it down in the bin. The tortoise, now out of its shell, looked up at him with an accusatory stare.

"What?" Frank said.

But the tortoise just continued to stare.

With some effort, Frank came to the likely answer. "Are you hungry?"

The tortoise stared.

"Oh, all right!"

Grumbling uncharitable remarks, Frank donned his jacket and stomped down the stairs, returning ten minutes later with a tired-looking, overpriced head of lettuce from the convenience store on the corner. He peeled a few leaves off and dropped them in the bin. To his relief, the tortoise promptly began munching on them. He sat down to watch as the animal consumed one leaf after the other with slow gravity. When it was done, it looked up at him again. He peeled off another leaf and held it forward, wondering if it would eat out of his hand. It stared solemnly back at him instead.

"Now what?"

He was at a loss. What else could you do for a tortoise? For want of a better idea, he picked it up and set it on the floor. It immediately lumbered under the couch and didn't reemerge. Well, if it was happy down there, so be it. He put all the boxes and wrapping paper back into the gift box, and he put that, along with the bin, in a closet. With a sigh of resignation, he picked up his laptop and returned to what he had been doing before Marla interrupted his solitary but settled life with her best gift ever. Within five minutes, he had forgotten all about his new roommate.

* * *

7

Guess Who's Coming to Dinner

T HE DAY HAD arrived when Frank had promised to "meet" Marla's new beau over dinner. It would have been awkward enough if he'd never met Tim before, but playing along with the current situation made him feel cheap and deceitful.

So there he stood, alone in front of a trendy restaurant in the Adams Morgan section of Washington, waiting for Marla and Tim. And now there they were, coming around the corner; Tim looked as uncomfortable as Frank felt.

"So! You're already here! Dad, meet Tim."

"Pleased to meet..." they both said, each starting and stopping at the same instant and then talking over each other again.

Marla laughed. "I said you were both a lot alike. Let's go inside."

Tim hesitated and then walked into the restaurant next to Marla while Frank trailed behind.

When they reached their table, Marla took a seat next to Frank so he could get a better impression of Tim. He decided that Tim was neither particularly good nor bad looking, although he knew Marla's opinion was more favorable. That was all to the good, Frank guessed, and anyway, he'd never understood how women looked at men, or anything else, for that matter. And Tim was very attentive to Marla; she led the conversation far more than he did, and Tim often nodded slightly in agreement when she spoke. Frank concluded that Slattery was a keeper from his perspective as well, and decided he should get to know him better.

"So what did you do your master's thesis on?" he asked during a lull in the conversation.

"Transparency and director responsibility in corporate governance."

"From what perspective?"

"I looked at instances where executives acted in socially undesirable ways and attempted to show that such activities were much less likely to occur in companies with boards that included outside directors who were actively engaged in board committees. I would have preferred to take a look at how politicians behave but couldn't sell that to my thesis advisor."

"Tim's very idealistic," Marla interrupted. "So before you get all grumpy and cynical, keep in mind that some people actually think they can make a difference."

"Okay, granted. But do you think it's even possible for things to get better these days? Look at all the polarization and gridlock. If you wanted to push for any sort of reform, how would you ever get it through Congress?"

"So? Does that mean everybody should just shrug their shoulders and do nothing?" Marla said, turning to Tim. "See? I warned you what a downer he can be."

"Not at all," Frank replied. "I'm just pragmatic. Can you name one person in the last ten years who's actually been able to change anything in Washington in a meaningful way? No? I thought not."

"Well, there's Edward Snowden," Tim interjected.

"Thank you!" Marla said. "There. How about Edward Snowden?"

"Okay, I'll give you that. He really did upset a lot of apple carts when he started releasing secret State Department materials. But did he actually change anything? Not that I'm aware of, and he's been paying for it ever since. I don't imagine that Russia is where he planned to spend the rest of his life when he decided to become a whistle-blower."

Marla realized, too late, that her father was headed down one of his favorite argumentative rat holes, and she wanted to change the subject, but Tim leaned forward and spoke before she could intervene.

"True, but if you want to make a difference, sometimes you have to be willing to make real sacrifices. Otherwise, like you said, things will never change."

"I grant you the guy has a lot of moral courage. But who elected him to decide what to expose to the world?"

"Nobody. But if he didn't let the public know what was happening, who would?"

"Maybe nobody again. And maybe it should have stayed that way for some of what he leaked. Before you put him on too high a pedestal, don't forget that he's no Daniel Ellsberg—the guy who leaked the Pentagon Papers to the New York Times back in 1971. Ellsberg kept to just one topic, exposing how the government was misleading the public about the Vietnam War. Snowden's been leaking information about all kinds of government activities all over the world. And he didn't stick around to see whether the courts would vindicate him, either, the way Ellsberg did."

"Sure. But why limit yourself to one topic, if the public is being misled on other ones as well?"

"But I say again—who was he to decide what to keep secret and what not? He was just an analyst who didn't know everything important. How could he know for sure that he wasn't causing real damage, or even putting peoples' lives at risk?"

"Because he didn't just release things willy-nilly. He enlisted two journalists to help him review the materials first, and then he released the ones they collectively believed needed to be revealed."

Marla tried again. "How about we call this one a draw and look at the menus?"

"Well, okay," Tim said, "but I still think people need to be willing to stand up for what they believe."

"Of course they do," she said, taking his hand. "See, Dad? I told you Tim is very idealistic. That's one of the things I love about him." She turned to Tim and continued. "And don't let my father's old codger act convince you. He's really a closet idealist himself."

* * *

Frank was walking home when his phone rang.

"Hey, Kid. What's up?"

"Like you can't guess," Marla said. "So what did you think of Tim, now that you've finally met him?"

He should have already thought of a good answer to that inevitable question, but he hadn't. "Uh, he seems like a very nice young man."

"Uhuh. 'A very nice young man.' Is that it?"

"I thought that was pretty positive, coming from me. Wasn't it?"

"I guess; I mean, no. I was hoping you'd say that you really enjoyed talking to him or maybe that you thought we made a cute couple—no, scratch that one."

"I'm sorry; yes, I did enjoy talking to him. And I liked watching the two of you together. Does that help?"

Silence.

"Look, I'm sorry," he added. "I don't want to disappoint you; I just don't know what you want me to say?"

"No, I'm sorry. It's just that I think he's pretty special, and I was really hoping you'd think so, too. Look, I've gotta go. Love you."

He stared at his phone and wondered whether he should call back. He decided he shouldn't and wondered whether he was just being a coward.

* * *

The next day, it was back to business as usual.

"How about we settle in over there?" Tim pointed toward a couple of empty couches facing each other at the CIA/Cloud Data office.

Frank nodded and followed him, looking vainly for anyone close to his age among the sixty or so people typing on laptops and engaged in conversation across the wide expanse of open office space.

Tim sent off a quick text when he sat down, and a minute later, a young woman stood up across the room and walked in their direction. Frank stood up to meet her, noting the small diamond piercing on the side of her nose and the magenta stripe that divided her black bangs, complementing her Kelly green blouse, albeit in a rather jarring way. She wore clunky, high-heeled boots.

"Pleased to meet you," Frank said, shaking her hand. She gave him a small smile that was somewhere between polite and "whatever" and sat down.

"I've already given Keri a high-level overview of what we're working on, Frank, so you can dive right in," Tim said.

"Great. Happy to have you on the team, Keri, because we want to come up with some new ways to look for useful information. I'm betting there are clues hiding in the data about Foobar that everyone's missing because they've already made up their mind what to look for. I want to figure out a way to analyze all the data from a fresh perspective, with no preconceived ideas about what might be important. Any suggestions about how to do that?"

"Well, I've got all kinds of data filters. Do you want me to focus on location? Subject? Relation to prior events? I can do pretty much whatever you want."

He shook his head. "No—that's the point. I don't want to tell you what I want, because I don't know yet what I'm looking for. What I want is to make it easy for something—anything—to jump out at me that I might never have thought was important or never even thought of at all. Can you do that?"

"Uh, like I said, I can do anything you want."

"How about this," Tim interrupted. "Why don't we start by listing all the different categories of data we have and then ask the same question again? Even if it doesn't suggest something immediately, it will at least help us figure out whether we need to use different techniques for different types of data."

"Good point," Frank agreed. "So what do we have?"

Half an hour later, they had a list of categories of data, each with subcategories—sometimes dozens of them. There were geolocations, personnel backgrounds, attack types and outcomes, communication relationships between individuals and between groups, educational vitae, travel histories, and much more.

Frank studied the list, trying to figure out whether there was a relatively simple way to address all of them. He picked one at random as a trial.

"So how about geolocation? How should we tackle that one?"

"How about a heat map," Tim asked. "We can use colors to show where the largest numbers of Foobar's people are. And we could do another map with colors showing where they travel and how often. That would make it easy to see something that might be significant, like whether there was a correlation between travel and the frequency and location of attacks."

"I like that," Frank said. "Why don't you make visuals as well as tables of information whenever you can. That will make significant data stand out so we can spot it more quickly and easily."

"I can do that," Keri agreed. "And do maps of other stuff, too. Where supplies are moving, and how much by type, linkages of his people abroad by their assumed role in the organization, and so on."

"Good. Let's try and map as many types of relationships as possible, and especially between data types that haven't been mapped and compared before."

An hour later, Keri and Tim had their marching orders, and Frank was on his way home, already impatient to see what Keri's maps and reports might reveal.

* * *

He had just unlocked his front door when the phone rang. It was Marla. He juggled keys, phone, and groceries as he walked toward the kitchen. "Hi, Kid. How're you doing?"

"I'm fine, but I just realized that I forgot to ask you something last night at dinner. How's Thor?"

Confused, he set the bag of groceries on the table. "Thor?" The name did ring some sort of bell, besides the mythically obvious one. Then his eyelids shot up. Of course! That damned tortoise!

"Oh, he's fine!" Frank skipped into his living room and got down on his hands and knees to look below the couch, trying to cradle the phone between his shoulder and face without dropping it. He was greeted by a number of sausage-shaped objects and a distinctly unpleasant odor but not by a tortoise.

"That's great! And are you two boys starting to bond?"

Frank was looking in the closet now, pushing the boxes around with his foot.

"Oh, you know, I guess as much as middle-aged men and tortoises are likely to. But hey, you caught me at a bad time—I was just about to send something off."

"Okay," she laughed. "You give Thor a big kiss for me, okay?"

"Very funny. Later."

He hung up the phone and stared at the small apartment. It was almost empty now. Where could the perverse creature be hiding?

He started by looking under the bed. No Thor. He tried the bathroom next, to no avail. It took hardly any time to check everywhere he could think of, and there was still no tortoise to be found. He tapped his foot on the floor and tried to reason it out, but he couldn't get anywhere. Where could a ten-pound reptile be when it was nowhere at all?

He gave up. The animal had been missing for a few days already and would just have to stay missing for another few hours. He had work to do, and anyway, maybe if he just sat still, it would get thirsty and come out of hiding on its own.

But it didn't.

* * *

He slept poorly that night, troubled by disturbing, improbable dreams. He imagined he was chained to the wall of a dungeon, imprisoned for a crime he didn't think he'd committed, and in any event didn't understand; he was haunted by strange scraping sounds that might have been rats or perhaps the chains of another prisoner fettered to the other side of the same wall.

When his alarm woke him, he felt dazed and grouchy. He swung his legs out of bed and began work on a serious yawn. But partway through his first step to the bathroom, he threw his hands up in the air and himself backward on to bed with a startled "Whoa!" He had placed his foot on something large, foreign, and cold that was moving to boot. He pushed himself back up to a sitting position and stared down into the critical, frosty eyes of Thor.

"You! You almost killed me! And where have you been?"

But the tortoise just stared back.

"Okay, Okay!" He got out of bed and headed for the kitchen but then caught himself.

"Oh no, you don't!" he said, returning and scooping up the tortoise. Only after it was back inside its bin did Frank procure several leaves of lettuce and some water for the prodigal reptile.

He stood and watched as Thor consumed the lettuce with deliberation. Frank thought he knew every inch of his small apartment after so many years of residence.

How could an almost foot-long animal hide itself where there was no hiding place to be found? He ransacked his apartment again. And once more, he could not find Thor's secret lair.

Throughout the next day downtown, he found his mind returning to the mystery. Eventually he concluded that the only way to solve it was to release the beast and keep it under surveillance.

That evening, he picked the tortoise up and held it at arm's length, looking it square in the eye.

"Okay, I've had enough. Show me."

But when he placed the animal on the floor, it promptly scuttled back under the couch again. Frank sat motionless and waited. Then he waited some more.

Clearly, this wasn't proceeding as planned. It was reptile two, mammal zip at the end of the second round.

Well, Frank wasn't giving up yet. He opened his laptop, selected the extended version of one of *The Lord of the Rings* movies, and settled in to wait out the miserable creature. An hour later, he fell asleep with the movie still playing.

The next morning, he awoke with a crick in his neck and no tortoise under the couch. And the odor in his living room had gotten worse.

All that day he worked away uncomfortably on one of his two kitchen chairs, peering from time to time around the doorframe into the living room, in the middle of which were the peanut butter top filled with water and the remnants of the head of lettuce. The stem of the now venerable vegetable was growing soft at its core, exuding what Frank hoped was an ooze irresistible to a tortoise. But Thor proved equal to the challenge, remaining perversely absent notwithstanding his lengthening fast. When Frank gave up and went to bed, the lettuce was still untouched. The next morning, all but the oozing core had disappeared.

* * *

8

Great Expectations

"FYI" WAS ALL the email from Roach read. Attached to it was a press release from the Responsible Technology Foundation. Mitty opened it and scanned the contents; the RTF had just announced that it had commissioned the Center for Infrastructure Studies, a respected research institute, to do a detailed report on the probable consequences of the physical destruction of data centers. He pressed his intercom button.

"Sue, get Paul Roach on the phone for me."

Five minutes later, she buzzed him back and he picked up.

"Paul, I just read that press release. I'm going to want weekly updates on this. I want you to find out everything that's going to be in that report so you can discredit it before it's public. And what about the release date they mentioned in the press release—can they really put a report like this together in just a month?"

"Reading between the lines of the press release, it looks like RTF commissioned the research a year ago. My guess is that they didn't commit to pay for the full, written report until they saw how the research turned out. They're obviously pleased with the results, so all the institute has to do is formalize what they've already summarized for the RTF. So yes, they should be able to release the report within a month."

"If that's the case, we've got to step things up a notch. I want you to get someone to hack into the RTF system so we don't get blindsided like this again."

"We can do that. That shouldn't be hard to do, if their system security isn't any better than most non-profits. But it will set you back fifteen or twenty K. We don't do that sort of thing in-house."

"Whatever. I want you to see and report to me on every email and draft of that report that passes between RTF and the Center for Infrastructure Studies. And I want to see your proposed talking points debunking it ASAP, as well as a list of who you plan to plant stories with during the couple weeks before the report is released. When can you get those to me?"

"I can get you the placement list this week. No sense working on the talking points until we get hold of a draft of the report itself, but we can turn those around quick when we do."

"Okay. And I also want you to send clippings of those articles to everyone on the Hill we care about. In particular, I want every congressman on Steele's Subcommittee to see a story talking about how all critical infrastructure software and data will be replicated across multiple data centers to ensure that no conceivable attack could take down the Internet in the U.S. or destroy every copy of any important data."

"Is that true?"

"Of course not. And neither was the claim that smoking doesn't harm your health. But your firm kept that one alive on the Hill for decades after the medical establishment was in unanimous agreement to the contrary."

"Just wanted to know where our strengths and weaknesses are. So don't worry, I'm on it."

* * *

There was a knock at Roach's door. He looked up to see Diana Sedgewick, his project coordinator.

"Is this a good time to talk about staffing the DCSA account?"

"Sure. Come on in."

"Great. What's the slot you want to fill?"

"I need someone to do deep research on cyber and physical security requirements for critical infrastructure, and in particular on an advocacy group called the Responsible Technology Foundation. No particular background necessary."

Sedgewick nodded without changing her expression. "Deep research" was the internal code word they used to describe going beyond normally acceptable professional practices.

"Let me see who we've got." She spent half a minute swiping through screens on the tablet she'd brought with her.

"How time consuming will this be?"

"We'll need most of someone's time for the next few weeks."

"Hmm. Looks like everyone who's done DR before is pretty swamped. I think we'll need to break someone new in."

That was unfortunate. Working someone new into that angle of the business was always a bit risky. You had to be sure you picked someone who wouldn't be hostile to the assignment before you got into the details. Roach rather enjoyed manipulating his employees, and liked to handle that conversation himself.

"You sure?"

"Sorry; otherwise, we're going to have to pull someone off some other project, and I can't think of any project where the account partner wouldn't hit the roof."

"Okay. Who do you suggest?"

"Can I get back to you?"

"Sure. It's worth taking the time to do it right. Try and give me two or three names of people who haven't been here that long."

Sedgewick stood up. "Will do."

"Today?"

"Today."

* * *

Roach looked at the summaries of the two candidates Sedgewick came back with. He hadn't known they had an employee by the name of Sean Lynch, but many of his particulars matched well against one of the profiles Roach often looked for in a DR candidate. Poor kid from South Boston. First in his family to go to college, much less grad school. Probably carrying a ton of student debt. Hard worker and hungry to get ahead. Bit of a temper. Already working without complaint on the accounts of two of the firm's most publicly unappetizing clients. Roach noted Lynch had recently changed home addresses, so he might be in some sort of transition and therefore more vulnerable. And he had granted access to his Facebook account.

Roach went to Lynch's Facebook page and clicked back through his posts and pictures. Nothing useful or remarkable turned up at first. Then he saw one that would either seal the deal or disqualify Lynch for the job. It was a picture of him at the beach with his arm around a young woman, and the young woman he had his arm around was Sara Ravitz.

He typed both names into his web search bar and requested an image search. Sure enough, while there was only a single picture of the two of them together at Lynch's page, there were lots to be found on other sites, apparently taken over a period of several years. On a hunch, Roach pulled up the profile that had been worked up on Ravitz and checked her home address against the one Lynch had recently changed. Bingo. They were indeed the same.

He leaned back in his chair. The fact that he'd only been able to find one picture of Ravitz on Lynch's Facebook page indicated that he'd tried to purge his page of every trace of Ravitz, but he had missed one picture. That suggested Ravitz had terminated her relationship with Lynch and he wasn't happy about it. Plus, he had anger management issues. There seemed to be much more to be gained than lost, provided he approached the situation carefully.

He buzzed his assistant. "Michele, book me a quiet table for two at the club tomorrow at noon, and ask Sean Lynch—he works for us—to join me … no, you don't have to check with him first. He'll be available."

* * *

Sean Lynch checked the time on his computer screen for the fourth time in five minutes. Any moment now, he would be meeting Paul Roach for the first time. Roach was not only the son of a founder of Roach & Drye but the partner with the biggest reputation in town. He had no idea why Roach would want to meet him, much less have lunch. But whatever it was, it had to be good.

He looked up to see Roach standing next to his cubicle.

"Ready for lunch?"

"Yes, sir!"

"Not sir—Paul. Sorry we haven't met face to face before."

Lynch shook the offered hand. "No worries … Paul. It's an honor."

Roach smiled. "I thought we'd grab a bite upstairs at the club. Sound okay to you?"

Of course it did. The Federal Club was the old-line, exclusive watering hole where the firm wined and dined its clients. Lynch had never been there before.

"Sounds great!"

So far so good, thought Roach. Obsequious deference to authority was another part of his favorite profile. They were welcomed at the club and immediately led to a table in the corner of the wood-paneled room.

"I don't know how your tastes run, Sean, but the fish here is usually pretty good."

When they ordered, Roach noted with approval that Lynch followed his lead, also opting for the baked haddock.

Roach chatted the younger man up amiably until their food arrived and then got down to business.

"So, Sean, here's the reason I asked you to lunch today. I've heard a lot of great things about your work, and I've been keeping an eye out for a good project that you and I could work on together."

Lynch almost dropped his fork. Like most of the recent hires, he had no idea how well or poorly he was doing. It was something of a sweatshop, with plenty of grunt work for junior staff to do. It took a couple of years before you got access to more challenging assignments, which was when the project managers began to cull the lesser lights from those allowed to advance to the next level. Thank God—he obviously must have made the cut. And he must be toward the head of the list if the big man himself wanted to work with him!

"That would be great. I'd be delighted to work with you on any kind of project."

Roach smiled. So far, so good. But they weren't quite there yet.

"I'm glad to hear you say that. One of the founding principles of this firm is that every type of business should have the right to get its story out to Congress and the public, even if that company isn't popular. People and legislators make snap judgments about lines of business all the time, you know. Take our coal clients, for example. America would never have achieved what it has over the last one hundred and fifty years without a dependable, affordable industrial energy supply. But now? A lot of people want to just shut down all the mines. They don't want to hear anything favorable about coal, even if it's accurate.

"Here at Roach & Drye, we don't think that's the American way. We firmly believe our job is to make sure that all the facts get out there, no matter what the business may be, and then let Congress and those people who still have open minds decide."

Lynch had heard the party line many times, beginning with his first interview with the firm. He nodded approvingly.

"That said," Roach continued, "we want to be respectful of the beliefs of our employees, and we also want to be sure everyone on every team is ready to do his or her very best for the client."

Lynch's glow of self-approval was ebbing a bit. He mostly viewed the conduct of business as an amoral matter and didn't spend much time thinking about the behavior of any particular company or industry. But he knew that not all of his friends looked at the business world that way. They enjoyed tweaking him about what they insisted on referring to as his "mercenary tendencies." And he was furious over being dumped by his long-time girlfriend because of his job.

"I'm sure I wouldn't have any trouble working on any account the firm decided to take on."

"I'm glad to hear you say that—I appreciate the show of faith. Still, let me tell you a bit about the client and then give you the names of some of the groups that are critical of it. It's called the Data Center Security Association. It develops and promotes physical and cybersecurity standards for the new data centers that are popping up all over the place to support cloud computing. An enormous amount of computing is already done in these centers. Give it a few more years, and just about nothing will run anymore on servers located at businesses, universities, laboratories, governments, trading floors, or you name it. I know your minor was computer science, so I expect you probably know more about this than I do."

Lynch was flattered Roach knew this much about his background. "Yes, I'm pretty current on computer trends. Cloud computing takes most of the burdens of security, updating, and maintenance off a business's shoulders and centralizes it where service providers can worry about all those things, maximizing efficiency and lowering costs for customers."

"Excellent! I'll have to run our talking points by you next time before we send them to the client."

Lynch was glowing again. He'd always heard that Roach was a tough guy to work for, but the man who was buying him lunch sounded more like his favorite uncle. But Lynch was also slightly puzzled; why would Roach think he might have any reservations? DCSA sounded like a Motherhood and Apple Pie association compared to some of the other accounts he was working on.

"Unfortunately, there's always someone out there that sees problems with everything. In the case of cloud computing, most of those people are expressing concern about security. Not that that's not a concern, of course. As a matter of fact, that's what DCSA was formed to address—it's a standards setting organization that develops holistic security standards for all aspects of running a data center, from setting up the systems to establishing and maintaining perimeter security to vetting staff. But that's still not enough for some people. One group is even worried that, somehow, someone's going to blow all the data centers up unless we bury them fifty feet underground, if you can believe that. Can you imagine how much that would cost?"

Lynch could, more or less, and it did sound absurd.

"So—any qualms so far?"

"Absolutely not." Lynch thought he'd show off a bit more. "The IT industry has been headed this way for years. Even Homeland Security has moved all of its software and data from thousands of locations to just four cloud computing centers. I expect that they ought to know something about security, physical as well as cyber."

"Excellent again. It sounds like you're an even better match for this team than

I imagined. So here's some more background. One of the things we've been doing is helping DCSA prepare the way for Congress to adopt the DCSA standard into federal legislation, instead of asking some agency that doesn't know what it's doing to draft detailed regulations for data centers. Congress references private sector standards into law all the time, although most people aren't aware of it. In this case, Congress was really quite interested in taking advantage of the good work DCSA has done, and the speaker of the house, no less, introduced a data center cybersecurity bill that incorporates DCSA's core standard verbatim. In a few weeks, we expect both houses to approve that bill and send it off to the president for signature. But groups are still trying to block it."

"Excuse me, but why? It sounds pretty straight ahead to me."

"It is straight ahead, but every bill has enemies. Maybe someone would make more money if there was no law. And another someone thinks their own business model will be threatened if the bill passes. And somebody else is a nervous Nellie that sees doom hiding around every corner. Make no mistake about it, some of these groups get pretty down and dirty. In fact, I'll share something with you confidentially that we don't tell most people in the firm."

Roach leaned a bit closer, and Lynch reciprocated with a thrill. The big boss was sharing information with him—a second-year employee—that more senior staff might not know!

"Nobody in our business wants it to become common knowledge in the press, but in this town, everyone's hacking everyone else's computers now, and that includes non-profits on the hacking side. If you're not playing the same game, you're going to get screwed. Most of our clients know that their computer systems are getting hammered, and if we can't help them stay ahead of the opposition, they'll go to one of our competitors. It would surprise you some of the questions I get asked when we're being interviewed by a potential client."

Roach stopped abruptly, waiting for a reaction to what he had just said. Non-profits hacking their perceived enemies was news to Lynch, but he tried to look like the kind of sophisticated man of the world who would have expected nothing less.

"I guess that's just the kind of world we live in today," Lynch said with a shrug.

"Indeed yes. Sad but true. So let me list a few of the organizations on our opposition list. These are the ones that we already know are against cloud computing data centers." Roach had made up the list to provide camouflage for mentioning the RTF, and he watched Lynch intently as he walked through it.

"First there's the Latter Day Luddites. They're kind of a guerrilla theatre fringe group, out of Berkeley, California, that's very anti-technology. Then there's the Citizens for Sane Technology. Same outlook, but a more conventional approach. And then there's the Telecommunications Industry Coalition. They've been serious trouble, because they see data centers putting lots of price pressure on their members. But we've been able to outflank them so far. And finally, there's the Responsible Technology Foundation. They're the nervous Nellie group I alluded to that thinks someone will bomb us into the Stone Age if we build data centers aboveground."

Lynch had been listening politely until he heard the last name. Roach watched as a range of emotions flickered across Lynch's reddening face, beginning with surprise, progressing to confusion, and at last settling on wide-eyed satisfaction. Success! That was the look Roach had been hoping for. Lynch had sensed the opportunity for revenge and liked the way it smelled.

"So are we good to go?"

"You bet!"

"Excellent!" Roach stood up and clapped him on the back. "In that case, let's go downstairs and get to work!"

* * *

A week later, Mitty received a hand-delivered envelope from Roach & Drye. Inside was a document with one of Roach's business cards paperclipped to it. In the upper right-hand corner appeared "DCSA Report – CIS Draft 1.3," and the title of the document read, "An Analysis of Probable Effects Arising from the Destruction of a Critical Percentage of Centralized Computer Data Centers."

"Sue, get Paul Roach on the line."

"Will do." Less than a minute later, she buzzed him back. "It's Paul."

Mitty spoke before Roach could say hello. "How bad is it?"

"Pretty bad. I haven't gotten a detailed readout from one of our own experts yet, but you don't get sloppy work from the Center for Infrastructure Studies. According to the executive summary, destroying any randomly selected thirty-seven percent of the big data centers would take down substantially all essential systems and services. If the enemy knew the right ones to hit, taking out as little as twenty-eight percent of the total would take everything down and keep it that way until the destroyed centers were rebuilt, which would be impossible with the Internet unavailable.

"On the impact side, they've concluded that an attack during the summer would result in the death by starvation, thirst, and other causes of at least half of the U.S. population within one month, with most of the rest to follow within three months. If we got hit any time from November through March, the one-month total would rise to seventy-five to ninety percent, depending on how cold it was. Then..."

"That's enough. I want everyone you've got with the right skills to pick apart every piece of data, and every assumption made, in this report. Find out about the individual authors, too—see if any of them has ever messed up in the past. And what about Ravitz—what have you been able to get on her?"

"Will do on the new requests. On Ravitz, so far, nothing useful. She leads a quiet, ordinary life. Never juiced her résumé. No drug use, even in college. Only drinks socially and then moderately. Highly regarded professionally and personally."

"Well, if she's never screwed up in her professional or private life, you're going to have to do that for her. I need something we can use if we need to that will make people question her motives and her credibility. Can you do that?"

"As you know, we've done that kind of work before."

"Good. Well it's time to do it again."

* * *

Lynch now had a brand new email stream to monitor: his ex-girlfriend's account at the Responsible Technology Foundation. He hadn't had to get his hands dirty, either. Someone else had done whatever it was that was necessary to set up a reflector on the RTF server that bounced a copy of every inbound and outbound email from her account straight to him. Better yet, they'd also set things up so he could not only impersonate Ravitz, sending emails the recipients would think came from her, but only he would receive their responses.

He was enjoying himself immensely. He'd been smarting mightily since she had given him the gate. The opportunity to get some payback on that humiliation was sweet indeed—especially since she'd have no idea she was being shadowed. If he was sufficiently clever and restrained in sending emails in her name, she'd never realize she was being impersonated either. He'd have to hold that tactic in reserve for when he needed it most.

Lynch found he had no qualms about what he was doing. Quite the opposite. After all, who was she to say she could no longer live with someone who worked for a lobbying firm with unsavory clients? It wasn't as if that kind of employment was against the law. And from what Roach said, these holier than thou non-profit groups were playing just as fast and loose as the people they were always trying to pillory in public. That said, he couldn't believe Sara would ever dream of hiring someone to hack into someone else's computer system.

So much the better. That would just make it easier to be sure his client won and she lost.

* * *

Several days after his last disappearance, Thor had lumbered nonchalantly out from under the couch while Frank was working there, as if the tortoise had just nipped in there a half an hour before to catch a quick catnap. After that, Frank and he reached a truce of sorts. Thor now spent most of his time in his bin in a corner of the living room, content, to the extent Frank was capable of judging his mental state, to reside within its limited, translucent confines. If Thor needed broader horizons, he would make scratching sounds, and Frank would remove him and set him down on the plastic bag, which now protected the cushion of the couch that was not already occupied by Frank. Then the nominally more cerebral of the two would place the usual lettuce leaves and water down as well, and Thor would enjoy his dinner. After that, he would stare at Frank for a while before going to sleep.

It wasn't much of a relationship, to be sure. But Frank eventually got used to it. After all, he'd had worse.

* * *

9

(Don't) Take the A Train

FRANK WALKED OFF the D.C. to New York air shuttle and hurried away from the gate. As usual, the flight was late, and naturally, the line to get a taxi was endless as well. When he eventually fidgeted his way to the front of the queue, he jumped in the cab and slammed the door. A minute later, the taxi was winding endlessly through the Byzantine exit pattern of the airport, and Frank was once again immersed in preparing for the meeting.

A half hour later, a rising tide of honking penetrated his concentration.

"Where are we?"

"Brooklyn. Traffic is messed up like I never see before. Nothing is moving on BQE, so I take side streets."

"To where?"

"I figure Williamsburg Bridge is best bet. We know in a minute when I turn up ahead."

The driver started speaking rapidly into his headset in a language Frank didn't recognize; he looked at the driver's picture and name on the license hanging on the seat back and guessed it was Arabic.

But nothing was moving when they reached Roebling Street either. So much for arriving on time at the first meeting of the combined Tiger Teams he'd flown in to attend.

The cabbie looked over his shoulder. "What you want I try next?"

"Give me a minute," Frank said, opening a traffic app on his laptop.

"Wow!" He pushed the map around with his finger. "Everything heading into Manhattan is solid red—there's nothing moving anywhere."

The light changed, and the cab driver crossed the intersection. "So?"

"Give me a minute." Frank studied his traffic app again. "Take your next left, and when you get to South 3rd Street, take a right. That street should take us all the way to the riverbank. Maybe we can see what's going on from there."

Damn it. He was sure to be late now. He'd better let someone know. He pulled out his phone, and as soon as he entered his password, it began rapping out a series of emergency news alerts.

> ***Ping!*** *NYT 9:39 AM: Section of lower deck of George Washington Bridge fails; scores of cars fall into Hudson River*
> ***Ping!*** *NYT 9:45 AM: Flooding abruptly closes Lincoln Tunnel*
> ***Ping!*** *NYT 9:48 AM: Explosion in the Holland Tunnel stops all traffic; flooding reported*
> ***Ping!*** *NYT 9:55 AM: Explosion on L Line subway may leave hundreds stranded below ground*
> ***Ping!*** *NYT 10:05 AM: Mayor declares state of emergency; asks all New Yorkers to await instructions*

Frank looked up in confusion at the quiet, neighborhood street they were following to the river; the driver was holding a rapid-fire conversation again over his headset. There was a muted TV on the seat back, and Frank saw the picture cut to video of the president's helicopter rising rapidly from the lawn of the White House. It barely cleared the trees before it leaned into a tight turn and roared off. Marine Two and Three took off a moment later, departing just as quickly. Two of them would be decoys, so no one would know which chopper carried the president. What the heck was happening?

Frank turned the sound up on the television just in time to hear a loud boom; the news camera swiveled up and around to catch a squadron of F-16s decelerating over the Jefferson Memorial before diverging to follow the helicopters off in three different directions. The announcer was saying something about trying to make sense of contradictory reports coming in from New York City.

At the end of the street, he and the cab driver got out. All up and down the river, helicopters darted and hovered, disappearing and reemerging like dragonflies over a forest pond, as they flew between buildings and over bridges. Along the FDR Drive, red and white lights on squad cars and emergency vehicles rebounded between the windows of the high-rise apartment buildings that lined the river, and countless sirens competed with the horns of stalled cars in a cacophonous din of impatience and fear.

As he tried to make sense of what he was seeing, Frank realized that the helicopters in the air weren't traffic and commuting aircraft but police and military choppers. On the river, police, Harbor Patrol, and Coast Guard Zodiacs were roaring up – and downstream to no immediately obvious purpose. And something seemed strange about the Brooklyn Bridge off in the distance; he thought he understood the angle that he was viewing it from, but it still didn't look right.

It took him several seconds to realize that one of its two towers was missing.

They got back in the car.

"What do they say on the television?" the cab driver asked.

"Nothing useful so far." He went back to fiddling with his laptop. "There's a restaurant on the corner a couple blocks back that's open all day. They probably have a couple of TVs in the bar we can watch. Let's go back there and try and find out what's going on."

Minutes later, they were entering one of the gentrifying neighborhood's trendy new establishments. The dining room was empty; a few tables displayed half-eaten meals. But they could hear a news broadcast coming through a doorway that led them into a bar room lit by dusty sunbeams streaming through a band of windows set high in one wall. The missing restaurant staff and customers were inside, staring up at the large screen TVs mounted on the wall behind the bar.

* * *

There was something surreal about sitting in a hipster saloon in Brooklyn as the first details of the horrors that had just occurred began to emerge. And yet there was no point in leaving. Every New York airport, and every subway, bus, and train station, was now shut down.

Just as on 9/11, employers everywhere in the metropolitan area were starting to send their employees home—if they could get there. The bar room gradually grew more crowded as released workers looked for a place to wait for the hopelessly gridlocked streets to clear. On the screen Frank was watching, the local network affiliate cut to a news team that was still setting up to broadcast from a riverside park in Hoboken, New Jersey. The skyline of lower Manhattan behind them provided a jarringly calm backdrop.

The reporter took the handoff and began to speak.

Chet, things are eerily quiet on this side of the Hudson. As you can see, it's a spectacular fall day—just like 9/11. The sun is out and the temperature's unseasonably warm. But underneath the Hudson and the East River, we're told there could be as many as ten thousand commuters drowned in their cars. And that's before you take the subway and train tunnels into account—they've been hit, too. We don't have any good figures yet on how many trains were targeted—all of the communications lines in the affected train tunnels were knocked out by the blasts.

We also can't guess yet how many may have been killed on the bridges leading into Manhattan. All of them have gaping holes in their traffic decks, and some have far worse damage. People stuck in cars near where the truck bombs went off never had a chance. It's just awful.

What about rescue crews, David? Have they been able to do anything?

I can't answer that, Chet. But I've got Irving Mandel from the New York City Office of Emergency Management Watch Center standing by, and he'll be able to bring us up to date. Mr. Mandel, can you hear me?

The screen switched to an archival still picture of the face and shoulders of a city worker.

Yes, I can.

Mr. Mandel, what can you tell us about the rescue operations that are underway? Have many people been saved from the tunnels?

Unfortunately, very few. We assume that everyone that was below water level who wasn't killed outright by the blasts died before they could figure out what happened or what to do about it. The only ones that had a chance were in cars near the ends of the tunnels opposite where the blasts occurred.

Do we know anything more about how the attacks were carried out?

Yes. The first stage of the attack began about 9:00 AM, when the terrorists drove dump trucks filled with explosives into the tunnels heading in both directions. These were the biggest explosions by far—the trucks might have held as much as six tons of explosives apiece. When they got close to the end of one of the tunnels, but while they were still under the river, they turned the trucks sideways to block both lanes. Then they waited for the traffic to back up. We can't be sure, but we're investigating whether they used spotters, or maybe even small drones, at the other ends of the tunnels to let them know when the cars were packed in tight all the way back. At about the same time, other trucks performed similar maneuvers on the main bridges connecting Manhattan to the other boroughs and New Jersey, and the traffic backed up there, too.

At rush hour, that wouldn't take long, would it?

No, traffic was already pretty slow in each tunnel to begin with. Same thing with most of the bridges.

Then what?

They detonated the explosives everywhere at close to the same time. Using dump trucks in the tunnels was obviously a deliberate choice: they have very heavy steel floors and sides, which helped direct the force of the blasts straight up, blowing through the tunnel casing overhead and the riverbed above that. Then the water rushed in.

The video cut to a shot of the New Jersey entrance to the Holland Tunnel. Huge emergency lights had been set up to illuminate the traffic lanes until they disappeared underwater. Divers were suiting up in an almost certainly vain effort to rescue survivors.

How many people would have had a chance to get out?

It probably varied. The Holland Tunnel seems to have filled very quickly—it could have been as little as ten minutes. The Lincoln Tunnel took longer, maybe twice as long. I don't know what anyone could have done to save themselves in either of those tunnels. The Queens Midtown Tunnel didn't flood at all—although it is completely blocked by the rubble created by the explosion. For most of the people in that one, it wouldn't have made much difference, though. In an enclosed space like that, the blast wave from the explosion must have been horrifyingly lethal for most of the way back to the other shore. And then it would still have shattered every windshield, as well as peoples' eardrums. The lights would have gone out immediately, too.

How about in the subway tunnels?

The video feed began sampling subway entrances around the five boroughs. Some were blocked by yellow police tape. At those near the river, teams of first responders wearing aerators and carrying stretchers and medical supplies were hurrying down stairs.

Those are a different story. The terrorists couldn't carry enough explosives onto a train to flood a tunnel without being noticed, so their goal was to block the tunnels and kill as many people as possible. Tragically, it appears that the bombs were also incendiary devices; we're getting reports that many of the subway and train cars were totally incinerated; it must have been horrible for the people packed into those trains with no way to escape.

That's terrible—were any of the trains able to evacuate before the bombs went off?

No. Again, all the bombs went off at almost the same time, and in any event, the explosions wiped out all means of communication. It took a while before the transit authority had any idea what had happened. And once again, the terrorists timed things for maximum effect. First, they detonated bombs on trains that were just about to arrive in Manhattan. We've only reached one of those trains so far, but the explosives on that one were powerful enough to derail the front car and turn it into a hash of metal blocking the tunnel. Then they detonated bombs on the rearmost cars of trains that had just left the last stops in Queens, Brooklyn, and the Bronx. Those bombs had the same effect, so both ends of the tunnels are clogged with wreckage. Until we can get that cleared away, we can't easily reach anybody or any other trains that are trapped in between.

How many commuters do you think are on those trains?

There are twelve trains unaccounted for. I don't have the exact number of cars yet, but trains typically have eight to eleven cars.

Okay, so let's say a hundred twenty cars. About how many people would that be?

Most of the trains would have been packed at that hour, so it could be ten, maybe even twelve, thousand people in all. Everything's an ungodly mess down there. We have no idea how many people were killed or injured or how long it will take us to reach all of them. We're trying to put crews together equipped with acetylene torches to cut a passage through the wreckage at each end of every tunnel, but that's going to take time; it's not the kind of situation we've ever trained to deal with at this kind of scale. It could be twenty-four hours or more before we're able to get to some people down there. I'm afraid that by then it may be too late for some of the injured. And we haven't even talked about the commuter trains and tunnels yet.

Frank tried to imagine the screaming terror and chaos reigning below ground. Some or all of the cars in the trains that had been bombed would have lost their emergency lighting, leaving wounded and unharmed passengers alike in total darkness, surrounded by the dead, with no idea how long it would take to be rescued. How many of them would die in the dark before they were?

This was beyond anything Frank had ever imagined—dwarfing even the carnage of 9/11. He glanced away from the screen. It was completely silent except for the voices coming from the televisions and someone sobbing quietly in the back of the room.

That's terrible. Things are hopefully better on the bridges though, right?

The video cut to live aerial footage, showing huge holes in the decks of bridge after bridge; on some, there was only a tangle of steel beams and cables where a supporting tower had stood only a couple of hours before.

Well, our ability to get to those who could be helped is better there, yes. But we have no idea how many cars went into the river, and these rivers are deep; we have to assume that everyone in those vehicles drowned immediately. That said, we believe the main goal behind all this may have been to cut off Manhattan as completely as possible.

Why do you say that?

We can't know for sure unless whoever is responsible tells us. But if they wanted to show what they could do to the strongest nation in the world, well, I think they've made their point.

Frank felt his skin grow clammy; if his flight had been on time, he could have been one of those wretched souls heading into the city who were talking on the phone or reading the news one minute and the next suffocating in a taxi in the pitch-black depths of the East River with no idea what had just happened.

Will it take long to get the bridges operational again?

It's too early to tell. We'll need to do a detailed engineering study of each one. On the suspension bridges, they stopped the trucks right next to the towers that hold up the roadways. We think they may have shaped the force of the explosives in some way there, too, so that most of the force this time would go to the side. The Brooklyn Bridge could be unsalvageable, and that may be the case for some of the others as well. I don't see any of them reopening for months.

Some of the people surrounding Frank began murmuring over that revelation; it was beginning to dawn on them that it could be a very long time before people could get on or off Manhattan in any normal way.

We'll let you go now, Mr. Mandel. Thank you. I'm sure you must be needed elsewhere.

You're welcome.

I see that we've just gotten through to Jules Olafsson, the medical disaster coordinator at Bellevue Hospital. Mr. Olafsson, can you hear me?

The camera cut to a grainy Skype feed of a man wearing a headset.

Yes, I can.

Thank you. Did I pronounce your name right?

That's fine.

Can you tell me, sir, what's being done to evacuate and treat the injured?

Well, as you know, we've made lots of progress preparing for disasters since 9/11. But it's hard to plan for every type of attack. One thing we never anticipated was that such a high percentage of our first responders and hospital staff might be unable to reach Manhattan, or heaven forbid, even be among the dead and injured. When current personnel come off shift, there won't be nearly enough trained staff to replace them. We'll have to ask anyone that can reach their hospital, firehouse, or ambulance station to keep working as long as they can stay on their feet.

What have you been able to do?

We've gotten to almost all of the injured on the bridges and started to move those most in need of care to hospitals. We've been able to do very little so far for anyone that may be injured in the subway and train tunnels. The mayor has asked that all cabs and private vehicles stay off the streets so that emergency personnel can get the injured to hospitals as quickly as possible.

Is that working?

For the most part, people on Manhattan are being pretty good. But it's still a challenge. We don't have enough ambulances, so we're transporting the ones first that won't survive without immediate care.

Will you have more help soon?

How? Manhattan's cut off! The terrorists hit every single one of the major bridges and tunnels that link Manhattan to the rest of the world! We don't have enough open beds in Manhattan to treat those we need to evacuate from this side, so we're starting to medevac patients out to surrounding hospitals, especially where they require special care. But there are only a few helipads on the island. Our disaster plans call for the Coast Guard to take charge of setting up additional landing areas in Central Park, but I don't have any information on how that's proceeding.

How about in the other boroughs?

Everything should be easier at the other ends of the tunnels and bridges, because there are more hospitals in the surrounding area where the injured can be taken. But people haven't been as good about staying off the streets there. A lot of folks are trying to get out of New York any way they can in case the attacks aren't over yet. But that's never easy even when you can go through Manhattan. Every road north and east is bumper to bumper, and there's no way to go west, except on the Verrazano Bridge.

Thanks very much for that important information, Mr. Olafsson. Chet, back to you.

The camera returned to a somber newsman seated at the network studio. Covering the screen behind him was a still picture of a fireman carrying a small, badly injured child in his arms.

What a terrible, terrible day. For those of you who may just be tuning in, as many as fifteen truck bombs, each believed to be carrying two tons or more of explosives, shattered the automotive tunnels and bridges leading into Manhattan today, beginning at approximately 9:20 AM. An unknown number of smaller bombs disabled or trapped at least twelve subway trains underground. Multiple commuter trains were attacked as well.

In an extraordinary feat of coordination, all of the bombs were detonated within five minutes of each other, effectively cutting off the more than 1.6 million people who live in Manhattan from the rest of the country and stranding as many as 2.4 million commuters that had already arrived at work. At least ten thousand people are feared to have died in the four tunnels serving Manhattan. A much smaller, but still unknown number, died on Manhattan bridges. Officials estimate that perhaps twelve thousand commuters may still be underground, trapped in subway and commuter train tunnels, an unknown number of whom have been killed or injured.

Coming up next: The president will address the nation at noon; ferries from throughout the metropolitan area and the surrounding region are pressed into service to bring much-needed medical supplies, first responders, and food into Manhattan and evacuate the injured; and what we know about the man assumed to be behind today's horrific attacks.

Frank had seen enough. He stood up to leave, and the cab driver followed him. They weaved through the crowd and entered the dining room.

"I wonder who did it?" Frank said.

"I don't want to think. I think about my family instead," the cabbie replied.

Of course, he would. Lots of kids commuted to school in Manhattan by subway. And everybody would immediately assume Foobar had just carried out his threat. The backlash against Muslims would start immediately, even if no one could tell for sure that the Caliphate was responsible. Frank fumbled for his wallet and pulled out fifty dollars.

"Here—don't worry about sticking around for me."

The cab driver nodded his thanks and plunged into the crowd outside. Frank stood alone in the deserted dining room, trying to figure out what to do next. With a shock, he wondered what the fate of the rest of the Tiger Team members might have been? Tim had taken an earlier flight—where was he? Frank dove into his pocket for his phone just as it rang—it was Marla—he should have thought to call her immediately.

"Thank God, you answered! Are you okay?"

"Yes, I'm fine—totally fine."

"Thank goodness! I've been calling you nonstop for the last half hour! All the lines have been jammed with too many calls! Where are you?"

"Brooklyn. I never got close to the bridge. How about Tim?"

She was crying now. "I haven't spoken to him, but I got a text from him saying he was okay before I even knew what was happening. But I didn't know what had happened to you."

"Where is he?"

"I don't know; somewhere in Manhattan."

"Why don't you try and reach him then. And don't worry about me. Really, I'm fine."

"Well, be sure you stay that way, and come home soon. I love you."

"Love you, too. I'll let you know when I can get home. Now go connect with Tim."

"Okay."

He stood there for quite a while, feeling numb and not knowing what to do or where to go.

Outside, crowds of people hurried by, each one totally absorbed by what they were seeing on the mobile devices clutched in their hands, trying not to believe that the horrors that seemed to be obliterating the world around them could possibly be real.

* * *

10

Foobar's Manifest Destiny

EVERYTHING WAS CHAOS in the days that followed. Confusion and fear reigned as families near and far sought to learn the fate of loved ones and the city struggled to get back on its feet. Rescue teams fought heroically to save victims who were almost certainly already dead. And federal and local officials wrestled with the challenges of a crisis of a magnitude they had never imagined could actually occur.

Forty-eight hours after the attack, several of the members of the multiple Tiger Teams were still not accounted for. The most recent one to be tracked down was unconscious and in critical condition at a hospital in Queens; she had been injured by the blast that took down the west tower of the Brooklyn Bridge. Gene Ensign, Hermann Koontz's Whiz Kid, was missing and feared dead.

Frank was on his way back to Washington by the evening of the day of the attack, courtesy of a CIA bus sent north to collect any Tiger Team members lucky enough to be outside Manhattan when all hell broke loose. They were picked up from the various points they'd reached before gridlock set in. As he gazed through the tinted window of the bus, Frank couldn't help imagining he was watching a World War Two news reel of citizens feverishly evacuating a city facing imminent attack.

Thousands of travelers were far less fortunate. As the bus moved slowly along side streets, he looked across highway barriers into the eyes of motorists stuck in their cars on roads leading to now-destroyed tunnels and impassable bridges, impatiently waiting their turn to back up a mile or more to an exit ramp. Some would certainly still be there after he had arrived home.

Overhead, he heard a constant stream of private and military helicopters shuttling the critically injured from the subway and train tunnels to any hospital that was able to accept them. The news stream he was monitoring told him that commuter ferries were hard at work at the Herculean task of draining the island of millions of commuters a few hundred at a time. Until they did, those still stranded would have no place to sleep and little enough to eat. On the return trips, the ferries carried whatever food could be rushed to the docks to feed the millions who could receive food no other way until the bridges and tunnels were restored.

But getting commuters, business travelers, and tourists back across the Hudson or the East River was just the first step; after that, they needed to somehow be returned to wherever they lived. For commuters, that could be as much as a hundred miles away. And for everyone else, it could be anywhere in the world. Passing a high school, Frank saw relief workers setting up hundreds of tents on football and baseball fields as a transit camp to warehouse and feed the evacuees until a way could be found to return them to their homes and families.

Later, sitting exhausted but alert in the darkened bus as it neared Washington, he realized for the first time how deadly serious his work for the CIA was. Until now, the enemy had seemed abstract and far away. Now, it seemed to be everywhere around him. When the cars were towed from the tunnels and raised from the riverbed, he knew that he would recognize names. Most of those he'd grown up with in his working-class Brooklyn neighborhood still lived there or nearby; many must have been victims or had relatives who had been killed or injured. All would be feeling the emotional and economic aftershocks of the bombings for a long time to come.

The next morning, Tim was still stuck in Manhattan, so Frank joined Marla to watch the round-the-clock newscasts covering the disaster. Most of the footage was simply a mind-numbing, repetitive montage of horrific scenes, accompanied by the same inadequate information that had already been repeated dozens of times before. But little by little, more details surfaced. They were watching as the most significant news broke.

We've just received word that a major announcement is about to be made on behalf of Mullah Muhammed Foobar. The expectation is that he will claim responsibility for the attack on New York. Please stay with us as we switch to a live feed courtesy of a CCB team filming on-site in al-Raqqa.

Frank recognized the dusty square instantly. He'd viewed the same one, vastly expanded in size, on the wall of the CIA conference room. As before, an enormous crowd was gathered, facing the high balcony on which Foobar's spokesperson invariably appeared.

Hello, Liz. Can you hear me?

There was a pause while the question and answer cycled halfway around the world and back.

Yes, Dick. Very well indeed, thank you.
Can you tell our viewers what we're looking at?
Yes, certainly. We're standing on the roof of the Hotel International overlooking the Place of the Martyrs, the new name Mullah Muhammed Foobar gave to the square after taking the city thirteen months ago and declaring it as his capital.
What are we expecting to hear today?
We anticipate that at any moment Sheik Tariq ibn Ziyad will appear on behalf of the Caliphate to claim responsibility for the New York attack.
Why do you think that will happen?
As you know, Dick, one of the reasons the Caliphate has been so successful is its mastery of communication. Indeed, one of Foobar's first acts after seizing al-Raqqa from ISIS was to announce the formation of a Caliphate Ministry of Media Relations. Earlier today, we were given a press release, under embargo until just a few minutes ago, and told to expect a full translation of the Sheik's address immediately following its completion.
That's rather remarkable, isn't it?
Yes, but that's not all. We're told that he will also announce that more attacks are on the way.

The news anchor paused, looking shaken.

More attacks! That's really bad news. Is there anything more?
Yes, but they're holding back on the details. All they've said is that we should expect an announcement that's even more momentous.

As she was speaking, a tall man in flowing white robes stepped on to the balcony above the square, and the camera zoomed in. The crowd rewarded him with a thunderous roar of approval that grew even louder when he drew a curved scimitar from the red sash around his waist and brandished it in the air.

Is that the sheik?

Yes. We're told that Ziyad is a member of Foobar's innermost circle.

Another figure appeared briefly on the balcony and handed something to the sheik. The crowd fell silent as he sheathed his sword and unrolled a scroll, holding it before him at shoulder level. When he began reading, his voice boomed across the square, broadcast by speakers on all sides.

Can you tell me what he's saying?

He's extolling the virtues of Foobar and condemning the evils of the West. It's sort of a warm-up act the Caliphate always uses to get the crowd energized.

What is he talking about, specifically?

Oh, the usual complaints about Western society: its decadence, its obsession with material wealth, its slavish reliance on technology. She paused. *Wait a minute. Here it comes…*

Wild cheers overwhelmed her voice before she could finish. When at last the din died away, she resumed.

Yes, that was it. He's just announced that dozens of martyrs who swore allegiance to Foobar carried out the attack on New York after months of careful planning. He said their success proves the righteousness of the cause. She paused again.

Now what?

He's saying that this is merely the modest prelude to attacks that will be even more devastating, followed by a final assault that will annihilate the West forever and herald the coming of the end times.

The end times? I thought that was only a Christian concept.

Not at all. Christianity, Islam, Judaism—they all share the same roots and honor many of the same prophets, including Jesus. Muslims don't believe he's the one that will return at the end of the world, though.

You say, 'not the one.' Do Muslims believe in a second coming of some sort?

Oh yes, quite. Almost all Muslims, Sunni and Shiite alike, believe in—

She stopped abruptly and turned her back to the camera, staring out over the square as the sheik finished speaking and disappeared from the balcony.

For a single moment, there was utter silence. Then the square erupted into bedlam, as the crowd cheered hysterically; some fired automatic weapons into the air.

The newscaster turned back and began speaking rapidly.

Sheik Ziyad has just announced that Mohammed Mullah Foobar has revealed himself to the world as the Mahdi. This will be viewed as truly momentous news across the entire Islamic world. At least, by those that believe him. According to...

Hold that thought, Liz, while we pause for a brief commercial break.

* * *

Marla turned to look at her father as the channel cut to a detergent ad. "What's a Mahdi?"

"He's the figure the newscaster was just about to talk about—the rough corollary to Jesus Christ in Islam, whose return was foretold not long after Mohammed's death. His arrival is supposed to lead to the defeat of evil in the world, leading up to the Day of Judgment itself."

She gave him a puzzled look. "And you know this why?"

He knew this because his briefing materials included a crash course on Islam, but he wasn't about to say so. "Why shouldn't I know this? You're not the only person in the family who's been to school you know. It just annoys you that I know something you don't."

Which was also true, but she wasn't about to say so, either. "Okay, so tell me more."

"Most Muslims agree that there is someone, referred to as the Mahdi, that will return, but there are a lot of variations on the theme. To Shia Muslims, the Mahdi is the Twelfth Imam, a direct descendant of the prophet Mohammed. They believe he disappeared around eight hundred seventy-three when he was very young and has been hidden ever since—they call this the Occultation—awaiting his appointed time of return. When he does come again, he's to rule for seven years, returning justice to the world, leading up to the Day of Judgment.

"If Foobar can get enough people to believe that he's really the one who has been awaited for so long, that could be real trouble; thousands, maybe even millions, of people might rally to his banner. Pretty shrewd move on his part, I'd say."

"I guess so. I wonder what happens next?"

* * *

The vast majority of Muslims throughout the world were appalled by Foobar's savagery and rejected his declaration out of hand. But his announcement was met with joy and celebration by some. Coming immediately after his stunning attack on New York City, it was particularly effective in persuading the desperate and disaffected Islamic youth of many countries to rally to his banner. Spontaneous celebrations broke out in cities and villages throughout North Africa, the Middle East, and across Europe. In France, thousands of young, unemployed men in downtrodden Arab neighborhoods poured out of their tenements and into the streets to riot throughout the night, burning hundreds of cars. For twenty-four hours, the police dared do no more than watch, for fear of inciting even worse violence.

Meanwhile, the administration found itself in an impossible position: the public expected the military to throw everything it had into an immediate and punishing response. But Foobar had prepared the Caliphate's forces well, dispersing his troops into the countryside and mountains over the days preceding the attack, leaving the U.S. with enormous firepower but almost nothing to target.

Frank spent most of the next three days watching archival video footage of the rise of the Caliphate and poring through the new briefing books the CIA circulated to the Tiger Teams, reading everything he could find about Foobar. Which, regrettably, was not much.

No one knew where he had grown up or what he had done before he emerged on the scene less than three years before. There was not a single confirmed picture of the man, or even a verifiable, firsthand sighting of him by anyone from the West. The CIA wasn't convinced he actually existed. One school of thought held that an inner circle of Islamist radicals collectively controlled the Caliphate and had concocted Foobar as a convenient fiction to fulfill historical prophecies in order to lend legitimacy to their cause.

Some of what Frank learned was even stirring, in a schoolboy adventure sort of way. Take Foobar's generals, for example. He watched footage from the Caliphate's site showing Foobar's commanders leading his armies into battle, each mounted on a pure white Arabian steed and armed with nothing but a sword—a scene straight out of first millennium history. The sight of such fearless warriors rushing pell-mell into battle against enemies firing state of the art modern weapons left Frank grudgingly impressed with their courage and conviction.

But there was a macabre element to the same story: each general demonstrated his unconditional allegiance to Foobar by sacrificing the little finger of his left hand, an act he was required to perform himself, using his own sword.

As Frank watched the evening news over the days that followed, he witnessed victorious troops in pickup trucks "liberating" city after city as joyous crowds lined the road and cheered. Each day the tide of red spread farther north, east, and south on the map displayed by the news anchors. And there appeared to be no end to their advance in sight but the sea.

* * *

11

To Catch a Thief

F RANK HAD A message on his phone, and the calling number wasn't Marla's. That was unusual, as his contacts with the outside world, such as they were, were conducted almost exclusively by email. He dialed up his voicemail and listened.

Hello, Mr. Adversego. My name is Sara Ravitz, and I'd like to discuss an issue I'm having at my business. I believe that someone is hacking my computer network, and I need to find out how to stop it. If you're able to take on any new business at this time, I'd like to arrange an appointment. My number is...

He scrabbled in his pocket to find a pen and replayed the message. How about that. A real client at last! He'd been so preoccupied trying to flush out Foobar's intentions that he'd avoided thinking about how he was going to make a living after the CIA project wound up.

Then he scowled. What right did he have taking on new business with Foobar on the loose? Still, right now, he didn't have anything to do until Tim and Keri got back to him with the results of their latest research. And that would likely take a few more days. Why not see whether this was a project he could fit in?

Then he scowled again. He'd been using Foobar as an excuse to put off finding a real office instead of admitting that avoiding interacting with anyone face to face was the real reason. Time to bite the bullet on that one.

* * *

Frank was feeling uncomfortably bogus as he waited in the small conference room for Sara Ravitz. It had cost him a five-hundred-dollar shared office facility membership fee for the right to sit for one hour in a room he might never use again. Promptly at 2:00, there was a knock at the door. It opened to reveal a dark-haired, earnest-looking young woman perhaps a few years older than Marla.

She held out her hand. "Mr. Adversego? Hi, I'm Sara Ravitz."

"Pleased to meet you. Did the receptionist offer you a cup of coffee or something?"

"Yes. I'm fine. Thanks for seeing me on such short notice."

"No problem at all. How did you find out about me?"

"I went online looking for a cybersecurity firm and ran into your site. I've read your book, so, of course, your name was familiar to me. I'm sure my problem isn't as interesting as what you're used to, but if you have time, I'd like to engage you to help me out."

He cringed at that; so she'd read the exaggerated account of his first adventure his ghostwriter had concocted. Thank goodness, she hadn't mentioned the imaginary wolverine.

"I'd be happy to. What is it that you'd like me to do?"

She frowned. "This isn't the kind of thing I'm used to dealing with. Where would you like me to start?"

This being his first client meeting, he had no better idea than she did.

"Wherever you'd like."

"All right. Well, I guess it would help for you to know something about the non-profit I run. It's called the Responsible Technology Foundation."

"Yes, that would be helpful. I've spent some time at your website, but I'm sure there's a lot more to know."

"Oh, good. Then you already know that our mission is to hold technology companies accountable if they don't operate in a socially responsible manner. In the past, we've focused on issues like the environmental impact of improper disposal of electronic equipment and exposing the exploitation of workers by contract electronics manufacturers in places like China and Vietnam. Most recently, we've started looking into the vulnerability posed by concentrating computing resources and records in cloud computing data centers. Is that something you're familiar with?"

If only she knew. "Yes, I'm very current on how vendors are trying to persuade customers to convert over from local to cloud hosting. I assume you're concentrating on cyberattacks?"

"Yes, we worry about that, but there are enough other groups covering those risks already. We think we can be most useful by making people aware that physical attacks could be far more dangerous, since a cyberattack doesn't usually damage the actual equipment. As, of course, you already know, an enemy conducting a cyberattack might be able to take the targeted system down for a while, but you can generally restore operations fairly quickly. True, an enemy could also delete or corrupt data, but if that data was backed up at a couple of other data centers, the attacker would have to attack almost all of them to have a catastrophic impact. We believe that physically destroying a much smaller percentage of the data centers would be sufficient to crash just about everything and keep it that way, so that's what we've been focusing on."

Clearly, Ravitz was going to get no argument from him, but it didn't seem prudent to dwell on the topic for too long.

"Thanks, it's helpful to me to have that context. Why don't you tell me a bit about why you think your systems have been compromised?"

"Sure. Well, first of all, shame on us—we haven't been as proactive as we should have about system security. We're quite a small organization, so we don't have any IT staff of our own. We use an outside service instead and let them worry about setting things up properly and keeping them secure. Until recently, we haven't been aware of any reason to be concerned. Now I'm not so sure."

"What have you noticed?"

"Nothing on the system itself—everything seems to be working just fine. But I'm worried that someone has been accessing our files to get information they can use against us."

"In what way?"

"As you might imagine, we're not too popular in some quarters, so there are always people out there who would love to see us slip up. We're very careful not to let that happen, but unfortunately, there are some vendors and groups out there that are perfectly willing to spread damaging disinformation about us. Usually it's pretty obvious and only gets believed by people who don't like us already. But lately we've been taken by surprise several times in ways that I don't think could happen unless someone had direct access to our systems."

"Are you sure someone that works for you isn't leaking information?"

"I expect everyone says that they're sure that couldn't be the case, but I really don't think that's it. We've only got a few staff, and they've been with me for years.

We're more like a family than a business. Plus, they're true believers in our cause, and I can't imagine any of them would want to damage our reputation."

"Sometimes people get into debt and do things they wouldn't normally do to get out of it. Or someone could be blackmailing one of your employees."

"I know, I know. And if we don't find another explanation, we should come back and look into that as a possibility. But I don't think we need to start there."

No problem, thought Frank. The first thing he'd need to do would be to figure out whether the RTF had been hacked, and if so, how. He could worry about who was responsible later.

"That's fine. It makes sense to start where the odds are high rather than low. So maybe you could give me an example of something that has aroused your suspicion?"

"We're planning on releasing a new report on the effects that the destruction of a significant, but not overwhelming, number of cloud computing data centers would have. We spent a good part of this year's research budget to commission one of the top computer science institutes to write it. We're very pleased—well, that's a strange word to use in this context—with the predicted results, which are even more disturbing than we expected. The report makes exactly the case we need to show Congress why it must require that all data centers either be limited to much smaller, more widely separated facilities, to make it much harder to destroy a meaningful percentage of them, or be buried at least fifty feet underground in order to make them much harder to damage.

"But—here's the problem. Other than issuing a press release a few weeks ago, we haven't shared any of the results or the methodology used to conduct the research with anyone yet. This week, though, stories started popping up that are targeted at debunking data center physical security concerns. And it's worse than that: the articles seem tailor-made to undermine the credibility of our report before it's even released. For example, some of the attack examples used in the articles are identical to those used in the report."

"Couldn't that be just a coincidence? I mean, there's only so many ways to stage an attack on a data center."

"Yes, but not in such detail. For example, one hypothetical scenario is that someone bribes a maintenance worker to take a couple of small incendiary devices to work every day for a month, and he hides them all over the data center he works in. After the devices have been installed, whoever is behind the attack sends a signal to all of them simultaneously. The resulting fires take out most, or all, of the servers in an entire facility; servers have a lot of flammable materials in them, you know."

He did know, but he'd never thought of this scenario. It was a pretty good one, too. He wondered whether Foobar had thought of it, too.

"You're right. If they got down to that level of detail, it would be a stretch to think that two different people would think of exactly the same scenario. Could you guess who might have hacked your system from where the articles appeared?"

"No. They appeared within a couple of days in several different media outlets and then got picked up and amplified in lots of others. It's hard to tell whether that was just the normal news cycle in operation or whether the same person that planted the stories also promoted them to other journalists and bloggers."

"Okay. So do you have any idea who might be likely to be behind the leaks?"

"I could come up with a list of people and organizations that don't like us, but it wouldn't be a short one."

"That's okay; this has been very helpful. It sounds like I should start by performing a forensic audit on your system. We can worry about who might be hacking it after we figure out how they did it. Can you set me up with an account, a password, and full admin access to all of your software and data?"

"Of course. I'll have our service provider email the information to you. Oh"—she caught herself—"Or maybe I should give them to you over the phone?"

"You're a fast learner. Yes, that would be a good idea. If you want to get in touch with me, don't text or use email. Do you have a personal phone as well as one you use for work? Good. That will be the best way for us to keep in touch. I should be able to get back to you within a few days with the results of my forensic review. Would that be quick enough?"

"That would be fine. Can you give me an idea of how much this would cost?"

"Let me take a look around your site first. That will give me a better idea. Would that be satisfactory?"

"That would be fine." She stood up and shook his hand again.

"I'll look forward to working with you," he said. "Oh, and one last question—do you know where your system is hosted?"

"Yes. I thought you might ask, so I called our IT service to find out. I guess it's no surprise, but it is kind of ironic. Our IT contractor uses a data center cloud service. It's called WeBCloud. Their prices are supposed to be great."

Ravitz turned to leave but stopped when she reached the conference room door.

"Oh! I almost forgot—I meant to tell you how much I enjoyed that scene where you were fighting off the wolverine at your campsite! I never realized there were any wolverines in Nevada!"

* * *

Frank was seated in the middle of his living room on his decrepit couch, the single item left in that room now that the search and destroy mission against his belongings had been completed. He'd begun by triaging everything he had accumulated: the largest category had been determined to be junk: unread magazines, out-of-date computer gear, paperwork of no current relevance, and objects with no remaining sentimental value. They had been immediately consigned to the dumpster.

The next category comprised items of nominal value for which he had no realistic use. These were somewhat more difficult to acknowledge, since it didn't make him feel particularly good to admit that a kitchen including two place settings and a one-quart soup pot would be adequate to meet his actual needs. He decided to compromise by retaining some extra place settings and never-used cooking gear in case someone ever opened one of his kitchen drawers or cabinets; there was a limit to how pathetic an image he was willing to present to the world, no matter how infrequently, if ever, he was visited by a human being other than Marla. Everything else in this category he dropped off at the neighborhood thrift shop.

Considering the little that was left, he wondered whether he should be moving into a rented room at the YMCA rather than buying a condominium. That would spare him the need—or worse yet, the urging of Marla—to go shopping for additional furnishings. Either prospect was dispiriting enough to direct him back from daydreaming to the topic at hand.

On the cushion next to him sat Thor, thoughtfully contemplating a stalk of celery Frank had placed in front of him. Together they were watching the evening news, a habit he'd acquired after the New York attack. Despite his direct access to high-level intelligence, he felt oddly compelled to be part of the shared experience of the population at large, who only learned of the latest terrible developments through the mass media. And it helped him keep perspective as well. Tonight, for example, the lead story focused on China's increasing bellicosity. He watched as its second aircraft carrier was commissioned while seemingly endless squadrons of fighter planes roared overhead. Meanwhile, Russia was voicing extreme displeasure over China's military buildup, and a growing chorus of nations along the Pacific Rim was calling for Japan to amend its constitution to permit it to re-arm to help offset China's increasing military might. The world seemed to be going to hell in a hand basket with even more determination than usual. If the U.S. weren't so preoccupied with the threat posed by the Caliphate, who knew what Washington might be doing in response?

Frank offered another piece of celery to Thor.

"Whadaya say, big guy? Is that enough identification with the masses for one day?"

Thor didn't seem to have a particular opinion on that topic but deigned to accept the celery. Frank figured that was close enough and switched off the news.

Watching Thor's slow but methodical deconstruction of the celery stalk, Frank reflected on where to go next on his project for Sara Ravitz. He'd just finished scanning the Responsible Technology Foundation website, which hadn't taken long. It was fairly modest, although it did have a back end that was password protected with different levels of access for major donors and RTF staff. As he had expected, the level of security the cloud service provider offered was fair but not impressive. Still, everything looked perfectly in order. He moved on to the virtual server at the WeBCloud site that hosted the other software the foundation used. The protection was no more robust, but everything seemed to be fine there, too. Not a back door to be found.

He drummed the fingers of both hands. If the site was secure, where could the issue be?

He realized he didn't actually know much about the leaks themselves—just that scenarios were getting to people who shouldn't have them. Where again did those scenarios come from? He checked his notes. Right. A research institute. So whoever it was could have hacked that site instead, and that would be a touchier investigation to pursue. If Sara didn't want to share her concerns with them, or if they were unwilling to give him a password, that would be the end of that line of inquiry.

Of course, if all the hacker was interested in was the report the institute was working on, he wouldn't have to hack either site on an ongoing basis—just intercept Sara's email or the email of someone cc'd on her email.

He used the administration credentials he'd gotten from Sara to access the RTF's virtual email server and scanned through the information he found there. Sure enough, there it was. Sara's email address had been converted into a group address so that any email sent to Sara's address would automatically go to anyone in the same group, which now included one additional address besides Sara's. That address had also been made an automatic bcc on every email Sara sent. He checked out the address and found it led to a server in Romania. But that might just be the first in a number of reflectors between Sara's account and the real address of the person shadowing her. And in any event, whoever was monitoring her could have hired a Black Hat to do the job rather than doing the dirty work himself. Frank could find someone on the dark Internet in fifteen minutes willing to set up such an elementary means of exfiltrating data.

Should he delete the extra address?

No. Not yet.

* * *

Frank was ensconced in his usual corner at the data center, surrounded by a no man's land of empty seats. He was pleased that the younger set had figured out that the unreconstructed curmudgeon who frequently took up residence there was best left alone. He booted up his loaner laptop and began working through the extensive spreadsheets and associated graphics Tim and Keri had put together and began reviewing them.

Three hours later, he finished poring over all the geolocation data and communications materials, pondering the nature of the Caliphate's suspected financial assets and those to whose care they had been entrusted, and puzzling over the travel preferences of its leadership. He was also knowledgeable now regarding the beard styles and tea brands favored by Foobar's inner circle. There seemed to be no type of information the CIA believed to be devoid of potential significance, and hence, everything made its way into the agency's infinite databases.

But instead of feeling better informed, he felt as if he had been stampeded by an endless wave of gerbils. How was he to find the right snowflake in the middle of such an avalanche of data?

He picked up another report, this one titled "Key Word Frequency," to see what words might stand out from the rest.

True to Frank's request, Keri had applied no filtering or judgment to her searches. All she had done was segregate a given type of data and then rank what she found. In this case, she had determined one of the words used most frequently of late by the management and minions of the Caliphate was "Hellespont." That word came in at number five this month. He flipped back in the report and saw it had first made the top one hundred words list three years before. Since then it had risen slowly but gradually, before rising dramatically this year and spiking to the top position on a recent date before drifting down again. The great majority of the other words were far less enigmatic, comprising places, objects, words of religious significance, and other everyday usages.

The date of the spike was the date of the New York attack. Finally, he might be on to something.

If so, the challenge would be to figure out what to do with this clue. He couldn't think of any explanation for the trending of the word other than that it was a code word for the New York attack itself. If that should prove to be the case, he should also be able to spot messages associated with Foobar's future attacks. But how would he know far enough in advance which word related to an attack and not something else? And beyond that, the knowledge wouldn't be worth much if the place name Hellespont had simply been randomly selected rather than chosen due to a particular association with the target. If the latter was the case, it might help him spot code words assigned to new attacks in preparation. That might be too much to hope for, but it seemed to be the best lead he had to work with.

So what could the connotation of that word be, assuming there was one? Hellespont sounded vaguely familiar, but he needed to go online to remind himself why. The answer was simple: it was the ancient name for the narrowest part of the waterway that connected the Black Sea and the Mediterranean, also known as the

Dardanelles. That seemed hopeful, as there were many historical connotations to that strait. He began to investigate them and soon learned there were too many possibilities to make divining the correct one an easy task.

For starters, the Hellespont was often referred to as the cultural boundary between Asians and Europeans. Was that all there was to it? Or had the word been chosen because the Hellespont was the site of the Gallipoli debacle during the First World War, where Great Britain and its Commonwealth allies suffered an ignominious defeat with appalling casualties at the hands of the Turks? Both possibilities were plausible, but in either case, the connection was too loose to suggest that New York City was the target.

Or did it relate to the doomed lovers, Hero and Leander? Legend had it that Leander swam the Hellespont every night to be with Hero, a priestess of the goddess Aphrodite. According to the legend, one night a storm blew out the temple light that guided him across the dark waters, causing him to drown, after which Hero threw herself from the tower to her death. If so, the connection escaped him completely. So also with the tale of the Golden Fleece, a passage of which held that Helle, the daughter of Athamas, had drowned there.

But then he read of a piece of history that intrigued him: the greatest historical event associated with the Hellespont was its crossing by Xerxes, the emperor of Persia, in the course of his failed attempt to conquer the Greek city-states. In order to reach them, his engineers had constructed a wondrous bridge supported by hundreds of ships anchored side by side—an astonishing feat, given the technology and materials of the day.

But a storm swept the entire enterprise away before his army arrived. According to the Greek historian Herodotus, the emperor was so enraged that he ordered his army to punish the waterway by giving it three hundred lashes, branding the swift currents with red-hot irons, and throwing hundreds of shackles in for good measure. After that, he had the bridge rebuilt and marched his great army across. But a violent storm destroyed that floating bridge as well, leaving the remnants of his now-defeated and decimated army stranded on the European side of the waters until the bridge was restored yet again.

That had to be it; Foobar had destroyed the bridges—and tunnels—of his arrogant foes, leaving them stranded. What better code name could there be for a plan to destroy the approaches to Manhattan? It all fit together perfectly.

He shut his laptop with a satisfying click. Now he was getting somewhere. The next step would be to get Keri started on looking for other words that had trended in a similar way in the past and, more importantly, any that were starting to take off now that didn't have a different reason for doing so.

* * *

12

Who? Me? Oh, Nothing

FRANK SAT ERECT in his seat at the weekly Tiger Team meeting, anxious to share the news of his discovery with the rest of the team. But anything that wasn't on the agenda would have to wait for the "other business" agenda item at the end—assuming there was any time left to get to that item. The most he had been able to do was let Henderson know that he'd like to bring up something at the end of the meeting.

Frank's tapping fingers beat a tattoo on his thighs while the voices droned on. The main item for discussion was how the planning and execution of the New York attack could have been carried out so effectively without detection. He could tell from Henderson's intensity in driving the discussion that the CIA and FBI must be taking a heck of a beating from Congress and the administration for failing to detect and prevent that attack. Frank would be the hero of the day when he finally got a chance to tell the team he'd taken the first step toward thwarting Foobar's next assault.

Or at least a potential hero. Tim and Keri had only had one day so far to pursue his theory, so there hadn't yet been time to discover any new code words. Still, they had discovered that every other paragraph directly following the one in which Hellespont appeared always had noticeable syntactic dissimilarities from the rest of the text of the communication. This suggested that the code word had two purposes: first, to identify the attack in question and second, to signal when the coded part of a message would begin and how it would proceed. Tim and Keri were now going back through the hundreds of Hellespont messages to analyze what each coded paragraph had in common as a first step toward cracking Foobar's cryptography. Frank had no idea how long this might take, since there could be additional layers of camouflage to be detected and decrypted before they had the keys they needed to extract the real meanings of the coded messages. But that would be someone else's job after Frank revealed his discovery.

The team finally reached the last regular agenda item, a presentation by Fermi, the NIST researcher. Despite his impatience to reveal his own discovery, Frank found himself listening with increasing attention as the computer architect described some interesting predictive ideas of his own. Fermi had worked up a program that identified suspicious activity in email traveling to and from U.S. recipients and diverted it to systems that could automatically strip out the flagged text before delivering the edited results to their intended destinations. The really clever part of the program he'd written was that it included an artificial intelligence component able to stitch the remainder of the email back together without leaving obvious holes in its syntax or structure. Given sufficient resources, Fermi said he expected he could create a beta system capable of handling heavy email traffic within a few weeks.

How great would that be, Frank thought. If you could intercept all of the Caliphate's most important communications with its hidden operatives in the U.S., you could combine Fermi's and Frank's work to discover and prevent any more attacks from occurring, and the Caliphate's embedded agents wouldn't even know it.

The team was clearly impressed with Fermi's initiative, especially after he was able to handle their questions and criticisms with ease. He finished with a request for a team of appropriately skilled developers who could help him turn his initial work into a usable program.

The chairman had been oddly silent until now. "That's very impressive, Bill. You're certainly to be congratulated for your ingenuity and insight. Based on what you've told us, I think that your concept has great promise."

"Thanks. How soon do you think I can get the additional resources?"

"That won't be a problem. In fact, I'll stick my neck out and say that I'll get this staffed within forty-eight hours. Ever since the hit we took in New York, we can get pretty much anything we ask for, and fast."

"That's excellent! Perhaps you could talk to the NIST director, too. He'll also need to make this a priority. I'll need his backing to expedite the administrative end of bringing the developers on board. We don't usually have to do anything on a rush basis over at NIST."

"Of course, you don't. That's why we'll need to handle this inside the Agency instead. We've got the security, the space, and the talent out at Langley that can support this right away."

"Uh, I guess that makes some sense. I'll have to figure out a way to explain my sudden absence at NIST, since no one other than the director knows I'm involved with this project. But that shouldn't be too hard."

"That won't be necessary. The role you're playing on this team is far too important to lose you now, as shown by what you've just presented. No, we need you to keep doing exactly what you're doing now. Who knows what breakthrough you'll come up with next? And I'll be sure your contribution will be properly acknowledged in our final team report."

Of course, you will, you toad, thought Frank. *You'll acknowledge it in the last footnote on the last page of the final report you produce two years from now, so long after you've claimed all the credit for a breakthrough so soon after the New York attack that no one will ever notice it.*

Fermi opened and shut his mouth once before finding his voice again. "But I think we'd make much faster progress if I personally supervised the project. Just turning a summary and some undocumented code over to people with no prior involvement will be terribly inefficient. They might even end up heading down the wrong track."

"I'm sure that won't happen, once you write out a detailed report of everything you've achieved to date, which I'll need by close of business tomorrow."

Frank felt sorry for Fermi. He was now slumped down in his chair with his daybook and Tiger Team materials still perfectly aligned in front of him but his plans in a shambles. His pocket had just been picked under his very own eyes, and he knew there wasn't a damned thing he could do about it.

"So that takes us through the formal part of the agenda," Henderson continued. "I know that there's something Frank wants to bring up. Does anyone else have any business to bring before the team? Nothing else? Okay, Frank. Over to you."

Frank made up his mind in an instant. "Thanks, but we ended up covering the same observations I wanted to make during one of the earlier agenda items."

"So much the better. We've all got work to do."

* * *

"So how long has this been going on?" Sara asked after Frank briefed her by phone on what he had learned.

"It looks like they made the changes to your email setting about two weeks ago."

"This is terrible."

"I hate to add insult to injury, but I should point out that the same person may have compromised your personal email account as well. I haven't done anything to check that out yet."

"Don't bother. I'll feel safer if I change everything immediately."

"You certainly can, although I haven't fixed your office email account just yet. Before I did that, I thought we should talk through the costs and benefits of making a change versus leaving things as they are."

"What possible benefit could there be to let someone continue to cyberstalk me?"

"Well, first of all, if I change the account settings back for your office account, he'll know that you're on to him. That would be okay, if the result was that he left for good. But it's also possible he'll just hack his way back in again and use a different technique to see what he wants. Then we'd be in a whack-a-mole contest, never knowing for sure when he's a step ahead of us and grabbing information until we find and plug the latest leak. Or, if all he's interested in is that report you're going to release, he could hack the institute's system instead. If he did that, you'd think you were safe, but in fact, he'd still be doing damage."

"But I still don't see the benefit of doing nothing."

"Sorry—I didn't mean to imply that you wouldn't do anything different. I was going to suggest that you set up new personal and work accounts with an unrelated ISP and use them whenever you want to keep things safe. The benefit I had in mind is that a situation might arise where you might want to use the old accounts to leak disinformation to whoever's trying to undermine RTF's mission."

"Okay. I get what you're saying, but I'm going to have to think about it. Not only is it pretty creepy thinking that someone's shadowing me, but it would be a pain to dual-track my email. I'd always have to think about when I cared and when I didn't about who would be reading it, and I might forget and slip up, too. For that matter, I wouldn't be able to use the new account very often, or the hacker would notice the drop in traffic."

"All true. So how about this. Just in case your personal account has also been compromised, why don't you switch that account immediately to an ISP with really strong security, so you don't have to worry about your personal communications at all. For the office account, we'll set you up with a second account with a different service provider, and you can use that for sensitive information."

"I take your point, but I'm still going to have to think this over. My main concern is plugging the leak, and I don't know whether I'll ever have a situation where I want to spread disinformation."

"So let's talk about that for a minute. You already know that they're trying to undermine your report before you release it, right?"

"So it seems."

"And also that you can't stop those stories from popping up, right? So that's another whack-a-mole problem, yes?"

"Well, I guess so."

"But if you change the scenarios in the report and work in new data to confront the FUD issues your opponent is planting, it would make the articles that have already appeared irrelevant."

"'FUD'?"

"Fear, Uncertainty, and Doubt. It's an acronym for what someone tries to inspire when they play this sort of game. Their goal is to confuse and worry those you're trying to influence and leave you constantly scrambling to address their criticisms rather than advancing your cause."

There was silence at the other end of the phone for a while.

"Okay. You've given me a lot to process. Give me a day or two, and I'll get back to you."

* * *

Sara not only decided to accept Frank's recommendation, but she rose to the challenge splendidly. She recruited the research institute to fork the current draft of the report in two directions. The first one, which they would continue to trade back and forth using her old email address, would modify the scenarios slightly to introduce flaws in reasoning and conclusions that her opponent would be certain to exploit. The second version, exchanged using a new email address, would introduce entirely new scenarios that did not incorporate those flaws and would rebut the FUD their opponent was already spreading in the technology media.

* * *

13

My, How You Do Run On

"SO, DAD, WHY don't you just stay with me? I can sleep on the couch, and you can have my bed."

"Won't Tim mind?"

"Please! First of all, that's none of your business, and second, he doesn't stay here every night. He's got his own apartment. If it bothers you, I can just go stay with him when we want to spend the night together."

"Maybe I should use his apartment instead."

"Would you please grow up? You're always bragging about what a rational modern adult you are, and here you are sounding like a jealous ex-husband instead of my father!"

As she expected, that was too weird for even a rational modern adult to deal with.

"Okay, okay, you're right. I'm sorry. I just don't want to be in your way."

"You won't be in my way."

"I know. But I'll feel like I am."

"So what's your alternative? Staying in your camper? You're not allowed to do that on the street, so what does that leave? The Wal-Mart parking lot? That would be too ridiculous even for you."

It wasn't, actually, but there was no need to admit it.

"I haven't decided yet. Maybe I'll take a bit of a vacation."

"You? A vacation? Since when do you go anywhere on vacation?"

"I don't know. I covered an awful lot of miles on my cross-country trips. I usually had to keep moving, so I drove by all kinds of interesting places that would have been fun to spend some time at."

"Name one."

"What is this, the Spanish Inquisition?"

"Maybe. I'm waiting."

"Well, maybe that island off the coast of Maine, for example. It was really beautiful up there, and I didn't get a chance to see everything."

"Like what? Like the only other restaurant on the island?"

"What a typical city girl response. People go to Maine from all over the country. It's scenic, it's peaceful, it's...well, that's enough. It would be the perfect place for me to—"

"Write a book? Sorry. Not buying it."

Damn! Why had he brought her up to be so good at this?

"Look. I'll think about it. But I know that you and Tim have a good thing going here, and you don't need your old man hanging around your apartment like a lost puppy for a couple of weeks."

"Don't you think I can handle that?"

Of course, she could. But he couldn't handle this charade of pretending he had no other contact with Tim than through her. What if they slipped up and started talking shop in front of her?

"Look, like I said, I'll think about it. Can we leave it at that?"

"Okay, yes. For the time being. When do you have to move out?"

"Pretty soon."

"Okay. I'll be in touch."

I bet you will, he thought. But he had other plans.

* * *

Frank was running in place, waiting for the light to change, when someone materialized at his elbow, also in running gear.

"Hey, Frank!"

"Hey, Tim. Do you run this way every day?"

"Not always. I like some variety, so I mix it up."

"Well, since we're headed in the same direction, how about we get up to date while we run? It'd save me a trip downtown today."

"Works for me." It more than worked for Tim; he'd sensed that Frank felt uncomfortable at the office and knew from Marla that her father ran every morning. It hadn't been hard to pull off the "accidental" meeting.

"So here's what I've been thinking," Frank began as they headed toward the National Mall. "I still think looking for a cyberattack is a waste of time. My latest thought is that it's also counter to Foobar's whole approach."

"In what way?"

"Well, according to the briefing books, a big part of his fundamentalist pitch to the faithful is that he doesn't accept anything developed after the Prophet's time. And he totally rejects the West's values and reliance on technology, right?"

"Right, but he also bends the rules whenever it suits him. He lets his troops use artillery and guns, for example."

"Yes, but in his writings he points out that the Chinese had gunpowder and cannons when the Arabs began conquering the world."

"And tanks? Trucks?"

"Okay, so yes, he bends the rules. But he doesn't have planes or drones. He says he rejects those."

"Well, he's only captured a few planes, and no drones. Plus, he doesn't have any trained pilots. I bet the anti-modern bit is just talk to cover up the fact that his army is way out-gunned and there's nothing he can do about it. And don't forget, his people use social media all the time to recruit more followers."

"Okay, I'll let that idea go then. But I still don't see the big risk as a cyberattack, as such."

"What does 'as such' mean?"

"It means I agree that it makes sense for him to attack our cyberinfrastructure, but not electronically."

"So you're still convinced he's going to attack the Internet infrastructure using explosives or some other physical approach."

"Right."

"But that could never be as bad an attack as he's been claiming he's going to pull off. Everything's too spread out. And according to what we heard at the last Tiger Team meeting, Foobar must have used up most or all of his stolen fertilizer on the New York attack. Even if he used ten times as many bombs as he did last time, the most he could do would be to take out pieces of the Internet. After all, it was designed from the start to route messages around any parts that go down."

"He wouldn't have to take the whole Internet down to prevent everyone from using it."

"What's that—some kind of riddle?"

"Well, maybe, in a way. But it's not hard to solve, when you remember that everything's run out of data centers, now that everyone's moving to cloud computing. Nobody has servers at their own facilities anymore—not even Hillary Clinton. Everybody's software is hundreds of miles away, and people just connect via the Internet without knowing or caring where their system is physically hosted. And it's not just their software, either—all their data's there, too. Take the data centers out, and the entire country shuts down immediately."

"But there must be thousands of locations out there, with built-in redundancy for each one, so if you took one farm out, your data would have been backed up at two or three other locations."

"Yes to the second. No to the first. It's not thousands, and it's not even hundreds."

"Really? Why would that be?"

"Because cloud computing hosting is a commodity business. There are only a few big providers, and it's more efficient for them to centralize their operations as much as they can. Why have hundreds of locations if you can have only a couple dozen? And don't forget—the electrical cost of running hundreds of thousands of servers is enormous. Over two percent of all the energy consumed in America is used by data centers, so if you own twenty percent of all those computers, you sure as hell want the cheapest power you can find. So that means putting the data centers near the cheapest sources of electricity."

"Okay. That makes sense."

"And then there are other concerns—unless you put your data center in the Arctic or at the bottom of the ocean, where the water is barely above freezing— which some providers are actually talking about doing, by the way—you also need lots of water for cooling, too. On top of that, all the big companies are being pressured to go green, because of global warming. So wherever there's cheap renewable energy, you see data centers popping up like mushrooms."

"Like where?"

"Well, think about it for a minute." Frank wished Tim would quit asking questions or run more slowly.

"Okay, I guess, hydro would be the best source, because it's cheap, green, and constant, and then after that solar and wind, cost-wise. And I guess you'd also want to have your operation as near to the highest use areas as possible, since data takes time to go back and forth and customers want instantaneous response times."

"You're on the right track. When you get home, go on Google Earth and scan your way up the Columbia River until you start seeing huge buildings with hydropower lines running to them. That's one of the first and biggest data center areas. But you can find them in other parts of the country, too. The largest buildings have over twenty-five acres of floor space. Sometimes they've got many times that in solar energy panels on and around them."

"So that's good, right? It sounds a lot more efficient."

"Efficient, yes—but vulnerable. The more servers, software, and data you put in a single building, and the more buildings you put near each other, the bigger the target you create. The more everything moves to cloud computing, the more vulnerable we get, especially since the servers that support the Internet and the electrical grid are all hosted in data centers, too."

"But still, how could a terrorist take out a data center that big other than with a cyberattack?"

"I don't know precisely how yet. But if I was a terrorist, I'd rather turn a data center into smoking junk than just take it off-line for a few days. I'm going to send you a link to a report on the impact of destroying data centers, and I'd like you to try and get an idea how few data centers you'd have to take out—and which ones—in order to take everything down. Got it?"

"Got it. Want to run together again tomorrow?"

"Tomorrow, no. I've got to get out of my apartment for a couple of weeks while they rehab it."

"Marla mentioned that. Are you going to stay with her?"

"No. I'm going to work on the road for a couple weeks. I've been in the city too long."

"Sounds like fun. I guess Marla forgot to mention it to me."

"Uh, it's possible I forgot to tell her. I'll give her a call this afternoon and bring her up to date." Or more likely, the next day, after he'd already escaped.

"Well, safe travels. I'll go through the data center stuff right away."

"That'd be great. Thanks." Frank split off and headed for his apartment. As soon as he was sure Tim couldn't see him, he stopped and leaned against the wall of a building, gasping for breath.

Damn kids. They were taking over the world.

* * *

14

A-Camping I Will Go

F RANK DUMPED HIS heavy duffle bag of camping gear in the trunk of the rental Jeep. His destination was the very same data centers along the Columbia River he'd referred Tim to, but he'd flown to Denver instead of Portland. There wasn't much for him to do for the CIA while Tim and Keri cranked away on the latest assignment he'd given them, and he'd been restless for a while now, anxious for an opportunity to spend a few days alone with his thoughts. Watching the romance bloom between Marla and Tim had unsettled him, turning his thoughts back to the enigma of his failed marriage. In a corner of Marla's apartment, there was now a plastic bin containing a tortoise, and in the backpack Frank used as a suitcase was the thick envelope of letters from Clare he'd discovered in his closet. He wanted some big skies overhead while he confronted whatever he would find there.

After Clare had left, he had obsessively analyzed and reanalyzed every element of their relationship in an effort to exonerate himself from any blame for the split. The process had driven him crazy. Only by forcing himself not to think about her at all, or to recall anything about their marriage, had he eventually been able to find any peace.

As he sat behind the wheel, he realized he'd been far more successful in that effort than he would have thought possible. Or perhaps it was simply the passage of time. Whatever the cause, he could now remember only the bare outline of the period between when he first met Clare and when she left him. He was torn now between the urge to understand what had really happened between them and the suspicion that some romantic bodies were better left un-exhumed.

Those somber thoughts carried him all the way through Colorado and across the border into Wyoming, where he took an exit off the highway onto a secondary road. That route led him to the dirt road he had selected as his near-term objective, and on that road, he set off to the northwest across the wide expanses of prairie that covered most of the state.

It had been an unusually wet fall, and in the shallow marshes spread across the undulating grassland, dense mats of dark green rushes grew, salted with vivid violet blossoms nodding in gentle winds. Overhead, as hoped, the sky was a flawless blue, complemented by masses of white cumulus clouds rimming the horizon. But the soothing effect of this gentle beauty was obscured by his building anxiety over confronting his past. Why couldn't he find the answers he wanted on the Internet, like everything else? That was something he knew how to do. Accelerating without thinking, he left behind a roiling cloud of brown dust that rose to obscure the brilliant blue sky.

Maybe he was just being silly, bringing those letters along. Clare had written them decades ago, back when they were much younger—just college undergraduates. So much had happened since then; how much could they matter to him now?

But they did. Clare was his first great love. Check that. She was the only great love he'd ever had. As well as the first girl he'd ever dated. What had followed that first date had bewildered as much as excited him.

At his school, a guy that didn't play sports didn't register on the social scale at all, and he'd been anything but athletic. But something strange happened during senior high school; his growth finally came in, and unbeknownst to him, girls who had never paid any attention to him before suddenly decided that he had become good-looking.

As it happened, many of the best-looking girls in his school were also the smartest. During his senior year, some of them tired of dating the same circle of jocks they'd passed around for years and decided to look around for someone different. Several of them let him know in ways that eventually even he couldn't miss that they wouldn't mind a date.

One of them proved to be particularly determined, and before he was quite sure what had happened, he'd not only asked her out—or perhaps it had been the other way around—but he and Clare were spending all of their time together. She was smart, talented, and pretty with big, brown eyes that unsettled him in a pleasant sort of way when they looked deep into his own and the kind of figure specifically designed to set a teenage male aquiver. Even better, he could talk to her and connect in a way he had never experienced with anyone before, male or female, family or friend.

The rest of senior year and the summer that followed passed far too quickly as their impending separation loomed ever nearer. He'd been accepted by MIT; she'd been accepted by a university down south. They would be far apart. Would their relationship survive?

It would not, at least for long. Just a page out of an old, old story that played out across college campuses every year. But unlike most relationships, this one settled into a pattern of fading and flaring that drove him to distraction. That much he still remembered.

He glanced at his watch; it was after six o'clock. Time to start looking for a place to spend the night. Ten minutes later, he saw what might do; a faint Jeep track angling off toward a rocky hill a half a mile off. He braked to a stop, backed up, and turned on to the track, sizing up his destination as he grew closer. It looked promising, dotted with junipers amid big, muscular granite knobs and balanced boulders covered with pumpkin-orange lichens set aglow by the brilliant, oblique light of the setting sun. Perhaps he'd find a spot with a good view to the west.

He slowly bumped and jolted his way along the track as it wound up and around the craggy hill and eventually crossed a small, flat area facing the sunset. Perfect. He parked the car and started to make camp—a brief chore, as he was traveling so light.

Besides what he'd brought in the duffle, he'd picked up a folding chair at a Wal-Mart near the airport along with his usual insubstantial camp fare of celery, peanut butter, canned pineapple, mixed nuts, bananas, granola bars, and coffee. A cheap Styrofoam cooler filled with ice and beer completed the items essential to the maintenance of Adversegoan existence. The final item was a rare extravagance in the form of a bottle of single malt scotch. He didn't usually bother with a fire, but a dead pinyon pine was conveniently located at the edge of his campsite, and its complex web of branches had shed their bark, leaving them ash-white and bone dry. In a few minutes, he had broken off all the fuel he'd need, and in a few more, he had assembled a fire ring of rocks.

With his chair and a lantern for later use facing the sunset, he popped a beer and removed the tops of a few stalks of celery with his penknife. He crunched away for a while, double-dipping his celery in the jar of peanut butter, and watched the shadows of distant mountains creep nearer across the prairie. Beneath his perch, two antelope kept casual watch over two fawns. From above, he could hear the urgent *cheeping!* of a night hawk that periodically swooped nearby in pursuit of its evening meal of insects. It was gratifying to be back in wide-open spaces, soothed by natural sounds and enjoying the smell of sagebrush carried on a dying breeze.

But now it was growing dark. He struck and held a wooden match to the little thatch of minute twigs he'd leaned against a larger branch and watched it bloom obligingly into a full-blown rose of flames. He placed progressively larger twigs and branches on the expanding fire until he was adding wood thicker than his arm, and then he walked back to the car to let the flames consolidate. He returned with the envelope of letters and settled in by the fire with the envelope in his lap and the bottle of scotch and a cup of ice at his elbow.

There was a date written in the corner of the envelope, something he hadn't paid attention to before. Noticing it brought back a rush of bitter memories. April tenth. He was surprised to suddenly recall that it had been a Thursday. That was the day during his sophomore year when he'd called Clare on the payphone in her sorority house hallway at the mutually agreed-upon time. But the person who answered was not Clare and told him she was out partying. It was the last straw. He sat down then and wrote Clare a letter telling her not to call or write him again.

At best, that had been a symbolic and ridiculous act; she was barely writing as it was and always took several days to respond to a phone message when she responded at all. He'd concluded that the certainty of no contact was better than the ongoing anxiety of waiting for such infrequent crumbs of attention as she might be willing to drop his way.

Looking down at the still-sealed envelope, he wondered whether that was what he had really wanted. More likely, it had been a vain attempt to assert some degree of influence over a relationship that was clearly outside his control. Or maybe he was simply trying to salvage some last shred of pride from the disintegration of their relationship. Most likely, it was both.

But he'd never sent that letter, and no longer remembered why. It made little enough difference anyway, as it was months before he heard from her again.

Whatever. Decades-old memories, who knew how reliable, probably wouldn't take him anywhere anyway. He took a sip of his drink and opened the envelope.

A cascade of close to a hundred letters dropped into his lap, each one addressed in Clare's tiny, precise script. The sight of the familiar hand and the small envelopes she favored brought him up short, giving him second thoughts again about the wisdom of the enterprise. Putting the letters back in chronological order, holding each one up close to his face to decipher the smudged date stamps next to the eight-cent postage, gave him time to regain his composure. Then he opened the first one.

Hey, stranger!

He immediately put the letter down again and stared out across the darkening prairie.

When he resumed reading, he was reminded that he'd left for college ten days before Clare had, and she'd written to him every day before she left for school. Each letter ran to two or three pages of tiny, perfect penmanship. He found that these were wonderful letters to read.

It was clear from them that falling in love for the first time had been a grand experience for Clare, and she'd plunged into it with the exuberance he now recalled she brought to every new adventure. The letters were perfectly reflective of her personality—witty, fun, affectionate, smart—all that anyone could ever want in someone who had come to occupy the biggest part of his life. He read each one slowly, pausing often to reflect on the memories streaming back of things he'd forgotten and puzzling over the references to those that did not.

During that summer, he now recalled, it mostly hadn't mattered what they did. They'd spent all the time they could enjoying each other's company and, whenever possible, each other's bodies. But as fall and their separation neared, she brought the topic of love up ever more frequently, expressing hers and waiting for an affirmation of his. A time-honored skirmish began with her advancing and him retreating.

Perhaps back then, their thoughts were simply holding true to their age and gender-assigned roles. She was ready to fall in love and willing to err on the side of believing that she had; he was wary and unsure what love was and primed by literature to believe that only some overwhelming wave of emotion would signal that he'd fallen victim to its attack. By the time the summer ended, they were mightily attached and secretly confused over what they wanted to happen next.

That last night before he left for college, after he had walked her home, after they had spent as long as possible making out on the front stoop of her building before she finally went upstairs to her parents' apartment, he'd been in no hurry to go home. Sitting alone in a park, he'd stared at nothing at all in sadness, assuming the odds were poor that their relationship would survive.

Staring now into the darkness that surrounded his fire, Frank yearned to experience once again what it was like to be swept along by the sensations of a first relationship, regretting that he had not appreciated it more at the time. He had taken that experience for granted, cavalier in the assumption that if this one didn't work out, there would be another one to follow and another after that. But he never again experienced the easy, happy abandon of that first phase of that first relationship, with Clare or with anyone else, or the complete connection they had experienced before she left for college and decided that her new friends, experiences, and loves were more satisfying in the moment than was his steady devotion from afar.

The campfire was almost burned out by the time he finished reading that first series of letters. He stared at the dying embers and gulped down the rest of his drink. That was enough reading for one night. He might not remember the details of what followed, but he knew all too well how the next act ended.

* * *

The next day he woke up tired and ornery. It had been a while since he'd slept on the ground, and he hadn't paid much attention to how often he'd topped up his glass of scotch the night before. Indications were that it had been often. All that day he tried to focus on the next steps he'd need to take to thwart Foobar, and he decided to stay in a motel for the night.

He found one in a dying town by a dead railroad and tarried over dinner at the only available restaurant for as long as possible. Returning to his room, he logged on to the Wi-Fi and caught up on the email that had accumulated that day. But there continued to be little for him to pay attention to back in Washington, and that took less time than he had hoped.

Should he go back to the letters or not? He was wide-awake. And it was only 8:30.

He brushed his teeth, poured himself a sensible measure of scotch, stacked a few pillows against the bedstead, and opened his laptop again after climbing in bed. But before long, he'd read as much of the day's news as he had any interest in absorbing. And it was only 8:50.

The hell with it. He got up, pulled the envelope of letters out of his backpack, and settled in again.

He couldn't recall what Clare's letters had been like after she left for college, except that he thought they had been as similar from letter to letter as his had been, and therefore rather boring. He found now that this was both right and wrong. Largely, Clare's letters were simply a daily diary of her experiences in an environment she was finding very much to her liking—the new people she met, updates on the ones she was growing most close to, and a seemingly endless round of keg parties, musical events, and swimming parties at the lake. But they were also as vivacious in text as she was in person and brought her back to life in ways he had not anticipated. And often enough they also confirmed how much she loved him or recounted how she would brag to her roommates about the wonderful boyfriend she'd left behind.

Meanwhile, he was struggling with an awkward adjustment to life at a school that gave numbers rather than names to its buildings and tended to attract the socially challenged. Fool that he was, he wrote to Clare every day. New to letter writing and not knowing what else to cover the pages with, he described how demanding his course work was; how many incredible things there were to do on campus but he had no time to do; and how distant the people were that he met. In other words, he portrayed himself as a drudge surrounded by drudges who were more studious than alive.

Toward the end of September, the mood of Clare's letters changed abruptly between one and the next. She continued to say the same sorts of things about their relationship, but it didn't ring true.

Their first and last visit of his freshman year followed two weeks later. From the moment she stepped off the plane, it became clear that their old, easy connection had gone missing. And the mutual loss of their virginity that night proved to be an uncomfortable disaster rather than the consummation they'd anticipated for so long.

After that, the daily letters came weekly for a while before becoming even less frequent. The weekend they had picked for his visit to her was now pronounced by Clare to be "not good" due to exams, as did the next date he suggested. Eventually, he received a letter in which she admitted that she'd been misleading him for weeks. She hadn't intended to date when she left for college, she said, but when she arrived, it seemed silly to limit herself when there were so many interesting people to meet and experience. She also pointed out, in so many words, that he had become a studious boor who was failing to flourish in his new surroundings as she was in hers. She provided full details, including ones about a young man who had become a particular soul mate.

He had just finished rereading that letter when the lights in the motel winked out and the ventilation unit along the wall shut down with a pronounced *chunk*. He opened a window and lay down, staring blankly into the dark, surprised to hear the faint, disembodied jazz that had been emanating unnoticed from the tiny speaker on his phone.

He tried to fall asleep. But the air was stale, and his mind wouldn't be still. He felt around on the night table until he found his phone, turned on the flashlight app, and went back to the letters. The battery ran down rapidly as he read awkwardly on, holding his phone next to his ear with one hand and a letter just below his nose with the other.

After that letter, he found that their relationship ceased to be a positive topic in the few letters that followed, when it was mentioned at all. The next week, a new very special male friend was mentioned. She really wished Frank would get out of the library and enjoy life more, the way she was.

He decided that reading the letters was like shuffling the pages of one of those flipbooks that featured one slightly morphing, acrobatic picture per page, creating a motion picture effect when you shuffled the pages rapidly from front to back. His face flushed as he visualized his tormented dance as Clare's marionette. And he was glad when he reached the last letter from his first college semester. The rest of the letters would have to wait to be read. Maybe forever.

* * *

15

P.S. I Love You

THE NEXT MORNING, he reached the data center. He slowed down as he approached the gate and took as much in as possible before turning onto a side street. He could have seen the same details using Google Earth and Street View without ever leaving Washington, but he wanted to get a more complete feel for the scene. Now that he was here, he was startled to see how insignificant the facility's defenses were. The tiny guardhouse next to the gate couldn't hold more than one person when it held anyone at all—which appeared to be never. Instead, only a video camera, a keypad, and a gate arm not much more substantial than you'd find at a tollbooth stood in the way of immediate access to the building. There weren't any tire spikes or the kind of barrier that could be raised from the road that protected federal buildings in Washington. A truck, or even a car, could easily drive right through the gate. And a large truck traveling fast should be able to barrel through the razor-wire-topped chain link fence on either side without even slowing down.

In any event, it would have been impossible to comprehend the enormity of the structure if he'd only viewed it online. It was one thing to read that a building was three stories tall and covered as much land as twenty football fields, but it was something else to see it rear up in front of you, with its cliff-like walls converging into points in perspective view far in the distance to the right and left. True, it was lightly defended. But it was also massive beyond his imagining. It would easily take ten truck bombs parked around the perimeter to hit just one building like this hard, and even then, only some of the servers around the sides of the building would be damaged.

One reason he'd chosen this facility to visit was because it was bounded by hills on one side. Ten minutes later, he was motoring slowly along a road running along the top of one of those hills, looking for a good view of the server building from above. But there were houses and trees everywhere, blocking his view.

Eventually, he found a small park and pulled over. He could clearly see the flat roof of the building in the distance, but it was almost a mile away.

The scenario he had been imagining assumed two or three terrorists armed with rocket-propelled grenade launchers. The world was awash with RPGs—more than nine million had been manufactured in various countries since 1961, and a picture of a terrorist was as likely to show him wielding an RPG launcher as an AK-47. He had to believe it wouldn't be hard to set up a few dozen U.S.-bound cargo containers in such a way as to conceal one or two RPG launchers and some ammunition in each. At one thousand yards, that kind of weapon wouldn't be very accurate, but it wouldn't need to be, given the enormous size of the target.

According to what he'd read, a small team of terrorists should be able to fire a hundred grenades in ten minutes, leaving plenty of time to make good their escape if they attacked in the middle of the night. That number of rounds ought to be enough to wreak some serious havoc, especially if they used incendiary grenades. But only if they could be fired from a location higher than their target, where the marksman could be sure to evenly distribute his fire across the entire roof of the target.

Maybe a mortar would be a more likely weapon? After all, most of the data centers weren't in hilly areas. With mortars, you lobbed your shells high up in the air and let them fall back down on the target. And instead of being fired free hand from the shoulder, a mortar was a piece of mobile artillery set up on the ground that could be precisely adjusted for direction and range. He put the car in gear and headed back down the hill toward the motels clustered around the highway exit, discouraged that a trip he had regarded as a simple confirmatory exercise had instead led to unexpected complications he would now need to resolve.

* * *

Frank set his Styrofoam plate on one of the empty tables in the "Free hot breakfast!" room of his motel. On the plate sat a yellow-white puck of microwaved scrambled eggs, two small cinnamon swirl rolls, and a tiny container containing something ominously identified as "buttery spread." He hadn't had the courage to try the biscuits and gravy; the latter had congealed into something that appeared primordial and life threatening. He went back for a cup of coffee and picked up a copy of the local paper next to the coffee urn.

He scanned the front page with the same degree of interest as his eggs merited, preoccupied by his failure the night before to reach any sort of conclusion about the desirability and feasibility of using black market infantry field mortars to destroy data centers. Not surprisingly, nobody had seen fit to write about it online yet.

In concept, a mortar seemed to be the perfect tool for the job he had in mind. Mortars were highly mobile, built in a variety of calibers, and could fire shells with varying payload weights and target ranges. But there didn't seem to be any manufacturers in countries he could imagine selling to the Caliphate, and they didn't appear to be as available on the black market as were RPG launchers and grenades.

That didn't mean mortars couldn't be what the terrorists intended to use. But it did mean he'd need to rely on the CIA's resources to evaluate their appropriateness for the kind of attack he had in mind. That could be a problem, since he wasn't supposed to be investigating mortars—that was the Kinetic Tiger Team's remit. It wouldn't surprise him if his and Tim's searches were being monitored, and it didn't sound like a good idea to be seen wandering so far afield if that was the case.

He flipped the front page of the paper over and scanned the second page with as little attention as the first, when an arresting picture caught his eye: it showed a close-up of the neck of a child with extraordinarily swollen lymph nodes. The brief story that accompanied the picture reported that the child also suffered from a high fever, muscle cramps, and vomiting. It was the second such case to appear in the local hospital, and the physicians were at a loss to diagnose what the children had contracted. Blood samples had been sent the day before to the Centers for Disease Control in Atlanta for analysis. Strange.

He dumped his disposable plate and utensils in the trash, picked up his backpack, and went to the front desk to check out and move on. But move on to where? He'd envisioned visiting several data centers to get a firsthand impression of each. But after seeing one, he wasn't sure what more there was to learn. Each would be enormous and barely defended. Some would be near cities, and some would be in the country.

Maybe he was foolish trying to figure out exactly how the terrorists might attack, anyway. For all he knew, they might be planning to fly ultralight airplanes on suicide missions, carrying leftover Soviet tactical nuclear weapons in their laps. That would be a way to go out in style. Maybe all those devices hadn't been accounted for after all. And you didn't even need a pilot's license to buy and fly an ultralight from a grassy field. Maybe that was too Hollywood to be realistic, but who knew? Maybe it wasn't.

He went back to the breakfast room to refill his coffee cup before leaving and noticed the newscast on the big television screen on the wall was showing a picture that looked very similar to the one he'd seen in the paper. He took a sip of his coffee and stopped to listen.

> *In a surprising announcement, the Center for Disease Control announced this morning that at least two cases of bubonic plague have been reported in Oregon. Both of the victims are young children. As of now, neither the CDC nor the hospital where the children are being treated has any idea how the children could have been exposed to infection by a disease that has only very rarely been seen in the United States.*

Frank didn't like the sound of that. He decided it was time to head home.

* * *

Frank tried to focus on news sites on his laptop as he flew from west to east. Below him, suspected new cases of bubonic plague were being reported everywhere now. But despite his best efforts, he couldn't get Clare's letters out of his mind on the long flight home. All he recalled about their relations during college was that after reconciling the summer after their freshman year, the same sad scenario had played out again. Being abandoned twice was a more than doubly painful and demoralizing experience.

He wondered whether they had visited each other, and if so, whether he had traveled south or she north. Most of all, he wondered why Clare had dropped him once again. Somewhere over Minnesota, he gave up and retrieved the envelope from his backpack in the overhead bin. He opened it and found the place during their freshman year where he had left off. After four months, her correspondence suddenly resumed.

Things were apparently not going so well for Clare; some of the female friends she'd bonded with most during her first semester now seemed less interesting. The two male soul mates she had mentioned most frequently during the fall had decided to remain true to their own long-distance heartthrobs. A best friend from high school was preoccupied with her own crises. Clare needed someone to share her qualms with regarding these new uncertainties, and she had evidently decided there was no one left to confide in but him.

Later, she lined up a summer office job at a resort in the Poconos, where she wouldn't know anyone. As the semester waned, her letters grew more frequent. During a visit back to the city between exams and starting her job, they ran into each other a few times at bars where their high school friends got together. In the absence of her college circle, Clare was once again appreciating the things about him that had attracted her to him in the first place. Or perhaps he was just an available emotional anchor to windward to keep her off the lee shore of a lonely summer.

Whatever the reason, soon she was getting into the city whenever she could and urging him to take a bus to visit her as well. And her letters became wonderful again.

Rereading them now, he recalled one night early in June during his first trip to visit her. They were lying on their backs in a field, gazing up at the moon, and she was telling him how glad she was they were seeing each other again. But he was thinking he was being a fool; he'd been here before and knew how that had ended. He came within a breath of saying that reconnecting was a mistake—that she shouldn't take offense—but he had decided he didn't want to get back together again.

But he didn't, just as later on he never mailed the letter telling her not to communicate. Instead, he'd been weak, or indecisive, or hadn't wanted to hurt her feelings. Maybe he just didn't want to be alone again, no matter what it cost him down the line.

But the letters that summer were wonderful; letters that made his heart ache now to read after so many years of solitude. How could anyone have ever thought so much of him, seen such wonderful things? And then, suddenly, not?

When the dates between the letters began to lengthen again after her return to college, he knew enough to quit. He spent the rest of the flight staring out the window.

By the time he got off the plane, the BNN announcer on the TV screen in the gate area was reporting that confirmed or suspected cases of plague had been reported in almost every state except Hawaii and Alaska. And the first fatality had already occurred.

* * *

16

How Sick is that Doggie in the Window?

FRANK, MARLA, AND Tim settled down in Marla's apartment to watch an hour-long newscast on the epidemic that was overwhelming all other news. As the broadcast began, they saw a map of the United States over the news anchor's shoulder, scattershot with red dots indicating the locations of the outbreaks. It gave the impression that the nation itself was covered with inflamed buboes.

Good evening, and welcome to this special broadcast on the unprecedented outbreak of bubonic plague that is gripping the United States and Europe. I'm sorry to report that the number of confirmed and suspected cases in the U.S. now stands at six hundred and forty-nine. Tragically, eighty-five individuals, most of them children, have succumbed to this terrible disease.

The camera panned out to reveal three guests sitting opposite the news anchor at his desk.

With us tonight are Dr. Clarence Trombley, assistant director for Domestic Incidents at the Center for Disease Control; Dennis Fairhaven, communications director for the Department of Homeland Security; and our regular terrorism commentator, retired Army Colonel Archie Brascom. Thank you all for joining us tonight.

Clearly, the country is badly shaken, and I know our viewers want to hear everything you can tell us about this latest terrible, terrible event. Dr. Trombley, let's begin with you. What does the CDC know about where this epidemic came from?

Tom, I'm afraid we have no idea who's responsible—yet—but as of just a few minutes before this broadcast, I am able to confirm that we do now know how it was spread.

Really? That's breaking news. Before you tell us how, can you share with us the clue that solved the mystery for you?

Actually, there was nothing subtle or difficult about it; it just took a little longer for us to identify a particular subgroup of victims. Once that cohort was identified, the mode of transmission became obvious.

How so?

There's one thing every area where an outbreak has been reported has in common: there's a mall or other popular shopping area with a pet store near the center of infection—one of those that has puppies in the window and allows patrons to play with a dog they might want to purchase.

Dogs were getting sick at the same time that people were, but unlike humans, the effects of plague on dogs are mild. And it's not at all unusual for something infectious to run through a pet store, so the canine outbreaks didn't make the news. It wasn't until we noticed that most of the first adults to contract the disease worked at pet stores that we learned about the dogs being sick. The pet store employees were the second subgroup of victims I just mentioned. Then everything fell into place.

So, Dr. Trombley, how were the dogs infected? And how could so many people become infected as well?

The answer to your second question is through fleabites.

Fleabites?

Yes. That's been the traditional means of animal-to-human transmission since the disease first appeared in Europe during the Dark Ages. Fleas provide an efficient vector for transmission of disease, especially when an illness isn't fatal to them, which is the case with plague. Throughout most of history, the mammalian vector was rats, which live in farms and towns everywhere and probably carried the plague to Europe to begin with when they came ashore from ships. In the current case, whoever is behind these outbreaks settled on dogs as a highly effective stand-in for rats, which thankfully aren't as common around people as they used to be.

But how would the dogs have become infested with infected fleas?

We don't know the precise details yet, but it's easy to imagine many ways someone could introduce fleas to dogs in stores with no risk to themselves. You can imagine packages containing some sort of hollow chew toys, each filled with infected fleas, being sent by air from the source of the bacterium to agents across the U.S. Each toy would have a hole in it with a cap that would be easily dislodged as soon as a dog began playing with it. The packages would seem totally innocuous to customs inspectors.

Then what?

Then the terrorists could just drop a chew toy filled with infected fleas into a window display area with four or five dogs, and the result would be inevitable. Pet stores usually rotate dogs through the window display, so dozens of dogs would become infected before the pet store owner realized it had a flea problem that needed addressing. Every time a child picked up a dog, there would be a very good chance that one or more fleas would jump onto her.

What a horrible image. So there you have it—and you're hearing it first right here on BNN. Please stay with us while we take a short commercial break.

"That's hideous!" Marla exclaimed. "What type of monster would even think of such a thing?"

"I guess the same kind of monster that would fly passenger jets into the World Trade Center or drown thousands of people in tunnels," Tim replied.

"Yes, of course, but still. I just can't believe this. What kind of attack will they launch next?"

"How can you know when you never could have imagined this one? Anyway, the news is back. Let's hear what else they've figured out."

Dr. Trombley, where would someone get plague bacteria to begin with?

Unfortunately, plague is still endemic in a number of places around the world, especially in Africa. For example, there's been an annual outbreak in Madagascar for several years now. It's even commonly found in some prairie dog towns in the American Southwest.

Really? Mr. Fairhaven, let me turn to you now. Does the Department of Homeland Security have any idea yet who is behind this appalling act of terrorism?

No, we don't, at least with any degree of certainty. As Dr. Trombley noted, the bacterium itself can be harvested from many sources. It's possible that we may be able to identify that source by matching the DNA of the bacteria in the current outbreak to existing records at the appropriate point source, but all that will tell us is where it came from, not who harvested the fleas. Or who sent them into this country.

But you must at least have a short list of enemies with the motive and ability to do something like this?

Of course, although it's worth recalling that it doesn't appear that the anthrax attacks after 9/11 were launched by anyone that was on the equivalent list drawn up back then.

But surely, this must be the act of a large and sophisticated terrorist group? And coming so soon after the New York attack, wouldn't the Caliphate be at the top of the suspect list?

Yes, of course. But even then, we need to be careful not to jump to conclusions. It could be another enemy, like North Korea, anxious to distract us while they plan some other mischief. Or it could be a different terrorist group entirely, possibly one competing with the Caliphate.

As to the size and sophistication of the organization, we believe as few as ten people could have contaminated all of the pet stores, based on the timing of the first reported infections. It would only take someone fifteen minutes to park a car, walk to the pet store, drop whatever it was that held the infected fleas into a play area or cage, and walk back to their car. The rest would just be driving time. One person could have infected all of the New England states in less than two days.

That said, due to the sophistication of the attack, we do expect the answer will be that the perpetrators are from a nation state or a very well-organized terrorist group.

Indeed. Setting aside the who for the moment, let's talk about the why—why would anyone want to start a plague epidemic?

Whoever is behind this almost certainly chose plague as much for the fear factor as for the ease with which it could be transmitted via fleas and infected dogs. Everyone has heard horrible stories since childhood about the black plague, so it's the most dreaded disease a terrorist could pick. And the fact that they hit every one of the lower forty-eight states, and every country in Europe, would certainly seem to indicate that their primary goal was to make sure that no one, anywhere, can feel safe.

Before Fairhaven could continue, the anchor held one hand up and pressed the other against his ear.

My apologies, Mr. Fairhaven, but I've just been told that a spokesman for the Caliphate is about to make a statement. Let's cut right now to a feed from our crack news team on location.

The scene changed to a now-familiar setting. The large and euphoric crowd in the dusty square roared with approval when Foobar's spokesman claimed credit for the latest attack. And once again, he promised that there would be far worse to come.

* * *

Frank was meeting with Hermann Koontz when he felt the phone in his pocket vibrate. Half a minute later, it vibrated again, and an email alert opened in the corner of his laptop screen. The subject line said *Call me—Urgent.* He interrupted Koontz in mid-sentence.

"Excuse me, Hermann, I've got to make a call. Something's up at home." He ducked out of Koontz's office and pressed the speed dial button on his phone. "What's wrong?"

"Oh, thank goodness, you're free. I tried to call you and was sent straight to voicemail."

"So I'm here—tell me what's wrong."

"It's Grandma. I just got a call from the home. An ambulance just took her to the hospital. They think it's the plague."

"The plague! How in heaven's name could she have gotten infected?"

"It must have been Lilly. She went to the groomer just when the first cases were being reported. She must have picked up the fleas from another dog."

"Oh my God. I never expected this." He tried to think what to do. "I'd better go to her right away."

"I want to go, too."

"Where are you?"

"On campus."

"Okay. I'll meet you at your place, and we'll leave from there."

"All right. I'll be waiting."

He rapped on Hermann's open door. "I've got to go. I'll be in touch."

"Is everything okay?"

"No. I'll fill you in later."

He caught a cab on the street, and fifteen minutes later, he was at Marla's apartment, where he found her waiting at the curb with a small suitcase.

"I threw some things together for both of us in case we decide to stay someplace overnight. I told Tim I thought just you and I should go to the hospital and that we might stay the night. Where are you parked?"

Huh! He'd dashed out of the office without even thinking to tell Tim what was going on.

"Around the corner."

He took the suitcase from her and led her to the beat-up, secondhand car he rarely used.

"Do you know which hospital they took her to?"

"Yes; I guess they've designated specific hospitals for all the plague cases to go to. Here—I've already mapped it." She handed him her phone.

"Did they say what her condition was?"

"Pretty bad. They think she may have been sick for several days."

"Several days! How could that happen?"

"You know Grandma. She probably didn't want people fussing over her. When she didn't show up for an activity she'd signed up for, they called to see if she was okay, and when she didn't answer, they let themselves in to her apartment and found her in bed. They said she wasn't too coherent."

My God, he thought. How long had it been since he'd called her?

* * *

"My name is Frank Adversego. We're here to see my mother, Doreen Adversego. Can you tell us what room she's in?" Frank shifted uneasily from one foot to the other as he waited for the person behind the desk to tap the name into her computer.

She found the entry and frowned. "I'm sorry, Mr. Adversego. She's in isolation. I'm afraid you won't be able to visit with her until they've determined which type of the disease she has."

"Which type?"

"Yes. There are three different kinds. The rarest of the three is contagious, and until they've completed a sputum test, she'll be under quarantine."

"Do you have any idea how long that will take?"

"I don't. But we've set up an area on the fourth floor for the families of plague patients. Someone up there will be able to give you more information than I can. Take one of the elevators over there, and then just follow the blue stripe on the wall until you reach a lounge."

"Thank you very much."

Marla took his hand as they navigated the bustle of the lobby toward the elevators. When they reached the lounge, they saw that only a few chairs were empty. Some people were reading magazines or watching the TV on the wall, while others were simply staring vacantly ahead, their faces drawn and anxious. A hospital staffer sat behind a window in one wall.

"Hi, we're the family of Doreen Adversego. Can you tell me what her condition is?"

"I'm sorry, I can't, but I'll see if someone can come out and tell you how's she's doing."

"Do you know how long that might be?"

"I'm sorry, I don't. But I'm sure someone will see you just as soon as they can."

"Come on, Dad. Let's take a seat."

He followed her to the last pair of side-by-side chairs available, facing the TV, where someone was talking about the epidemic. It was still getting worse.

It seemed like forever before someone in scrubs entered the room and called their names. They stood and met her in the middle of the room.

"Hi. I'm Doctor Franzen. Let's go in here." They followed her into one of the small rooms that lined one side of the lounge.

"How is she doing?"

"We started her on intravenous antibiotics as soon as she was admitted. She's running a very high fever—over one hundred and four degrees—but it hasn't risen since she was admitted. I'm hoping it will start going down by tomorrow."

"Downstairs they said something about a sputum test. Are the results back yet?"

"Yes, and we've also gotten back her blood work. The good news is that she doesn't have pneumonic plague—that's the deadliest and fastest-acting type. From what I read on the chart, she's been symptomatic for several days. If she'd had that type of the disease, we probably would have lost her by now. And she doesn't have septicemic plague. That's good, too, because that can lead to gangrene and the loss of fingers and toes. But she's had the last kind—bubonic—for longer than we like before she started receiving treatment, and that's bad. We should have a better idea tomorrow how she's going to do."

"Does that mean we can see her?"

"Yes, they've moved her out of the isolation unit, but you won't able to talk to her. I stopped by her room before I came out here, and she's sleeping, which is exactly what I want her to be doing as much as she can."

"That's fine. I understand. Can we go back there now?"

"Sure. I'll show you where her room is."

They followed the doctor onto the ward.

"She's down that hall in room four-eighteen."

"Thank you, Doctor."

"Of course. I'm afraid I can't say don't worry, but I can tell you we've got a fine group of doctors and nurses here, and we'll do everything we can to make your mother as comfortable as possible and to get her through this."

They walked down the hall, glimpsing the families of patients through the open doors, standing or sitting by beds. From some rooms, they could hear the sound of television programs and conversations, but from others, there was only deathly silence. Through one doorway, they heard a feeble voice moaning in a way that made the hairs on the back of Frank's neck rise.

They paused at the door of room 418 before entering; it was a double room divided by a curtain. The person sleeping in the first bed wasn't Doreen. They moved past, and there she was, hooked to sensors and hanging IV bottles, her ashen face tilted slightly back and her mouth gaping open. Frank caught his breath; she looked like she was dead.

Marla must have had the same impression, but she handled it better.

"She's okay, Dad," she whispered, pointing to the jagged lines blipping their way across the monitor.

He realized he was still holding his breath and exhaled deeply.

"Go ahead and sit down," he whispered back. "I'll find another chair."

She did, and he borrowed the one on the other side of the curtain.

Neither of them could think of anything to do or say, because nothing they could do or say would make any difference. So they did what the families of plague victims had done for hundreds of years: they sat at the bedside of their loved one and waited, hoping for the best.

* * *

Frank was still sitting at his mother's bedside the next evening, exhausted, anxious, and be-stubbled. He'd persuaded Marla to go back to her apartment around midnight of the night before, promising that he'd let her know as soon as there was any change in his mother's condition. Since then, he hadn't broken his vigil except for a quick trip to the hospital cafeteria to buy food to bring back to the room. The only bright spot in the otherwise bleak ordeal was the completely ridiculous picture of a very indignant, shaved corgi that Marla had texted to him. Someone from the retirement home had called to ask her to take custody of Lilly while his mother's apartment was fumigated. The morbidly obese, hairless animal reminded him of a miniaturized Jabba the Hutt.

Frank fretted the dinner hour away, waiting for Dr. Franzen to stop by on her evening rounds. When she finally arrived, he waited silently as she studied his mother's chart and watched as her vital signs marched their way across the monitor screen next to the bed. At last, the doctor nodded toward the door, and he followed her into the hallway.

"I think the worst is over. Her fever's been below one hundred and two all afternoon, her pulse is stronger, and her lymph nodes aren't as hard or warm to the touch, so the antibiotics are clearly doing what we want them to. She's not completely out of the woods yet, but I'm optimistic now that she'll make a complete recovery."

"Thank goodness! How much longer do you think she'll be in the hospital?"

"Not as long as I'd like, to tell you the truth, but we've only got one section of the hospital properly set up to treat plague victims, and the case count is still rising. I understand that your mother's retirement home has a secondary care unit, which would be adequate to the task. If she continues to improve and gets through tomorrow night without any problems, we should be able to discharge her into their care the next morning, assuming they're willing to take her."

"That's wonderful, Doctor. Thank you."

"No thanks necessary to me; it's the staff that does all the hard work. Can I make a suggestion?"

"Of course."

"Why don't you go home and get yourself some sleep. You look like you could use it. We'll take good care of your mother."

* * *

17

Doodlebug, Doodlebug,
Come out of your Hole

ALL HELL HAD broken loose when the public absorbed the reality of the first Western epidemic of the plague in almost five hundred years. On top of the horror came hysteria and an overly zealous public response: in some states, thousands of people were quarantined who had, or might have had, some contact with someone who was infected, even though most of them had no chance whatsoever of contracting or communicating the disease. Shopping malls—even those without pet stores—stayed closed for lack of business despite extensive and unnecessary fumigation efforts. Hospitals stood half-empty, as anyone who could survive without medical care avoided them for fear of contracting the dreaded disease. And anyone with a dog was well advised to walk it in the middle of the night, when no one was watching. Frank decided that maybe there was something to be said for owning a tortoise after all.

All this irrational behavior continued unabated, even as the number of new cases of plague plummeted two weeks after the first case was diagnosed. Public health officials sought to reassure the populace that without infected fleas, the further transmission of disease would be entirely eliminated. And community leaders took great pains to spread the word that every reasonable—and many unreasonable—means had been and would continue to be pursued to ensure that the very last infected insect would be hunted down and destroyed.

But the truth was that this goal was impossible to achieve, because hundreds of flea-bearing dogs had already been taken home. Some of these had been abandoned by their owners as soon as the news broke, allowing the disease to spread to feral dogs and cats as well as to rats, raccoons, and other wild creatures. And some human cases of plague transitioned to the communicable, pneumonic form of the disease, which could be spread the same way as the flu—through sneezing and physical contact. When pressed, public health officials were forced to admit it was possible the disease might establish itself in pockets of infection that might take months, or even years, to eradicate, especially in southern states, where fleas could survive on wild animals through the winter. Meanwhile, demand for curative as well as precautionary doses of appropriate antibiotics overwhelmed available supplies.

The governments of stricken countries were under overwhelming popular pressure to strike back immediately against those responsible for the epidemic. But mounting the type of attack that could eliminate the widely distributed forces of the Caliphate would be no small undertaking, demanding the mobilization of tens of thousands of troops. Even with unanimity of purpose among the coalition, the sheer logistics of assembling and transporting sufficient troops, weapons, and supporting infrastructure into position would take months of preparation and implementation.

The predictable result was that any affected country that owned even a single military aircraft was scrambling to do whatever was necessary to get that plane somewhere over Caliphate territory where it could kill someone, even if that meant shoving a bomb by hand out the hatch of a cargo plane. The United States and its coalition allies, of course, were capable of bringing far greater firepower to the cause and did.

All of which seemed to leave the Caliphate curiously unconcerned. Wherever possible, his troops shamelessly co-located in hospitals and schools or melted back into the mountains. In his increasingly frequent public addresses, Foobar's spokesman mocked the West for the futility of its preparations for war. Not one soldier, he promised, would set foot on the territory of the Caliphate before the West was defeated on its own soil.

Following on the heels of the attack on Manhattan and the chaos wrought by the ongoing epidemic, many radical extremists in the Arabic world were prepared to believe him and flocked to his flag in spite of the accelerating Western preparations for war.

* * *

Frank was having no problem saving his breath as they ran this morning; he could scarcely get a word in as Tim reported the results of his latest research. Or, more accurately, reacted to it.

"I can't believe that we're going down the road we are! If the government isn't going to stop industry from warehousing everything it takes to run anything in just a small number of data centers, then they should force the private sector to put data centers fifty feet underground! All Foobar has to do is seriously damage about a third of them, and everything crashes, and there won't be any way to set the Internet back up again."

This was no surprise to Frank; he had recognized the folly years ago of moving computing from millions of widely dispersed locations to just a few. It was equally troubling that just about nothing important existed on paper anymore. If the electronic versions disappeared, the information would be gone forever. He'd even come up with a cynical slogan for it: "Vulnerability by Design."

"It's even worse than I thought," Tim continued, "because everything is way too interconnected for all the big users, like multinational companies, government agencies, and financial market makers. What's going on in one data center depends on what's going on in lots of the others, so even if you don't take them all out, you'll still disable the surviving programs trying to operate somewhere else.

"But even that's not the worst of it. I hadn't realized it before, but with the explosion of data and the increased reliability of systems, cloud providers have decided they don't need to do traditional, archived backups. Instead, they just mirror the data on more than one site in real time. So if you take out a primary server as well as its mirror server at another site, whatever data they were hosting is gone forever."

That really was the worst of it, Frank thought. Almost no one knew everything about anything anymore. There probably wasn't a paper copy in existence of the design of a single computer chip, or of the manufacturing details needed to create a silicon wafer, or to etch the circuits on it, or even to build any of the machinery necessary to perform those tasks, or to mine or refine the silicon to begin with. And the same was true for every other modern device or consumable, right down to making and filling a Pez dispenser.

"I mean, this is criminal!" Tim said. "We already run the risk that Foobar will bomb us back into the Stone Age. And if we get to him first, it will only get worse—every day, the data centers will get bigger, and more information and software will be relocated there. We'll just be hanging around, waiting for the next enemy to take us out. What the hell's the matter with Washington?"

Tim had picked up speed as he grew more emotional, but it appeared that he was waiting for an answer to what Frank had hoped was just a rhetorical question.

"Same thing that always has been," Frank huffed. "Politicians are politicians, and all politicians care about is not getting beaten in the next election. That, and coming up with campaign funds to make sure that doesn't happen. So they never want to annoy the big contributors—some of whom happen to be building and investing in the data centers. And the rest don't want to pay a nickel more than necessary to cloud service providers. So we're talking about just about everyone in business being on board. Once you think in terms of politicians not wanting to be beaten, it all falls into place."

"How about not getting annihilated? Who's going to elect them when all the voters are dead?"

"I guess that concept is a bit too abstract for most legislators to grapple with. But the cost of burying a data center fifty feet underground isn't. If anyone even suggested he might introduce a bill to force telecom and high tech companies to do that, he'd be swarmed by so many lobbyists he'd disappear from sight. And don't forget—while there may not be that many data centers, they're in enough states to be sure that a bill like that would never get adopted."

"So what are we supposed to do, just sit around and wait for something inevitable and horrible to happen?"

"You mean, kind of like global warming?"

Tim came to an abrupt halt. With relief, Frank jerked to a halt as well and turned around.

"Have you seen the projections of what would happen if a third of the big data centers were significantly damaged?"

"No," Frank lied, "What do they say?"

Tim turned on his heel and began running again. "Everything powered by electricity stops, because the grid is controlled by computers over the Internet.

"Everything moving stops, too—the planes, the trains, and the automobiles—once they use up whatever fuel is in their tanks when the Internet and the grid go down. That's because the refineries and the pipelines are down now, too, and the gas pumps at the local gas stations don't work, because they need electricity, and there isn't any. There's no air traffic control system either, because the control towers and the radar systems use electricity, computers, and the Internet, too."

Their footfalls slapped out a supporting tempo to Tim's staccato tirade as he continued to pick up steam.

"There's no food after you use up what's in your warm, dark refrigerator, or in the local store, because there's no way to deliver it from a farm or a factory to a store. There's no water coming out of the tap, either, because the distribution system is computer controlled and relies on electricity, so that's down, too.

"There's no heat, if you use gas, because that distribution system has shut down—you know why. And no oil heat after you use up what's in your storage tank.

"There's no financial system, of course, because it's all computerized—not even a working ATM. So what's in your wallet is all you've got. And all of your bank accounts and savings are gone anyway, because all they amounted to was computerized financial records, which no longer exist.

"There's no police, because they use gas-guzzling squad cars to get around, and the cops can't get to work anyway. So there's no public safety. And you couldn't call for help anyway, because neither your landline nor your cell phone work.

"There's nothing you can call a government left outside of small towns, because there's no way for government employees to get to work or to communicate with anyone anyway, other than through emergency radio signals. And they quit working after the backup generators ran out of diesel fuel.

"And on and on through everything else society relies on. Hospitals? No staff, no electricity, no medicine after the cupboards are bare.

"There's no way for anyone to grow food, because all the seeds for the next crop are stored in just a few locations, and there's no way to transport them anywhere else. Even if you still have some of your last crop in a silo, you can't replant it because the agribusiness companies these days make sure last year's crop will be sterile so you'll have to buy more seed to plant every year. But hell, there's no fuel for the farm machinery anyway, and almost no horses or old-fashioned plows to use, either.

"What there is in the U.S. is looting and fear and hunger and more guns than people. According to the report, if the attack comes in the winter, most of the population will die of exposure or starvation within a month—if they didn't die of thirst within the first few days. If it comes in the summer, it would just take a little longer, with more people starving than freezing to death. If Europe is gone, too, who's going to save us? Russia or China? Fat chance. Most big countries have trouble feeding their own people and import food from us. They'll be hard-pressed to help us out if their own people are on the verge of starvation. And even if they did, there's no way they could transport enough food and fuel to the U.S. to help many people before they died.

"Whoever attacked us could just walk right in. It would be like the white men coming to the New World after smallpox wiped out eighty percent of the Native Americans. Back then, the Europeans took over the best town sites and cleared fields, all of which were now empty. But this time it will be even better, as there'd be all this great physical infrastructure in place. Whoever hit us could just waltz right in and take over our homes and our public buildings and our cars and our tractors and everything else and treat any survivors however they wanted to—turn them into slaves, even.

"And all of this isn't in a report from some left-wing organization with an agenda. It's from a government report. A *government* report—this is what our own experts predict will happen if someone launches a serious attack against the data centers. So what are we supposed to do? Just stand around and do nothing?"

Frank gave it up and skidded to a stop, mopping his brow with the bottom of his running shirt. He figured this would not be a good time to point out that at least a Christian prophecy would be fulfilled—the one about the meek, in the form of the Amish walking behind their horse-drawn plows, inheriting the earth.

"I guess not, no. I guess if we're aware of something like this, we should support an organization that's trying to do something about it, or write op/ed pieces or organize demonstrations or something."

"And how much good would that do?"

"I don't know; I guess as much good as anything else. People have made a difference with political issues before. Look at civil rights and environmental protection. There's been a lot of progress made there."

"Sure, and look at how long that took. And how about poverty and fixing the educational system, where things are getting worse? What happens in the meantime? Every new data center that gets built aboveground makes us more vulnerable and makes it that much less likely that Congress will act. Who's going to want to take an already operating ten-billion-dollar facility apart and put it back together again at the bottom of a hole?"

"Look, okay—of course, you're right. Something's got to be done, or we'll be just as vulnerable after catching Foobar as we are now. But first, we've got to catch him, right? The targets are already out there in plain view, and we're not going to bury them in the next two weeks. So we've got to figure out how to stop the Caliphate damn quick or everything you read in that report is going to come true."

"Fine. But we're going to have to come back to this. Are you with me on that?"

"Sure thing. How about we head home?"

Tim nodded and started to lope off. They ran for a while in silence, each thinking his own thoughts.

* * *

Tim might have been energized by anger against the establishment, but Frank was haunted by the view from the top of the hill along the Columbia River, gazing out over the roof of the enormous, defenseless data center. He'd started to have a recurring dream where a couple of doughboys from World War One used the mortars of their day to blast a hundred craters into the roof of a data center in ten minutes' time, each large enough to swallow a truck and collectively sufficient to turn the computing resources of thousands of servers into smoldering wreckage. He was not willing, like some politicians, to dismiss Foobar's promise to conquer the West on its own turf as pure grandstanding. There was, after all, an uncomfortably feasible way to do the job. He realized with a shock that it would be January in a few weeks—the perfect time to trigger such an attack to maximum effect.

But assuming he was right, how exactly did Foobar plan to attack? There wasn't a lot of time left to figure that out, and he had only a few enigmatic hints tweezed from mountains of data to work with.

Tim and Keri hadn't made a lot of progress decrypting the coded portions of messages, but they had produced something interesting on the code word front as they continued to refine the series of search algorithms they had developed. Now they were looking only for non-common words that, like Hellespont, were used a single time in a message and had low relevance to the rest of the text. This allowed them to screen out almost all the words that were of no interest. Using this search technique, they concluded that "Venice" was the code word for the plague attack and learned that Foobar's henchman had begun to grow fond of the noun *asad al-naml* about three years ago. Its use had risen sharply over the past five months, and it was now the second most used word on the list of possible code words they had compiled.

Translated into English, the word was "antlion."

Frank looked up from the report. What was an antlion, besides an oxymoron? He started browsing on the CIA's extensive intranet to find out.

The first thing he learned was that an antlion was a really ugly-looking insect, at least in its larval stage. Later on, it would emerge from a cocoon looking like a dragonfly with its second set of wings at the wrong angle, and with a more elegant name as well: antlion lacewing. Apparently, antlions could be found in sandy areas all over the world, and their name derived from their reputation as voracious consumers of small insects, particularly ants. He also learned that antlion larvae were "unusual among the insects" due to lacking an anus. Instead, they stored up their waste internally throughout their entire larval stage. No wonder they were so mean.

But why would Foobar's men have chosen the name of an ill-tempered insect for what might be their big attack? Hopefully, the name would provide a clue, as Hellespont and Venice had. But what could that clue be? He kept on reading.

After hatching underground, an antlion would look for an appealing area of sand and begin digging down, moving backward, and stacking sand on its head.

Periodically, it would toss its head backward, hurling the material out of the cone-shaped pit it was excavating. Once that pit was two or three inches wide by a third of that in depth, the insect would bury itself deeper. All that extended upward into its pit would be its enormous, sickle-shaped jaws, each equipped with sharp, hollow tines it used to suck the soft interior out of any prey unlucky enough to find itself in their embrace. Clearly a lifestyle that only someone like Foobar could appreciate.

Engineer that he was, Frank was fascinated to learn that the secret to the antlion's success was setting its trap in loose sand and then constructing its pit in such a way that its sides would assume the "angle of repose," meaning steep enough to be on the verge of collapsing inward but otherwise stable unless disturbed. An insect wandering over the edge of an antlion's pit would upset the equilibrium of the sand particles on the cone's surface, turning them into the equivalent of ball bearings that would begin sliding away beneath it. The hapless insect would be left scrambling ineffectually to escape, while the remorseless beastie waiting below used its formidable jaws to fling yet more loose sand around its intended prey. Eventually, the doomed visitor would tumble downward into the maw of its hideous executioner. Frank watched the process unfold in a video clip, and was grateful he was not the size of an ant.

That was all very interesting, but what did it mean? It sounded promising, what with the ferocious reputation of the antlion, the fact that it set traps for the unwary, and lived a secretive life underground, ready to pounce, but was that all there was to it? Perhaps if he looked into how the word was used in context, he would discover a more useful clue. He looked up the archive of translated Caliphate intercepts and performed a word search. As promised, there were several hits.

Apparently, "antlion" was also a nickname for an improvised electronic device, the kind of bomb a terrorist would bury under or beside a road and trigger when an enemy vehicle was passing by.

He snapped his laptop shut in disgust. Just a dead end.

* * *

But over the next week, the usage of "antlion" by the Caliphate continued to rise, and at an ever-steeper angle. If it continued to mimic the arc of the use of Hellespont, it would peak in just a few weeks' time. Frank decided he'd been too hasty in rejecting it. But what could the clue be that was lurking in the choice of an obscure insect with a bad attitude?

He decided the answer wasn't likely to be gleaned from analyzing Big Data. He'd have to figure this one out the old-fashioned way, hoping that if he stumbled on the right information, his intuition would come to his rescue. He prepared the way by having Keri compile a list of every common association with the word "antlion" she could find. The result was a list of bulleted ephemera that covered elements as diverse as the origin of the insect's scientific name, mentions of the bugs in folklore, and references in gardening manuals. He worked his way through the list, roving out onto the CIA's extensive intranet when an item seemed promising, in hopes of uncovering some bit of additional information that would allow the connection to spring into view.

In the course of that quest, he learned that while crossing Cape Cod, Henry David Thoreau had likened the landscape to a "bleak and barren country, consisting of rounded hills and hollows" in which he "might tumble into a village before we were aware of it, as into an ant-lion's hole, and be drawn into the sand irrecoverably." Interesting, but not likely what he was looking for. Foobar didn't seem like the Thoreau type.

He also discovered that the insect was parasitized by other arthropods, including a horsefly larva that cohabitated with antlions in their lairs and lived off their crumbs, as well as by a species of wasp that stabbed antlion larvae with a sharp, egg-bearing spike on its rear end called an ovipositor. Thus planted, the wasp's larvae would hatch inside, and feed on, their host. The wasp angle sounded like it had the potential to suggest a connection, but he couldn't make it out.

Then there was the fact that antlions were in the habit of tossing the lifeless, drained carcasses of their prey over their shoulders and out of their pits. Frank hoped that wasn't what he was looking for. He wasn't too keen, either, on the fact that if a winged adult had the ill luck to land in an antlion pit, it was likely to become dinner for the next generation of its own kind. And he didn't at all know what to make of the fact that the antlion mating technique called for the adult male to attach itself to an adult female, after which the male "hung below her, suspended only by his genital apparatus." And for up to two hours, to boot. There was even a picture.

Interestingly, although antlions lived almost everywhere around the world, he learned that they were still usually called antlions in the local language. But not everywhere. Malayalam speakers in India called them pit-elephants. Hispanics in the American Southwest called them *toritos*, meaning little bulls, and in Tennessee, they were sand lions and ant devils. Meanwhile, they were ancient earth cattle in Mandarin, but backward-moving bulls in Cantonese. In Korean, they were ant demons, and in Slovenian, little wolves.

Could any of these variants have a secret meaning to the Caliphate? He felt like he was getting nowhere but persevered, discovering that antlions had long been referred to as doodlebugs in the southeastern states of the U.S., for some reason inspiring many variations on a single bit of doggerel that was to be recited as the observer tickled an antlion's pit with a piece of straw. The object of the exercise was to provoke its owner to throw sand in the direction of its hoped-for dinner. One version went like this:

Doodlebug, doodlebug, come out of your hole

I'll give you ten dollars and a bag of gold

In other renditions, the doodlebug might be offered some pie, bread and butter, a grain of corn, or a barrel of sugar; most often, it might be informed that its house was on fire and it had better come home or its children would burn. It might also be asked to make a cup of coffee or catch a blade of grass.

All of that was pretty devious, but at least not as threatening as the warning intoned in Afrikaans by the children of South Africa:

Joerie, Joerie, bread and butter,

if I get you, I will kill you.

Hmm. That didn't sound like a particularly convincing argument to use to motivate the desired behavior.

Even Mark Twain had climbed on board, tasking Tom Sawyer with consulting a doodlebug for advice on a spell. The doodlebug's resulting thrashing about confirmed Sawyer's suspicion: the charm had been the work of a witch!

Frank was despairing of ever making the right connection by the time he learned that in *Episode VI* of the *Star Wars* saga, Sarlacc, an enormous and dreadful animal living at the bottom of a sandy pit, was inspired by the antlion. Could Foobar, like North Korea's Kim-Jung Il, be a closet Western movie freak?

He gave up with that last bit of information, feeling extremely well versed in the *gestalt* of antlions in various civilizations but no closer to his goal. What could he possibly do with all of this information?

He brooded on that for a while. He had to start somewhere, so why not work with the American variant of the name, given that the United States was Foobar's biggest threatened target. Delving deeper, he learned that the word doodlebug could also apply to an early self-propelled rail car, a 1950s scooter, a 1930s tractor, a midget racing car, and several aircraft, one of which was the pilotless, jet-powered, German V-1 flying bomb. Apparently, the Brits had exercised their traditionally mordant wit to give the V-1 that nickname as tens of thousands of the early drones rained down on London. Which, if any, of these usages was he looking for?

He worked his way down the list, spending the most time on the V-1, not because it seemed to be a stronger lead, but simply because he had always found the V-1 and its successor, the V-2 rocket, to be fascinating examples of early, cutting edge technology. Eventually he found his way to the site of a small post-war museum built on the ruins of a factory in Nordhausen, Germany, where slave laborers from a nearby concentration camp had been compelled to build thousands of both weapons. While browsing around that resource, he stumbled upon a news article reporting that three years before, persons unknown had broken into the museum. Among the items stolen was the museum's unique collection of original V-1 plans, specifications, and operations manuals.

* * *

18

Antlion Has Landed

F RANK WAS REPORTING his discovery to Tim as they ran through Marla's neighborhood.

"So, on the plus side, the timing is perfect—about the same time the word doodlebug starts to show up in the messages, the plans get stolen. Add to that the fact that we're talking about seventy-five-year-old technology, so the weapons could be made just about anywhere in the world. And while the original V-1s had pretty primitive targeting controls, you can buy GPS-aware navigation units online to steer model airplanes. Using the output of one of those units to control a full-size aircraft-1 wouldn't be challenging at all. Do that, and you've got a pretty close approximation of a modern cruise missile. It can fly low to avoid radar detection; it's got a range of one hundred sixty miles—probably a lot farther if they used modern aircraft fuel instead of kerosene—and can deliver almost a ton of explosives. You'd only need a few of those to take out each data center."

"Sounds interesting. Any negatives?"

"On the downside, you're talking about a jet plane over twenty-seven feet long, weighing almost two and a half tons, that was designed to be launched from either a large bomber or a land-based ramp up to one hundred sixty feet long. The ramp was manufactured in pieces to be portable, but individual sections were made out of iron and were twenty feet long. So we're talking about a big jump here from an RPG launcher or a mortar. If you were trying to transport all that stuff to locations within range of the targets, you'd need several full shipping containers for the launch ramp and another container for each V-1."

"Right," Tim replied. "Foobar doesn't have any planes to launch anything from, and if he did, they'd be picked up on radar and shot down before they left Caliphate airspace. And you could never get all that equipment into the U.S., much less set up launching ramps without being noticed. Too many of the data centers are near populated areas. So that sounds like a dead end to me."

"But you could launch them from ships."

"Hah! Good point—and nobody pays a lot of attention to ships until they're at the dock. I wonder how he'd go about doing that?"

"I don't think it would be too hard. You could put the launch rails above decks and cover them with tarps, but I think I'd put two side-by-side rails inside with a blast wall between them and some sort of doors in the bow of the ship that I could open when I was ready to launch. Above each launch rail, I'd have another, longer rail running the whole length of the ship. I could have an entire fleet of V-1s hanging from those rails, where I could get them fueled up and ready to be rapidly moved forward, like on an assembly line. Finally, I'd have big, curved blast deflectors separating the firing section in the bow of the ship from the storage and preparation area amidships. The deflectors would direct the launch exhaust out the sides of the ship.

"If you set things up that way, each ship could pack a heck of a wallop. If you had a six-hundred-foot-long ship and allowed two hundred feet for the launch area, that would leave four hundred feet for the preparation area. That would mean you could have twenty-six V-1s all fueled up and ready to go, plus the two in the launch area. Add an elevator to the deck below, and you could have another forty ready to bring up two at a time and add to the launch line. That would mean about sixty-eight V-1s per ship."

"That's a lot of firepower."

"I'd say so. If you targeted each data center with six V-1s, you could take out eleven data centers per ship."

"How long would it take to launch that many drones?"

"Once you opened the bow doors and launched the first two, I figure the launch sequence would go like this: open the blast deflectors like a pair of gates, move two more V-1s forward, close the blast reflectors while you're lowering the V-1s onto the firing rails, and then launch. I expect if you set the whole thing up well and had the launch crew really well trained, you could fire a pair of V-1s off every five minutes."

"Wow! That's something. If they launched at night from five miles off shore and set the drones to fly below radar, I bet it would take quite a while for anyone on shore to figure out what was happening, or where the V-1s were coming from. And then they'd still have to figure out what to do about it."

"That's right. Every ship might not succeed in launching every V-1 before we were able to counterattack, but then again they very well might. It's not like we keep fighters or bombers at the ready to defend against coastal attacks anymore. So even after we figured out what was going on, we'd have to scramble flight crews, fuel up our jets, and then get them however far we needed to fly them to reach the ships. And meanwhile, those V-1s would be closing on their targets at more than four hundred miles an hour."

Tim was clearly impressed. "I wonder how many data centers would be in range?"

"A lot, I bet, but don't get so excited—I can't run that fast. Anyway, I've calculated that more than half the population of the U.S. lives within range, so that means you'd expect half of the data centers, more or less, to be within range, too."

"Frank, I think you may have hit on it. Head for home and see how far we can take this?"

"Yup. But don't run me into the ground on the way."

* * *

It didn't take long to sketch out the rest of a feasible scenario. Frank tackled the ship aspects while Tim researched the targets and logistics side of the investigation. Frank learned that the most common size ship in use was referred to as a Handysize, and more than 2,000 vessels in this category were spread out across the globe. Most were set up as freighters and were equipped with large cranes and hatches on deck to allow a wide variety of cargo types to be taken on board and then removed again—just right to load and unload the flying bombs. With a typical width of eighty-eight to ninety-eight feet, that meant that launch doors wide enough to let two V-1s pass through could easily be cut through the bow of the ship high above the waterline. Other doors could be cut through the sides to vent the jet exhaust. And it wouldn't be hard to pick up a few old, worn-out vessels without attracting attention.

For his part, Tim confirmed that the great majority of the data centers were indeed near large coastal cities. Anyone working for Foobar wouldn't need more than a laptop computer and a Wi-Fi connection to grab the targeting data using

Google Earth. Tim also found several websites that tracked global commercial shipping, showing the points of departure, destinations, owners, and much more for every ship in operation.

Everything continued to fall in place almost effortlessly as they took their investigations deeper into the details. The necessary modifications to the ships could be carried out at shipyards in numerous ports located in out-of-the-way developing nations like Bangladesh and Cameroon. There was an active market not only in purchasing used ships but in leasing them as well under terms that assigned maintenance and upgrading responsibility and costs to the lessee. And almost all commercial ships were registered in countries like Panama and Liberia that had next to no regulations applicable to ship operation, and therefore no nosy inspectors snooping around the ships under their jurisdiction.

But proving that their scheme was feasible didn't prove anything more than that. They'd have to actually find a ship that had been altered to launch V-1s in order to know they had cracked the Caliphate's plot or succeed in decrypting communications that confirmed their suspicions. But so far, they hadn't been able to crack the Caliphate's code.

"So I guess it's time we tell the Tiger Team what we're thinking, right?" Tim asked.

"That should be the right decision, but I'm not so sure."

"Why? We don't have a lot of time to work with here. As a matter of fact, we don't even have a clue how much time that is. And none of us is a codebreaker."

"I know. But I'm not confident anyone is going to believe us. We've been told often enough that if there's a danger to cyberinfrastructure, it's going to be through a cyberattack and not to waste our time on any other theory. Henderson keeps insisting that if anyone is going to worry about any kind of traditional attack it's going to be the Kinetic Tiger Team. Except that they've been told that any kinetic attack will be against people or power stations or the like. And finally, if we claim we've found something the Kinetic Team hasn't, we make them look bad and they'll say we're crazy."

"But still—what if we're right and we don't tell anyone in time? Then what?"

"I don't have a good answer for that, except that if we go too soon, they'll probably ignore us. So let's set a deadline of the next weekly Tiger Team meeting to come up with everything we can, and whatever that is, we'll take that to them. That gives us five days."

"Fine, but what can we do in that amount of time that's likely to be worth waiting for?"

"How about this? We can assume that every ship would need some sort of structural changes in order to serve as a launch platform. Even if it's not as dramatic as a below decks launch facility, they'd still need to modify their above decks area to accommodate launch ramps—and also get rid of any obstructions between the bow of the ship and the other end of the ramp.

"I have to believe that the CIA or the Department of Homeland Security has a database with satellite photos of every ship of any size. Assuming that the photos get updated periodically, Keri could do a search for any ship where the forward two hundred feet of its hull has changed significantly. Then she could analyze the results and see if any of those changes were similar and made at the same shipyard, or a couple of shipyards. If she finds a group of ships where that's true, we can look at the changes and see if they're consistent with what we would expect to see in order to accommodate launching ramps."

"Okay, we can do that. But what if the modifications aren't on deck? A satellite taking pictures from above isn't going to show doors in the bow of a ship."

"That's true. But there are other kinds of data we could use instead, like how long a vessel has stayed in port, and where. A ship that isn't moving isn't making money, so unless it can't find a cargo, it's got to have a reason for staying in port longer than it takes to load and unload. If we find that some ships have been idling in the same ports rather than working steadily, maybe they'll have something interesting in common that would support our theory.

"Sure, but like you said, what if a ship just can't find a cargo, or isn't sailing for some other reason? I read the other day that with oil prices down so low, energy companies are buying up old tankers just to use as floating storage facilities until the price goes back up."

"Keri should be able to weed ships like that out by pattern analysis. If there are a lot of oil tankers hanging around oil production facilities, then she can ignore them. But if a port has a lot of ships coming and going all the time and just one ship is there for a month, then that would be interesting. And I'm betting that the shipyards we're looking for are in out-of-the-way places, not in major ports that cater to supertankers. It might take some work, but if we keep at it, we should be able to find what we're looking for—assuming, of course, there's something there to find."

* * *

Five days later, Frank had what he thought he needed. The satellite pictures hadn't panned out, but the pattern analysis had. They'd found thirteen elderly freighters that had each spent eight to ten weeks in one of three small shipyards, one in Mauritius and the other two in Malaysia. All of the ships were owned by the same company, which was owned by another company, which was finally owned by a company in which the CIA suspected the Caliphate had invested. Each had also visited a port in Myanmar that was not far from a company that built airframes for an Indian cargo aircraft company, and the CIA believed the Caliphate might have invested in the airframe manufacturer as well. The Myanmar company didn't normally make engines, but it had a division that made high-pressure industrial boilers, so it had all the necessary equipment and adequate experience to build the primitive jet engines used by a V-1.

It would be great to have more to go on, but it seemed like enough to Frank. If his Tiger Team chair endorsed the V-1 theory, the CIA should be able to check it out quickly using its global resources.

Not wanting to risk rejection before he had time to explain his theory fully, Frank waited to ask to be added to the agenda until he walked into the meeting. As before, he also waited impatiently for his turn. When it arrived, he carried his laptop to the front of the room and connected it to the projector. Accepting the remote from the chairman, he took a deep breath and began.

"So, as most of you realize from my comments in earlier meetings, I've been kind of skeptical about the concept of the Caliphate being able to mount a serious cyberattack against the U.S. or one of our allies. Nothing we've heard from the field suggests they have the capability to do that or that they've been trying to acquire the assistance of those that do. For example, no one's been able to find any evidence of recruiting efforts targeting people with cyber skills, and I haven't been able to find anything anywhere on the dark web that suggests that the Caliphate has been trying to hire that kind of talent.

"That doesn't mean, though, that I'm skeptical that the Caliphate might want to take down the Internet by physically destroying the infrastructure it depends on. If the web and the Internet went down all over the Western world, it would be disastrous for us but have almost no impact on the Caliphate. So I can't imagine anything that could fulfill Foobar's threats better than that."

Barbara Travers, the liaison with the Kinetic Tiger Team, interrupted. "Hang on a minute, Frank. The Kinetic team is already covering that contingency. According to their threat analysis, the most realistic scenario would involve cutting telecommunications fiber optics in as many chokepoints as possible. There are dozens of places in the country where you could open up a manhole and in an hour cut off a city or more using just battery-powered hand tools. Or just toss a grenade in and run like hell."

"I agree that's a very credible risk. But we could get everything up and running again in a few days, so the impact would be less dire than what the Caliphate has been threatening.

"But now consider this: according to the calculations in an analysis the

Department of Homeland Security performed, if you took down about a third of the largest data centers, the Internet would collapse. And if you used kinetic weapons, you wouldn't be able to repair the damage."

Virgil Cooper, the former Navy SEAL commander wasn't buying it. "Don't you think that's a bit of an exaggeration? Sure, you could do a lot of damage with explosives, but what's to stop you from just hauling in new servers and setting everything back up again?"

"Because everything would have stopped—without the Internet, there'd be no gas, fuel oil, or food deliveries; no trains and no planes operating; no electricity to run the factories that make the tens of thousands of servers you'd need to replace, and so on. That's in the DHS report as well." Frank divided the stack of reports he'd carried to the front of the room into two stacks and handed them to his left and right.

"He's right," Dr. Fermi said. "I've read the same report."

"So for the sake of argument, I'll accept that," Travers said. "But why are you bringing up something that's another team's responsibility?"

"We weren't looking for this specifically. How we got there was by trying to get more information out of the intercept data than we were finding on the Internet."

"Also not your responsibility," the chairman cut in, checking his watch in a way that Frank was intended to notice.

Frank decided to speed up in case the chairman decided to cut his presentation off entirely. "Well, let me just briefly summarize our methodology, and then I'll jump ahead to what we uncovered."

Frank woke the projector up and started running quickly through a slide set that started with tables of code names and then progressed to charts of the frequency of the use of the suspect words they'd tracked, to pictures of data centers, and then to maps of their locations, providing a running commentary along the way.

"Through data analysis, we found what we believe were the code words for the Manhattan attack and then for the plague attack, based upon context and juxtaposition of peak usage leading up to the dates of those attacks. We've also come up with a third word that's skyrocketing towards levels that neither of the first two ever reached. We think, in each case, the code word is used to identify the sections of coded messages that relate to the specific attack the Caliphate is working up to and that the code word that's taking off now refers to the really big attack that Foobar has been promising. It's possible that other trending, suspect words relate to other pending attacks, or it may be that they're just camouflage, in order to confuse anyone trying to decode the messages we think relate to the big attack."

It was clear he had their attention now, so he pressed on. "So the next thing we tried to figure out was whether a given code word could give us any clues to what kind of attack was being planned. The code word for the Manhattan attack, which involved taking out bridges and tunnels, was "Hellespont," which suggests the nature of the attack because the Hellespont is where the Persian emperor Xerxes tried to cross from Asia into Europe to attack Greece on a bridge of boats two thousand years ago. But storms kept destroying the bridge, just as the Caliphate took out all of the bridges to Manhattan. And for the plague attack, they used the code word Venice, because that's the port through which the plague is believed to have entered Europe during the Middle Ages."

To everyone's surprise, Frank now switched to an archival photo of a V-1 flying bomb on its launcher. "We believe that the code word for the big attack is antlion and that the clue in that word is its association with the German V-1 rocket, which the Brits called a doodlebug, which is another word for antlion. And a set of plans and manuals for the V-1 was stolen three years ago from a museum in Germany."

The SEAL commander jumped in again. "So you're suggesting that Foobar's big plan to conquer the U.S. and Europe is to attack us with World War Two weaponry?"

"Yes, but not in the same way. Remember that where I started was noting that all someone would have to do is take down fewer than a hundred data centers to knock down the Internet and the Web."

"Brilliant. All he has to do is ship all those flying bombs and launch ramps and everything else to the U.S., ask everyone to look the other way while he sets them up all over the country, and then fire them. By George, Adversego, I think you've got it!"

Frank ignored the resulting laughter and kept forging ahead. "Actually, we think there's a much easier way available to him." He started working his way now through satellite shots of the specific ships they had settled on and the shipyards they'd visited, followed by a global map showing the routes of the ships over the last twelve months.

"So that's what we think. It all fits together. We've got no coastal defenses to protect us from an attack like this or any security program that inspects ships before they're at the dock. If you look at where those vessels are right now, each is on a course that, within a few weeks, would take it to a port near a major, in-range concentration of data centers in the U.S. or Europe. If we intercept those ships before they reach their destinations, we can head off Foobar's assault. He would have no reason to plan any attacks after this one, so if we stop it, we'd have enough time to take out the Caliphate before it could plan and launch anything else."

Frank stopped and waited for a response. Koontz was staring at him with deeply furrowed brows, while Fermi looked intrigued. The commander's face radiated disdain. The rest were staring at the chairman to see what he would say.

"So that's it?" the chairman said.

"Yes. That's what we think."

"Based on the facts that someone stole a set of V-1 plans, that some old ships needed repairs, and that in two weeks each of these ships could reach the U.S. or Europe, or, I might observe, just about anywhere else in the Western hemisphere."

"Well, not just that—"

"Oh—of course not. Excuse me. How could I forget. You've also got the fact that a Western colloquialism for an antlion is 'doodlebug.'"

"Uh, yes. That is where the V-1 part comes in."

"Okay, Frank. It may be that you've stumbled on something here that's important, by which I mean the code words and your theory that they identify related information contextually. If that proves to be true, that will be useful enough for me to forget about the cock-and-bull nonsense you just wasted our time with and perhaps even the amount of time you and your team spent concocting this fantasy when you were supposed to be saving the Homeland. Of course, if you'd shared the code word information with us however long ago you discovered it, we'd all be better off."

"But—"

"So in summary, I don't want to hear another word about your nonsensical V-1 theory or learn that you're wasting another minute of your team's time on anything other than what you were hired to work on, which is averting the possible catastrophe of the Caliphate launching a major cybersecurity attack. Do you understand?"

"Of course, I understand, but what about the ships? Isn't anyone going to check one of them out to see if we're right?"

"If you're inviting me to repeat what I've just said, you're making a bad decision. So I ask again: do you understand?"

Frank flapped his hands helplessly at his sides. Having no other choice, he said, "I understand." But his mind was already racing ahead to figure out a way to prove otherwise.

* * *

19

The Long and the Short of it

WITH THE CYBERSECURITY bill close to being signed, Mitty was getting ready to spring the trap he'd been preparing ever since his board of directors had adopted its growth at all costs strategy. The first step was to announce WeBCloud's acquisition of Cyber IP Holdings LLC. For the last two years, that company had been quietly filing patent applications and buying up patents owned by others for the sole purpose of eventually demanding license payments from anyone who might be infringing them. To those that approved of this business model, that made it a "non-practicing entity," but to everyone else, it was a "patent troll."

The marketplace was unaware of CIPH's activities, as CIPH had thus far operated in what venture capitalists referred to as "stealth mode," meaning that it had no publicly announced purpose and only an "under construction" web page. It had not, for example, issued a press release when it sold ten percent of its stock to WeBCloud several years before, nor had it revealed that, as part of the transaction, WeBCloud also received the right to buy the balance of CIPH's stock for a set price on the second anniversary of its initial investment. Although there was nothing in writing to indicate CIPH was operating under the control of the larger company, it was nonetheless a fact that virtually every patent in the CIPH portfolio would necessarily be infringed by anyone building or maintaining a cloud computing facility that complied with the DCSA data center security standards.

"Stuart Danforth is here, Nate."

"Thanks, Sue. Please tell him I'll be with him in a few minutes. Oh, and tell Lou as well."

"Already done that."

He smiled. "Of course, you have, Sue."

Mitty wasn't particularly busy, but he made Danforth wait for ten minutes anyway before joining him in the conference room.

"So," Mitty said, sliding a piece of paper across the table, "what do you think of this?"

The investment banker frowned slightly as he leaned forward to pick up the paper, expecting it to be the CIPH acquisition press release. Mitty looked a lot more confident than Danforth thought he had a right to be. This was going to be a rough meeting if Mitty thought yesterday's announcement that WeBCloud had purchased some unknown startup would make investors more interested in participating in the WeBCloud offering.

But the piece of paper wasn't the press release. Instead, it was a form letter on WeBCloud stationary with the address of the recipient left blank. It began:

> *Dear ,*
>
> *I am the licensing officer for WeBCloud, Inc., which has recently acquired Cyber IP Holdings LLC ("CIPH"), an intellectual property development and licensing company focusing on cloud computing security technologies, facilities, and services. According to your website, your company is principally or significantly active in one or more of these areas.*
>
> *As you may be aware, on January , the President of the United States signed a bill into law popularly known as the Cloud Computing Cybersecurity Act ("CCCA"). Under the CCCA, all vendors of cloud computing equipment and software and all providers of cloud computing services will be required to fully comply with the CCCA within six months of the CCCA's effective date. Substantial penalties will apply for non-compliance, including being barred from offering products or services if non-compliance is not rectified within the established grace period.*
>
> *Enclosed with this letter, you will find a list of thirty-seven granted patents that will be necessarily infringed by any cloud computing installation that is in compliance with the CCCA, as well as a table of the fees required to obtain a license to gain access to the technology*

represented by these patents. For your convenience, we have included an estimate of the fees you would pay to obtain such a license, based upon your publicly reported disclosure information.

After you have had an opportunity to review the table, please contact me promptly at the address below so that we can prepare the necessary paperwork and final fee schedule to permit you to comply with the CCCA.

I look forward to speaking with you or one of your employees at your earliest convenience.

Danforth looked up from the letter. "What kind of money would we be talking about for one of your big competitors to get a license?"

"Well, we don't want to be too greedy here. Say, about 1.25 billion dollars per calendar quarter."

The investment banker's eyes lit up. "And these patents—how solid are they?"

"Rock solid. Even if someone successfully challenges one or two of them, there will still be dozens that will stand up. But in any event, I'm not worried."

"Why not? If the patents are solid, we could take you public this summer. But if they're successfully challenged, whatever you paid for CIPH is money down a hole."

"Of course. But the patents will never be challenged while we own them."

Danforth frowned again; he knew that Mitty was no fool, but his answer didn't make sense. "Because?"

"Because supporting the validity of those patents will be worth far more to whoever is the winning bidder when we sell WeBCloud."

So that was it; Mitty had been planning all along to stick up the marketplace. Between his trade association and this acquisition, he'd have all of WeBCloud's competitors over a barrel. Mitty was looking very pleased with himself and clearly expected a reaction.

"Aha! I always knew you were a smart guy, Nate, but this is brilliant. My hat's off to you."

And indeed, it was brilliant, Danforth thought. There was no way Orinoco and the other big cloud service providers could outlast him if he could become profitable by charging patent royalties from everyone else. WeBCloud had already pushed cloud hosting margins down to almost nothing. Adding big new fees on top of existing operating expenses would drive every other cloud services provider out of the market entirely—except for the one that succeeded in buying WeBCloud. That would be sure to inspire a spirited bidding war and generate one hell of a big sale price—as well as one hell of a big commission for the investment bank that managed the sale.

Danforth found that his mouth was growing a bit dry as a new thought occurred to him. "That's tremendous news, Nate—we'll have no problem closing the round at a nice premium over the last one now. What would you think about a dual-track strategy? We could shop the market for a buyer at the same time we're soliciting funding from investors. That way we'll get competition between both groups as well as within each one. You could take the best offer you get, whether it's a lot more money at a much better valuation or a sale right away for the right price."

"No, Stuart, I don't think so. I think it's time for us to reap what we've sown. Cloud hosting is still going to be a tough business no matter how things play out. Speaking just for myself, with eight percent of WeBCloud's stock, I think I'll be able to get by with my share of a hundred-billion-dollar sale, and I expect that's how our investors will look at it, too. That's not a bad return on three years' work, even if there were a lot of late nights along the way."

Danforth couldn't tell whether Mitty was bluffing or not. They both knew the agreement between WeBCloud and Silicon Valley Securities only covered fundraising—not a sale of the company. There was nothing to stop Mitty from terminating their agreement while they were sitting there right now and then signing up one of SVS's competitors to sell WeBCloud. If that happened, Danforth wouldn't see a penny of the hundreds of millions of dollars the other investment bank would make on the sale.

His mind was racing now; who knew what calls Mitty might have already made to those competitors? He decided he couldn't take any chances. "Well, I can understand that. And if you want us to cancel the financing effort, we'd be just as happy to work with you on a sale. It won't take any time at all to convert the private placement memo we've been using for the financing round into a sale book. We'd only need to add a few sentences to our agreement with WeBCloud to cover a sale instead. And I hope you agree we've always given you exceptional service."

"Yes, we've always been happy with you and your team. But as you can appreciate, choosing the right investment bank for this transaction is going to be one of the most important decisions I ever ask my board to support. I expect they'll be leaning on me to pick one of the big, safe, well-known national outfits instead of taking a chance with a West Coast boutique firm like yours. And I'm sure that they'll grill me on the commission, too, just as they should. I'll need to have good answers to those questions, so several weeks ago, I asked Lou here to contact all of the top investment banks to collect their best offers. I must say, some of them were astonishingly favorable to WeBCloud. Right, Lou?"

Lou nodded enthusiastically. "Absolutely. I was very pleasantly surprised."

"And, of course," Mitty continued, "with the data center security law about to be signed and our acquisition of CIPH, our stature in the marketplace has risen considerably since we signed our current contract with SVS."

Danforth tried to maintain his best game face. He didn't want to give up an inch he might later regret, but he didn't want to risk losing the deal, either. "I'm sure you've done your homework, Nate, as always. And of course, you owe that to your shareholders. But keep in mind that we know your company inside out. That can make a big difference in negotiating the deal—if we can't get you a ten percent higher sale price than any other investment bank, I'll be amazed. Plus, we've always been there when you needed us."

"Indeed you have. That's why I've had our lawyers draw up an amendment giving you the transaction, at the lowest commission we were offered by any of your competitors. If you'd like to take the deal on those terms, just sign here."

Mitty slid a document and pen across the table. Danforth reached over to take them, and without further pretense, he turned to the page where he knew the commission terms would be found. Mitty was offering him half the usual rate. He flipped back to the first page and leaned back in his chair, thinking.

Mitty smiled. "Take your time. I don't have another appointment until 3:00; one of your competitors insisted on delivering a new bid personally."

Danforth glanced at his watch. It was 2:53. It was a struggle not to let his emotions show. This was what really sucked about being a service provider. It didn't matter if he was a dry cleaner or an investment banker wearing a two-thousand-dollar custom-made suit or that he'd always done great work for WeBCloud in the past. To Mitty, he was just another fungible tool to be used or tossed aside depending on the price.

Mitty looked down at his watch and began lightly tapping the table with his index finger.

Damn! Danforth wished business hadn't been so slow; he'd love to call Mitty's bluff. But it was, and he couldn't. He picked up the pen and examined it, trying to buy even a few more seconds to think before Mitty stood up to leave. On the side of its sleek barrel, it read *Goldman Sachs*.

The single crumb of satisfaction Danforth salvaged from the miserably demeaning experience came from snapping Mitty's pen in half before signing the amendment agreement with his own firm's pen.

* * *

"You're looking perky. Good meeting with Mr. Danforth?"

"Good enough, Sue. Let's just say eventually he came around to my way of thinking."

"I'm glad to hear it. If you don't mind me saying so, you've been looking run-down lately."

"Really? Well, I'm feeling just fine today."

"Good! Oh—Mr. Roach called while you were in with Mr. Danforth. He said it was important and hoped you'd be able to return his call today."

"Thanks."

So much for his good day. He dialed the lobbyist's number himself.

"Paul Roach."

"Nate here. What's up?"

"Nothing we can't handle. But Ravitz is at it again. We just saw in her email that she's persuaded Congressman Titus Steele to hold a hearing on data center physical security before the president can sign our bill, and she'll be one of the experts on the hearing panel."

"You have got to be kidding me! I've spent two years and ten million dollars in campaign contributions to get that bill adopted!"

"I know—who do you think told you how much to pay, and to who?"

"Listen—it's worse than that. After buying the rest of Cyber IP Holdings, I've only got three months' cash left. If we don't get financed or bought within the next two months, we'll have to declare bankruptcy."

"Take it easy. I don't think we need to go crazy here. I've already been in touch with Steele's chief of staff. Benno's met with him twice in the last six months, and he assured me he'll put Benno on the panel."

"Who else?"

"I'm pretty sure I'll be able to get your chief security officer on, too. Obviously, he'll say the right things. I can't imagine they won't be able to run rings around Ravitz."

"If it was anybody's committee other than Steele's, I wouldn't care. But he's so anti-business we didn't even bother to contribute to his campaign."

"I know, but he's no liberal, either. He's not likely to give much credence to a Chicken Little claiming the sky is falling."

"So why's he holding a hearing? Especially now?"

"My guess is just for the publicity. He's up against a primary challenger from his own party for the first time in ten years, so he's been trying to keep his name in the news as much as possible. And don't forget—we're all set to debunk Ravitz's fancy research report, so why not think of this as an opportunity to publicly shut her down? Let Tight-ass go ahead and rant for the cameras. If we just keep calm and carry on, everything should settle down then and the president will sign the bill."

Mitty stared at the phone. He was too close to the end of the road to take chances. And he was definitely not feeling calm.

"That's not good enough. When we were interviewing lobbying firms, you assured me you could be 'creative' when the situation demands. Well, the situation is demanding. What can you do to discredit Ravitz?"

"Nate, I really don't think we need—"

"Well, I do. Get back to me tomorrow with an airtight plan for making Ravitz look like a fool in front of that committee."

* * *

President Henry Dodge Yazzie considered the advice he'd just received from Carson Bekin, his oldest advisor and now his press secretary.

"You know, Carson, this isn't what we came to Washington for six months ago. We were going to be different—that's what we promised the voters, remember?"

"Sure, Henry. Problem is, we're here now, and it's a whole different ball game from what we expected."

"That's bull, Carson. If anything, I thought it would be worse. I didn't expect to be able to believe anything anyone said if they were asking for something. And everybody's always asking for something."

"Of course. But that's not what I meant. What I'm realizing is that if we're going to deliver on any of the promises we made to the voters, we're going to have to hold our noses and support more things on other peoples' agendas than I expected. Sometimes even special interest agendas."

"If that's a surprise, Carson, you were kidding yourself. But either way, there's a difference between supporting something and just not getting in the way, and that ought to be good enough. I'm okay with not vetoing something that has strong support in both houses of Congress, provided it's not outright counter to the public interest, or contrary to an issue we campaigned hard on. But I'm not going to publicly support a bill I don't believe in just because one group or another wants us to."

"This isn't some special interest group, Henry. This is a bill introduced by Bill Taylor—the speaker of the house—and one that a company called WeBCloud has lobbied hard for! Taylor's got a tough election coming up, and he could really use WeBCloud's support. It's one of the bigger employers in his state. Why should he help us on a bill we care about if we don't support him on one of his?"

"Because it's a bad bill! Did you see that report on the vulnerability of data centers to physical attack? There was a reference to it in my daily briefing yesterday, so I asked for a copy. It's from some public interest group Bill Ravitz's daughter started, and it turns out that DHS had already done a similar report that came to the same conclusions. Anyway, Ravitz's father sent advance copies to the White House and a lot of other folks on the Hill, and it scared the hell out of me. You ought to read it."

"Most of what's in your daily briefing scares the hell out of me."

"Yeah, but this is something I can do something about."

"Such as?"

"Veto that bill."

"Henry, you can't."

"Of course I can. Haven't you read the Constitution?"

"Don't be cute, Henry. I'm serious. Don't forget you ran as an independent—neither party owes you anything. In fact, quite the opposite, given that you beat their own candidates in the election. If Taylor wants to turn his back on you, nobody in his party is going to complain. Then we'll never get anything accomplished. Look, why don't you let me at least make a favorable comment on your behalf. Then we can figure out some kind of executive order you could issue after the election that will address your concerns. How about it—can we look into that?"

Yazzie frowned and swiveled around to look out a window of the Oval Office. He hated this part of the job the most. But maybe Bekin's idea had some merit. "Okay, Carson," he said finally. But he felt unclean.

* * *

Sean Lynch was standing by a copy machine, waiting for one stack of paper to become four, and he was no longer enjoying himself. The early glow inspired by his lunch with Roach had faded almost immediately. For starters, he was being supervised by someone only a couple years' his senior instead of by Roach. And when he did have any contact with the big boss—say, sitting in a chair against the wall while the other team members traded ideas with Roach across the conference room table—he might as well not have been there at all.

The experience of monitoring Sara's account had also quickly turned sour. It was difficult to maintain his righteous anger while following her familiar way of expressing herself. By turns serious and cheerful, her messages reminded him all too clearly what had drawn him to her, leaving him lonely and regretful. And the contrast of her high-minded efforts, regularly reported in the news media with his own tawdry activities left him feeling soiled and cheap. Lately, her parting words kept springing back to mind: "You're too good to be doing what you're doing." She loved him, she'd said, but she wouldn't stand aside and watch him promoting causes she knew he didn't believe in just to make a lot of money. "I'm doing this for your sake more than mine," she'd said. Maybe it would wake him up. She hoped so, but if not, then they had never been meant for each other to begin with.

The voice of his manager on the DCSA account just outside the alcove he was standing in brought him back to the present.

"Hey, Rob. Just on my way to see you."

"What's up?"

"Fire drill on DCSA in conference room three."

Lynch took the stacks of paper out of the copy machine and hurried back to his cubicle. But there was no blinking light on his phone and no meeting invitation to accept in his email. That was strange; he might be the most junior person on the account, but at least he was always invited to team meetings. He walked down the hall to conference room three, hoping he'd be noticed and invited in. But the door was already closed.

What could that mean? He searched his mind and couldn't think of anything he'd screwed up.

* * *

Roach started speaking as soon as the third and last invited team member arrived.

"Okay, so here's the situation. We're just about across the finish line on the cloud computing security bill. But now, at the last minute, the chairman of the House Cybersecurity, Infrastructure Protection, and Security Technologies Subcommittee has decided to hold a hearing on data center security. Go figure.

"You'd think the client should be pretty happy that I've sweet talked the DCSA executive director onto the hearing panel, along with WeBCloud's own chief security officer. WeBCloud, you'll recall, is the company that's been funding DCSA and pulling all the strings from the beginning.

"But—and here's the catch—the third person on the hearing panel is going to be Sara Ravitz, and WeBCloud thinks she'll be presenting a fat report from a research institute that, taken at face value, would indicate that Congress would be crazy to adopt a bill based on the DCSA standard."

"But I thought we were all set to neutralize that report?" the team project manager asked.

"That's what I told Nate Mitty, the WeBCloud CEO. We should be able to start to undercut it at the hearing and trash it pretty convincingly in our written testimony, which is what really counts. We'll have lots of third party support for what we say, too, through the articles we've planted and a white paper that the DCSA funded. But Mitty doesn't want to leave anything to chance. He wants us to take Ravitz down, too. So I'm looking for ideas here."

There was silence for a while.

Finally, the project manager spoke up. "What do we have to work with?"

"Not much. She's a pretty straight arrow."

Another pause.

"Anything from deep research to work with?"

"Nope. I should have said a really straight arrow. But we can spoof her email address."

The project manager brightened up considerably. "How far can we run with that?"

"As far as the client is concerned, as far as we want. But emails leave tracks, so that's farther than I want to go if we can avoid it. I'd like us to come up with something that gets us where we want to go but doesn't leave any bread crumbs back to us."

Silence again. Then another team member spoke.

"Okay, so how about this. We get a rumor started that she's shorting the stock of one of the big cloud providers—say Orinoco. That way it would look like she's using her non-profit as a front to manipulate the stock market for her own profit."

"'Shorting?'" one of the other team members asked.

"Sorry. It means you sell shares you've borrowed, say, from your brokerage firm, when the price is high, and then cover the sale when the stock drops to a lower price, and make a profit on the spread."

"Pardon my ignorance, but I didn't understand a single word you just said."

"It means you're betting against a company's stock price. If it drops a lot, you make a killing. If it goes up instead, you lose your shirt."

"Okay. Thanks."

"Anyway, and better yet, just by starting the rumor, it would probably lead to other investors climbing on board and shorting the stock as well. The markets track changes in short positions, so that would make it look like the rumor was actually true. And the more people hear the rumor, the lower it drives the price."

"Isn't that stock manipulation? Can't you go to jail for that?"

"Not if we do it right. There are lots of stock trading chat rooms online. We can have one of the people we work with set up a few aliases out there to plant the rumor. Once it takes off, we can anonymously tip a few financial reporters to the posts in the chat room, and they'll be sure to write up the story."

"But what if we get caught?"

"We won't get caught. The way they catch stock manipulators is see who the big buyers and sellers were before and after the fake story hits the market. And we won't be doing either."

"But in fact, neither will Ravitz."

"That won't matter. She'll deny that she's shorting the stock, which is what everyone does when they're accused of gaming the stock market. But it's pretty darn hard to prove the negative. By the time she convinces everybody that she's innocent, the bill will already be signed, and then who cares?"

Roach said nothing for several seconds and then said, "I might be able to buy into that." Another pause. "Okay, let's run with that. The hearing's in ten days, so you better get moving."

Lynch saw Rob and the project manager walk past his cubicle, and grabbed the same stack of paper he'd copied fifteen minutes earlier. He followed the pair, hoping they'd pause to chat at Rob's cubicle again. They did, and he glided unnoticed into the copier alcove to listen.

"So I can get Sean to help me plant the rumor about Ravitz shorting the Orinoco stock, right?"

"Not this time. Turns out Ravitz is an old girlfriend of his. Roach thinks asking him to help take her down might be pushing things too far."

"Ah—got it. That's makes sense."

Lynch had only laid the paper in the feeder so the sound of the machine wouldn't make it hard to hear, but he jabbed the start button now. His head was awhirl with cascading realizations. He hadn't understood everything he'd just heard, but it was clear that the "pushing things too far" comment meant the only reason he'd been assigned to the team—and to do the dirty work—was because Roach had guessed he would leap at the chance to get back at Sara. That meant Roach hadn't had his eye on him at all. And now Sean didn't know whether he had a future at the firm or not.

The machine was done copying, but he still stood there staring at the blank wall behind the copier. Now what?

There were now no voices to be heard behind him. He picked up his copying and returned to his cubicle, trying to remember exactly what he had heard— something about taking Sara down by starting a rumor that she was "shorting" Orinoco stock, whatever that meant. It didn't take him long to figure that out online. Clearly, Roach was taking things up a notch, trying not just to counter what the RTF was doing but to destroy Sara's reputation as well.

He leaned back and the same question pushed its way forward again.

Now what?

He grabbed his coat and left the Roach & Drye office. It took two hours of walking for him to come up with the right answer.

* * *

20

Why Didn't you just Say so the First Time?

FRANK PEERED OVER Tim's shoulder as he called up the SlipMeFive.com website.

"It works like this," Tim said. "All you have to do is sign up as a user and then describe what you want someone to do. Just about everyone who signs up to provide goods or services is from a developing country and agrees to charge just five dollars to take on your project, whatever it is. People use the site to buy custom logos, or book cover designs, or just about anything else that can be delivered on a virtual basis."

"Including drone services in Myanmar?"

"You'd be amazed. Anyway, it can't hurt to find out, right?"

Right, Frank thought. Because they might not have enough time to hop on a plane and hopscotch their way to Myanmar and back before Foobar launched his attack.

"How does this sound? Wanted: quad drone with video camera operator for harbor assignment in Yangon, Myanmar."

"I guess that pretty much says it. Here's hoping someone bites."

When Tim emerged from the bathroom the next morning, Frank was standing by Tim's computer like a cocker spaniel next to an empty food bowl. Tim suppressed a smile, half-expecting Frank to use his nose to nudge the laptop forward.

"Okay, okay. I'll check."

There were three responses.

Frank whooped. "That's fantastic! How fast can we get moving?"

"We'll have to see. Don't forget, we're talking to people on the other side of the world who just finished dinner. What do you want me to say?"

"Let's send the same response to all three of them and say that the first one that gets back to us gets the job."

"Good idea. Here—why don't you enter the job description."

Frank took the laptop and thought for a minute. Then he typed:

> *You must speak English, have Skype or a similar program on your phone, and have a drone with at least a half hour's flight time. You will need to get within visual range of a ship that we will identify which is docked near the cargo container terminal in Yangon. We will provide the URL of the site to which you will broadcast the live video feed from your drone. When your drone gets close to the ship, we will direct you where to send it. The first respondent to this message gets the deal.*

They got their first response almost immediately. By the end of some spirited negotiation, their contractor had moved the price from five dollars up to twenty dollars, supposedly to cover the rental of a boat so that he could be sure to be able to get within his drone's fuel range of the ship. They decided on three o'clock local time the next afternoon for the flight, when the crew might be taking a mid-day break from the heat.

* * *

Frank and Tim were huddled around Frank's laptop this time, waiting for the Skype call to come through in the wee hours of the morning. It was already fifteen minutes late. At last, the signal sounded, and Frank accepted the call. They were looking at the face of the drone operator, taken by his mobile device's camera.

"Sorry; the ship is farther from where I expected."

"Okay. Where are you?"

The drone operator's face disappeared, and the image on the screen turned into a smear of colors; when it once again came into focus, they were looking at a ship that was growing larger by the moment. They were almost able to read its name before the picture swung around again to show the phone's owner.

"Great," Frank said. "Slow down and see if you can tell whether there's anyone on deck."

They could hear the small boat's engine fade. "Cranes are not moving. I am too far down to tell if anyone is on deck, but no one looks this way anyway."

"Great. Is there somewhere you can get out of sight to launch the drone?"

There was a pause. "Yes. I see empty slip near the ship. I launch there and keep drone close to water until I get to ship. Remember—you promise we not stay long. If I lose drone, you pay for."

"Right—don't worry. This shouldn't take long. Let us know when you're ready to launch."

Frank drummed his fingers on his thigh and looked at his watch. He looked twice more before the voice returned.

"Okay. Hovering over water. Let me know when you get video feed."

They stared at Frank's laptop, which was set up to receive and save the feed.

"There! We've got it. Now head to the bow of the ship. When you get there, take a slow wide angle shot of the bow from the waterline to just below the deck."

Frank was drumming with both hands now as the video climbed the hull; as they hoped, they could see eight feet of darker paint below the fully loaded waterline. The ship was carrying a light cargo.

Frank pressed the mute button. "There it is! Just like we hoped!"

A thin line had appeared that extended for what looked to be about forty feet in each direction across the bluff bow of the ship before making a right angle turn and extending vertically. A third vertical line equidistant between the other two was at the exact center of the bow. As the drone rose, they saw a second horizontal line appear at the ends of the three vertical lines, closing the tops of the rectangles that represented the launch doors they had been looking for. That meant there were two doors that would open like window shutters.

"What now? Are we done?" Tim asked.

"Not yet. We're going to need to do better than that before anyone believes us." He unmuted the phone. "Now pull back two hundred yards and then go up to five hundred feet and move slowly from bow to stern over the ship. I want to get a look from above."

The video feed pulled back farther and farther before moving up into the sky. The camera swiveled down, and they stared at water until at last the bow of the ship came into view.

"We hit pay dirt!" Frank whispered. "Look!"

There was an open hatch.

"Stop when you get over that hatch and zoom in as much as you can."

The image swooped downward, but as it did, the image got fuzzier and darker. Frank pressed the mute button and squinted at the screen.

"We can't see anything from this height. The inside of the ship is in shadow. Damn it, I should have thought of that and scheduled the flight for noon."

He unmuted. "Okay, we need to see what's inside the ship, and it's too dark to see from this high up. Bring the drone down."

"I can't too far; I won't be able to see it."

"That's okay. Just take it slow and we'll tell you what to do from the video feed."

"I don't like. What if you crash my drone?"

"We won't."

"What if I get caught?"

Frank thought quickly. "How about we pay one hundred dollars instead of twenty dollars?"

Pause. "Okay. I wait while you go to SlipMeFive and make payment."

"You're kidding!"

"Hurry up. Only fifteen more minutes of flight time."

Frank punched the mute button again. "Who says piracy is dead? What's that password again?"

Frank scrambled to open the SlipMeFive.com site and logged in while Tim coached him.

"You push that button—right—now in the menu, select 'My SlipMes.' Right. Now 'Add service.' You can skip the description and hit enter. You're good."

"Okay—we made the payment. How long do we have?"

"Eleven minutes—twelve, maybe. Let me check account."

Frank put his laptop down on the table and held his head in his hands, moaning softly as he rocked back and forth. At last, the image began to get larger. He grabbed his phone again.

"Okay, keep it coming down—okay, a little more slowly. And bring the resolution back."

The dark square below grew gradually larger. Eventually, it began to change from black to dark gray. Finally, indistinct outlines of objects began to appear.

"Okay. That's great. Now bring the camera around to ninety degrees so we can see ahead. Keep going down slow."

The camera swiveled and they could see they were just about at deck level.

"Okay. Slowly…slowly…slowly—and stop." It was still too dark to see much. They'd have to move out of the sun and under the deck.

"Go forward very slowly. Don't worry, we're not going far."

The picture lightened considerably. They were looking at the side of the ship from the inside. Racked against the hull were large tanks containing who knew what. Thick hoses were coiled on the floor.

"Is time to leave. Only have six more minutes of fuel."

"Not yet! Do a slow three-hundred-sixty-degree turn with the camera first."

"Okay, but then go!"

The video panned around toward the stern of the ship. They watched as huge crates, marching in rows back into the darkness, came into sight and then disappeared from view, followed by oversized forklifts, after which the video at last moved toward the bow. As the camera continued to turn, it picked up what looked like the end of a board, extending parallel to the deck, that continued to lengthen until it connected to a long torpedo-shaped body mounted on a rail extending off toward the bow. Above the body was a long canister mounted on struts, and another board extended away from the body toward the other side of the ship.

Frank grabbed Tim's arm. "Did you get it? Are you sure?"

Tim nodded vigorously as he fiddled with the laptop.

"Now! Which way to get out!" called the voice from the phone.

"Okay. Swivel the camera until it points straight up. Good. Now go backwards—a bit farther—a bit more—and you're good to go!"

The sky swallowed the video feed as the drone shot upward.

"Great! We got what we wanted! Thanks a lot."

"No problem. You need more help, you get in touch. I give you good deal."

* * *

21

You Don't Say!

WHEN HENDERSON, THE chair of the Cyberattack Tiger Team did not respond to his calls by 11:00 the next morning, Frank decided to take a different tack. He attached a twenty-second video clip to an email showing the V-1 in the hold, as well as an updated executive summary of the plot as he had described it at the Tiger Team meeting, and sent it to Lieutenant Travers. Then he just sat on Marla's couch, waiting for the phone to ring. And waited. He was so nervous he was making Thor fidgety, too.

Tim had left for work as usual, bleary-eyed from their middle of the night aerial adventure on the other side of the world. Frank called him when he couldn't sit still any longer.

"Have you heard anything there? What's Koontz up to?"

"Nothing. He's been in a staff meeting all morning."

"Okay. Let me know if you hear anything."

Finally, at 3:30, his phone rang. There would be a meeting at CIA headquarters the next morning where he and Tim would be debriefed. The details would be worked out over the next several hours, but they should expect that a car would pick them up no later than 7:30 AM.

"So how do we handle a debriefing?" Tim asked.

"Dunno. Maybe George can give us a quick coaching session. I'll give him a ring."

George not only could, but he'd just been asked to help them prepare. He suggested that he meet them at the office in half an hour.

By the time George arrived, he was up to date on how plans for the next day were developing. Due to the urgency of the situation, the CIA would be departing from usual protocols.

"It sounds from your report like the attack could come in as little as a week or ten days, so the analysis and decision process is going to have to be radically compressed. What they're talking about is quizzing you in front of a lot of high-level decision makers instead of debriefing you first and then summarizing your information in reports that would take days to prepare before they could be reviewed by the higher-ups.

"The last I heard, they'll want you to give short presentations on the key elements: how and why you think the code words identify the surrounding text, why you think the data centers are the targets, how you decided which ships were involved, and why you believe that the ships are already loaded with the V-1s. They're putting together a team of subject matter experts to ask questions after each presentation. There may be questions from the audience as well. I expect you'll want to divvy up the subjects between the two of you since you don't have a lot of time to prepare."

"How are they going to explain the fact that the only new information we've submitted since we got laughed out of the Tiger Team meeting is the video from the ship?" Frank asked.

"They've already papered that little detail over. Instead, they'll be stressing how quickly the CIA moved from a theory to confirmation."

"The CIA!"

"Of course. What did you expect? I know it sucks, but they are paying your salary, so it's not a totally inaccurate statement. If I were you, I'd toe the Agency line. There's nothing to gain from making a big deal out of it, and don't forget you sat on the code word information longer than you should have if you were a good team player."

"Huh!"

"Anyway, keep the game plan in mind, and there's no need to be nervous about the debriefing or to worry that anyone's going to give you the third degree. They know you've pulled their chestnuts out of the fire. If you guys hadn't figured this out, there would have been hell to pay inside the beltway."

"Hell to pay!" Tim gasped. "Most of the people inside the beltway would have ended up dead!"

"Yes, but now they won't, and that changes everything. Now they can take their time planning the invasion of the Caliphate without worrying that Foobar might strike first."

"How does that change everything? We're still just as vulnerable as we were before. Anyone else could stage the same kind of attack. And someday somebody certainly will."

"True. But for now, all the administration has to do is capture some old ships offshore and sink them."

"I don't understand—why would they want to sink the ships?"

"Because if word gets out about what almost happened, people will expect the government to do something right away about all those data centers."

"Of course, they would! And they'd be right! They've all got to be buried or broken up before someone else tries the same thing!"

"Sure. That's what you or I would say. But we're not politicians. The biggest high tech companies in the world own those data centers, and they retain some of the country's highest paid lobbyists."

"So what? What about the voters?"

"More than a third of the congressmen and senators come from states where those data centers are located."

"I know. Frank and I've already been over that. But if the voters knew what the risks were, the politicians would have no choice but to act."

"Exactly. And now we're back where we started, and now you know why I'm expecting them to decide to sink the ships to be sure that no one ever knows what they escaped."

"Come on!"

"Sorry. But just think about it. Pass a law saying that existing and new data centers have to be buried fifty feet underground—or that no data center can be larger than a convenience store, if you prefer that approach instead—and everything on the cloud computing front will grind to a halt until the government writes the detailed regulations and the vendors figure out what it will cost. That will take years. Then they'll need to redesign the data centers, and then get all the permits they'll need before they can start work. And that will take years. Then they have to actually dig the holes or build thousands of mini-data centers and fill them with servers—more years. By the time all is said and done, we're talking about the better part of a decade here."

"So they'd better get cracking then!"

"Hold on—I'm not done yet. Don't forget that cloud computing is brand new.

One of the main reasons it's grown to be so popular so fast is because it's cheaper than running traditional, on-site systems. Burying or massively dividing up data centers would dramatically increase the cost of the service, and the whole business model might collapse."

"Great! Better a few vendors have their business model wiped out instead of the entire developed world! Before the cloud service companies had their bright idea, everything was spread out everywhere, and there was no way to destroy it all short of a nuclear war. Congress ought to make us go back to that model before it's too late!"

"Just like Congress put the Glass-Steagall Act back in place after the Great Recession so it wouldn't happen again, right? Oh, right. Somehow, that didn't happen, did it? My bet is the president's political advisors will say that going public on what almost happened will advertise how vulnerable we are, and the public wouldn't like that or the fact that almost all of the data centers got built on this president's watch. And they'll say that none of our enemies would dare try such an attack, since the nuclear submarines we always have at sea could annihilate anyone that attacked the data centers."

"Really? How would they know who to fire at? Foobar's using a bunch of old ships owned through three layers of shell companies. After an attack, there'd be no way to figure out who hit us, and anyway, everyone would be too tied up defending their family from someone trying to steal their last can of beans!"

"All good points. Who knows—maybe I'm wrong and instead we'll be listening to the president ten days from now taking credit for saving us all from attack." He looked at his watch. "Anyway, you boys better get ready and then get some sleep. You're putting on a command performance tomorrow."

But Tim wouldn't leave it alone as he and Frank walked to the Metro stop.

"Do you think George is right? Wouldn't the president want to make a big deal about saving the country?"

"I don't know. The infrastructure report you read is secret, but it's not as if data center vulnerability isn't obvious to anyone if they think about it. I shouldn't really be telling you this, because it involves another client, but in just a few days, a non-profit is going to release a report that has everything important in it, even if it doesn't have quite as detailed a description of the aftermath of an attack. I even ran into an article the other day by a technology reporter out in Silicon Valley who's been trying to get people to think about data center vulnerability for two years now. But no one seems to have paid much attention to him. Hell, any wannabe thriller-writer with a decent knowledge of high-tech trends could figure all this out and self-publish a book that would make your hair curl."

"Then how can they keep ignoring the danger?"

"How do they keep ignoring all the other dangers they keep ignoring? Maybe they like living on the edge. Or maybe politicians really are as detached from reality as we always thought they were."

"Yeah, well, I'm not."

* * *

The next morning, the Agency car and driver arrived on schedule to deliver Frank and Tim to the CIA's headquarters at Langley, Virginia. Despite George's comforting words to the contrary, Tim continued to fiddle with his presentations on their way out of town. On arrival, they were escorted to a meeting room and asked to sit at the smaller of the two tables that stood on a platform, angled toward each other and the audience. In front of each chair was a microphone, as well as a revised copy of Frank's executive summary.

He skimmed the summary as he waited, determining that the information was largely intact, despite the CIA's urinating on it enough to be sure that anyone sniffing it would conclude that the CIA had pulled off a near miracle by saving this great nation from imminent destruction by a cruel and merciless foe.

The room quickly filled with what they had been told would be top brass from each of the service branches as well as upper level agency and administration personnel. A few minutes after the scheduled start time, an assistant director of the CIA entered the room. He was followed by seven individuals, some in uniform and some not, who took their places at the second table on the platform. To Frank's surprise, one was Virgil Cooper, the former SEAL team leader from his own Tiger Team. The assistant director stepped up to a lectern behind Frank and Tim, and the room immediately fell silent.

"I'd like to thank you all for making yourselves available today on such short notice. On your way into the room, each of you should have received a high-level briefing paper summarizing the situation we will be learning more about today. If that's not the case, please see one of the personnel by the door.

"As you've already been informed, late yesterday afternoon we received the first concrete evidence confirming that the Caliphate is in fact preparing to attack the Homeland. More importantly, we believe that we now know the nature of that attack and will therefore be able to thwart it before it is launched.

"However, we also believe that time is extremely short—perhaps as little as one week. Due to this urgency, we have taken the unusual step of debriefing the individuals who secured this information in your presence so that all decision makers likely to participate in planning, approving, or executing the military response will have firsthand data as quickly as possible. You can be assured that the

CIA is already dedicating all needed resources to filling in the remaining details relating to the anticipated attack, and will continue to do so during and after this meeting.

"In just a moment, I will turn the meeting over to the experts we've asked to conduct the debriefing. I trust you'll understand if most of these individuals are not introduced. For similar reasons, no photography will be permitted. But first, I'd like to play a brief video that should bring home the nature and potential extent of the disaster that we are now about to avert. Would someone turn off the lights, please."

The room grew half-dark, and a projector bathed the screen behind the platform with light. Frank swiveled in his seat and saw a freighter surging through a suitably dramatic seascape as a commanding voice proclaimed that the vessel was controlled, through multiple shell companies, by the Caliphate. The image switched to a satellite picture of a manufacturing facility, identified by the voiceover as another similarly disguised resource of the Caliphate. Frank realized that the hastily thrown together video was providing a condensed version of the more dramatic parts of his original executive summary.

Jarringly, the video cut to grainy black-and-white footage of V-1 flying bombs coming off the production line in Germany in 1944 and then being launched from Belgium. The next image showed firemen training their hoses on the smoking ruins of buildings in London's East End.

In a cut back to color, the audience was introduced to aerial shots of enormous, sprawling data centers, then to an edited version of the feed from Frank and Tim's drone as it zoomed in to the bow of the ship in Yangon, and then into the hold of the ship itself. When the camera completed its 360-degree sweep, the video cut to footage of an actual blackout rapidly knocking out the lights of a major city building by building, like a row of dominos, until the screen and the room itself was totally dark. The only sound came from people shifting uneasily in their chairs before the room lights came up once again.

"I hope that gives you a more immediate sense of what we're dealing with today. Thank you for your attention. I will now introduce Colonel Derek Henderson, the chair of the Tiger Team that made these discoveries. Colonel Henderson, please take over."

Henderson strode—no, Frank decided, he strutted—to the podium.

"Good morning. As the chair of the Tiger Team responsible for uncovering the catastrophic attack that will now be averted, I'm pleased to introduce you to two more Cyberattack Tiger Team members."

Frank and Tim rolled their eyes in spontaneous synchronicity.

"Today you will be hearing information from Agency contractor Frank

Adversego and employee Timothy Slattery. Our Tiger Team was commissioned earlier this year to search for any evidence that the forces of Mullah Muhammed Foobar might be planning a cyberattack on the Homeland.

"We have asked Mr. Adversego and Mr. Slattery to make a series of short presentations addressing how the plot was discovered, how we believe the Caliphate executed the major elements of its preparation, and how and where we believe it will be targeted. Opposite them on the stage are Commander Virgil Cooper, a National Counter Terrorism Center operations officer and former SEAL Team commanding officer and a member of my Tiger Team, and several other gentlemen whose identities and positions I will not share. Although everything remains fluid at this moment, our working assumption is that a joint task force of Navy and Air Force units under the command of the Joint Special Operations Command will be formed to intercept and take the Caliphate ships. The SEALs would play an important role in that effort, and Mr. Cooper will help brief them in preparation for that operation.

"As this is a debriefing, we expect that this morning's proceedings will be more free form than rigid so that we can be sure to gain as complete and clear a picture as possible. At the end of each presentation, my colleagues and I on the stage will ask follow-up questions, after which we will allow questions from the floor.

"With that, I'd like to ask Mr. Adversego to make the first presentation."

Frank reprised in greater detail the presentation he'd given the week before to the Tiger Teams, noting as he did so that the slides he'd presented at the Tiger Team meeting had now been turgidly translated into minutely detailed MilSpeak.

As the morning progressed, there was little that either Frank or Tim had to say that was not extensively questioned and examined. Each of the experts who grilled them across the stage had obviously been coached not to call out the fact that all of the revelations Frank had just presented originated from his and Tim's unauthorized, and indeed explicitly forbidden, extracurricular efforts. Instead, everyone acknowledged the revelations had originated from the coordinated efforts of the entire Tiger Team, inspired by the extraordinary leadership of Colonel Derek R. Henderson.

After four hours, Frank and Tim were totally wrung out and welcomed the delayed lunch break when it was called. As they waited for the audience to file out of the room, the assistant director of the CIA approached them and held out his hand.

"I'd like to thank both of you for this tremendous breakthrough and for your fine presentations and responses today. You can be sure that your roles will be recognized at the highest level. I expect we'll be in touch in the days ahead as we develop and then implement a plan to intercept the ships."

Frank and Tim looked at each other. "So we're not needed after lunch?"

"Yes, but not in this meeting, where we'll be moving into a discussion of response options. We've scheduled one-on-one debriefings with each of you for the rest of today and tomorrow so that we're sure we've got one hundred percent of the data we need to finalize the interceptions. My assistant will escort you to another part of the building where that process will begin."

"I guess we shouldn't be surprised," Frank observed as they followed their guide through a series of hallways. "After all, this isn't the movies. There's no need for us to be sitting in the Chinook when the SEALs slide down the ropes onto the decks of the ships, or whatever they'll be doing."

"You're right. It's still a bummer, though. Can you get in touch with George tonight to find out how the rest of the meeting went?"

"Good idea. I don't know whether he'll be able to tell us everything, but it can't hurt to ask."

* * *

22

Man Doth not Live by Code Alone

T IM WAS FURIOUS when he heard what Frank had learned from George. The administration had indeed indicated it might order the military to take out Foobar's ships in secret, never revealing to the public that an attack with horrific consequences had been narrowly averted.

"How can they try to just brush this under the rug, like nothing ever happened?"

"Didn't you ever read *Catch-22*?"

"Yes. But what does that have to do with this?"

"Well, what *was* catch-22?"

"That if you didn't want to fly because it was too dangerous, you couldn't be crazy, and if you weren't crazy, you weren't entitled to a psychological discharge."

"That's what most people think. But the way I read it, the real, big picture catch was this: they can do anything to you that you can't stop them from doing. That's how they can sweep this under the rug as if nothing ever happened."

"Well, then we've got to stop them."

"Interesting concept. How do you propose we go about doing that?"

"Well, I'll blow the whistle on them. Call a reporter. Leak some files. You know, what people have done before."

"And then what happens? Remember Snowden? I bet Moscow is pretty cold this time of year. And how about Chelsea Manning? She won't be out of Leavenworth 'til she's in her sixties."

"Well, Daniel Ellsberg never went to jail for leaking the Pentagon Papers during the Vietnam War."

"Not for want of trying by the government. As I recall, he only went free because the judge tossed the case out of court due to egregious misconduct by Nixon's prosecutors."

"So what do you suggest we do?"

"I don't know. But I do know that the first thing we need to do is everything we can to help stop Foobar from bombing us back to the Stone Age. After that, we can talk about how to get the word out without violating the nondisclosure agreements you and I signed that say they can toss us in jail forever if we violate them."

"Sure. And who's going to listen to us after the danger's past? Remember you told me about that journalist who's on to the danger and can't get anyone to listen to him."

"Okay, okay. But I still say let's come back to this later. If we blow the whistle on this now, Foobar will just tell his ships to turn around, right? We'd look like a couple of cranks. No one would even notice when we got tossed in the clink for as long as the CIA felt like keeping us there."

"And if we blow the whistle after they sink the ships, why won't we look like a couple of cranks then?"

"I can't answer that yet. I just know that we've got to stop Foobar first."

Tim threw up his hands. "Fine! Just fine! But I'll tell you, not worrying about this until the whole thing's over is making less and less sense to me."

* * *

Things were progressing rapidly now, as indeed they needed to with the ships steaming inexorably closer to their targets. Multiple, hastily assembled teams of engineers and analysts were scrubbing the data Tim dumped from their laptops into the CIA's system, testing their assumptions and crosschecking them against the updated information streaming into CIA headquarters from satellites, field operatives, and NATO sources.

One group was reviewing everything the CIA was learning about the Caliphate's financial and contractual relations to determine how the new V-1s had been manufactured, and by whom. Another was trying to determine as much as possible about the flying bombs themselves. Was there evidence anywhere that they had been tested in actual flight? Could they have been modified to use modern fuels to extend their range? Should it be assumed that each one would reach its target? There was so much to learn—like the total number of prehistoric cruise missiles that had actually been built and whether the ships might have V-1s stowed on multiple decks instead of just one—but very little time.

Another team was crunching the data necessary to refine the list of most likely targets, an area Frank and Tim had not had time to address in more than cursory fashion. The last team was taking apart Tim's data relating to the Caliphate's ships to confirm that each ship he had identified as being a V-1 launcher was indeed a threat.

In every case, all the significant data held up. The target and ship teams were now tracking the routes and speeds of each ship in order to match their current courses against the presumed targets and determined their expected arrival date off shore of those targets. Day by day, the whole picture became clearer.

Meanwhile, a dozen SEAL platoons were feverishly training off San Diego, readying for the rapidly approaching day when they would come alongside the freighters in small speedboats with muffled engines before throwing grappling hooks aloft and swarming aboard. Once they had secured the ships' bridges and locked the off-duty crew in their cabins, the rest of the team would arrive by helicopter to take the crews into custody and remove all the computers and other evidence they found. All but one of the ships would then be scuttled; the last one would be diverted to Guam for more detailed study of the weaponry aboard and anything else of interest.

* * *

"Hello? Remember me?"

Frank's and Tim's heads swiveled up from their laptops in unison to face a pajama-clad Marla standing in the door of the living room of her apartment. They stared blankly for a moment before Tim replied.

"Oh—sorry!" Tim said. "I didn't think you'd still be up. It must be 12:30. I just got in."

"Yes, I'm still up. If I didn't stay up late these days, I'd never see you at all. And all I see of my father lately is the back of his head. What's come over the two of you?"

"Things are just really busy on my government project," Frank replied quickly, giving Tim a minute to think. "But things will start slacking off a lot after Friday."

"Friday?"

"Uh, yeah. I've got a deadline I'm working against. If I'm not done by then all hell will break loose."

"And how about you, Tim?"

"Hmm, not so sure." Tim looked down at his laptop again, hesitating. "I just learned I may have another project waiting for me as soon as this one is done. It may start with some meetings out of town."

"You've got to be kidding—after all the hours you've been putting in?"

"Yeah, I know. But they're telling me this is a real plum assignment—a reward for all I've been doing and a big career advancement opportunity. I didn't know how to turn it down."

Wow, Frank thought. *That's harsh.* You'd think the CIA could give the kid a breather after everything they'd done and still come up with a great assignment for him later on. And anyone looking at Tim could tell he needed a break. He'd been looking progressively more tense and haggard ever since Henderson had finally taken them seriously.

"Well, okay," Marla replied. "But I hope it really is and you're not just letting them take advantage of you. But either way, if this is what life is going to be like going forward, I'm not sure how I feel about that."

Tim frowned and looked like he was about to say something but then thought better of it.

"Time for a beer," Frank interrupted. "Let me know if anyone else wants one."

As expected, they ignored him, and he evacuated the living room for the safe haven of the kitchen. When the sometimes unusually loud voices in the other room finally subsided, he peeked around the corner and found the room empty and the bedroom door shut.

Propped up against pillows in the unfolded convertible couch in the living room, he read almost a whole page of a novel before falling asleep.

* * *

He woke up to the first light of morning and someone touching his shoulder.

"Dad?"

"Sounds right. What can I do for you?"

"Can we talk?"

"Sure. What's on your mind?"

Marla was still in her pajamas and sat down on the foot of the bed.

"You and Tim seem to have gotten to know each other really well—which is great. Do you know what's going on with him?"

"What do you mean?"

"Everything had been going so well, and then he started getting busier and busier, and then suddenly things got so different."

"Different how?"

"Well, at first it was just that he was busy. When he did have time, everything was still the way it had always been. But then he started getting so uptight. I told myself he was probably just tired or maybe worried about how his job was going. Or probably both. But lately he's been getting really distant, and last night he was even irritable and short with me, and he's never been that way before."

Well sure, he might be getting distant, and even a bit testy, with all he had on his mind, Frank reflected. He remembered with a twinge that he'd done the same thing once, when he was about the same age. It hadn't ended well. He'd grown to like and respect Tim, and he very much didn't want that to be the case for Marla and him.

He patted her knee and adopted what he hoped was his most reassuring voice. "I expect you've diagnosed it just right. You know, a first real career job can be terribly stressful. Everything about it may be new, and you want to look like everything you're asked to do is no sweat, even though you and everybody else who's new is sweating plenty, trying to figure out what the hell they're doing without ever asking a question, even when they haven't got a clue what's going on. I remember one Friday night at my first job after MIT. It was about 7:30 and a bunch of us new guys were still hard at work, and I looked up, and all of a sudden it all seemed pretty silly. I rapped on my desk and said 'It's okay—we can come out now! All of the grownups have gone home.'"

Marla giggled. "What did they say?"

"They all looked at me like I had two heads. But I felt a little better."

She gave him a quick hug. "Thanks, Dad. I needed that. I hope you're right."

She got up. "Gotta get ready for class. Will you be working here today?"

"Yup. I may go out to check out my condo—they said it might be all done today—but I should be here when you get home."

"That's great. It's been getting lonely around here."

Marla returned to her bedroom, leaving Frank happy to have taken the edge off her concerns. But he was worried, too. Tim had been growing uncharacteristically terse with him as well.

* * *

23

Now We'll all just have to
Sit Around and Wait

DHS, THE CIA, and the FBI had all interrogated him at length and were now satisfied that not a single bit of useful information remained to be wrung out of CIA contractor Frank Adversego. It would be another four days before U.S. and allied forces would be prepared to strike, and Frank suddenly had nothing to do. He decided to use that time to leave Washington for a couple of days and get back to his own personally apocalyptic thoughts.

Three o'clock on a Monday afternoon should have been early enough to beat the Washington D.C. traffic, but no. For two hours, he crawled westward in the company of hundreds of frustrated commuters, all inching their way past accidents and road work. Finally, he made his escape onto a secondary road. Two hours after that, he was still looping his way through slow turns as he crossed West Virginia across the grain of the Appalachians, plumbing the depths and scaling the sides of successive mountain hollows. He was counting on a tiny state park campground to be empty on a weekday at this time of year and grateful to find out on his arrival that it was. He parked his car at the most private of the campsites and pitched his tent, missing the dry, insect-free expanses of the west where a tent was just so much useless baggage. This campsite might be cold and damp, but it certainly was isolated. Maybe this would be a good place to hole up for a while if they didn't catch Foobar in time.

His camp made, he sat down beside the fire that this time he'd built for warmth rather than psychological comfort. It was time to get down to the contemplative business at hand. Watching the progress of Tim's courtship of Marla continued to bring him both pleasure and trepidation. He knew Marla was a much more grounded, sane individual than he had been at her age. But he also knew that to him the feminine psyche remained a mostly impenetrable black box. And while he was comforted by the respect and affection Tim always displayed for Marla, he also knew that reactions in human chemistry did not exhibit the predictability of laboratory experiments. After two generations of divorce in the Adversego family, he fervently hoped for better success for his daughter.

All of which had impelled him to this cold and solitary place to read the last of the letters from Clare. He no longer expected to discover any dramatic clues that might help him fully understand the troubled course of his own failed marriage. But having undertaken the painful task of excavating his emotional past to the depth he had, he wanted to see the process through.

Now that he was here, though, he found he was in no hurry to get started. The remaining stack of letters was small, but he expected its contents would be the most painful of all to rediscover. At some point, he knew, he would reach the letter in which he would sense Clare once again beginning to slip away.

But the winter days were short now, and it was getting dark. He turned on his camp lantern and opened the first letter, dated just after they had each returned to school their sophomore year. Just as before, the letters regaled him with the wonderful people and the great times she was having: swimming parties until all hours at the lake, and midnight bike rides under a full moon. And once again, their frequency soon began to decline, week by week.

Now that she was again surrounded by a vibrant circle of friends, Clare had found a balance point where her need for him could be satisfied with occasional letters and telephone calls. And for a while, she seemed content to think of their love as just as perfect and complete as ever, no matter how little time she assigned to its maintenance—perhaps like a favorite piece of jewelry that could be worn on special occasions but left in the dark in a drawer the rest of the time. He was painfully aware that he was reading only half the script, though. He had no copies of his letters to her, and therefore, no way to know how he was responding to her neglect. Had he sounded petulant? Demanding? Irrational?

He must have been transmitting his concerns in some way, as from time to time, Clare would try to reassure him. Eventually, there was a letter from her that informed him that if he wasn't comfortable with the life she was leading, then her choice would be clear and not one he would like.

Then there were almost no letters for quite a while. He couldn't recall whether they saw each other over Christmas break or whether any single event had brought things to a climax. All he could recall was that her neglect had made him wild, ending with the letter he had written and never sent and his sealing up her letters for over a quarter of a century before opening them again.

After that, he had heard nothing from, or about, Clare, except for any tidbits of information he might overhear in conversations with mutual friends; he had been too proud to ask any of them outright for information about what she might be up to. As far as he could tell, her interest in him had simply evaporated when his needs had become tedious.

He slid the last of the letters back into the envelope that had preserved them for so long. So that was it. No bang and scarcely even a whimper. His inquiry into the romantic disasters of his past through the examination of ancient, recently discovered texts was complete. He wondered what the best word to summarize the emotions that lingered was, and settled on mourning. Mourning for the fact there had been no more secluded waterfalls to skinny dip in together and no more stifling dorm room nights making love heedless of the heat, aware only of the completeness they found together for a brief while and the irrelevance of anything else.

Over the years that followed, an occasional letter from Clare would arrive unheralded in his mailbox. As always, they focused on the events of her day and the people she was fascinated by at that point in her life. The letters asked no questions of him and suggested no need for, or for that matter necessarily any interest in, a response. It occurred to him that her letters had always been rather like diary entries, more to herself than to him. Perhaps these random apparitions from later years were only the product of a lingering habit, each sparked by a moment or event in her day that in the old days had always caused her to pick up a pen and record a few events that called out for a witness. Or maybe they reflected an effort to maintain some manner of connection. If so, they represented the smallest possible investment of effort that ran the least risk of leading to anything more.

Apparently, he hadn't saved those letters from her. And he had been careful to take a long time answering them and to be equally superficial in his responses. Never again, he vowed, would he permit himself to show any sign of weakness or need. He wondered whether that was an attempt on his part to reassure himself he was over her.

It was four years before he received a different sort of letter from Clare. It said that she missed his friendship and had often wanted to get in touch on a more serious note, but she didn't feel entitled to it, given how things had ended between them. She was going to be visiting a friend in Cambridge and wanted to apologize in person. Could they get together and catch up on what they'd been doing with their lives?

The letter arrived at a vulnerable time. He was coming down hard from a serious relationship that had just failed and answered yes. When they got together for dinner, he learned that so was she. And that she would be moving to Boston. They drank too much, and it was almost like old times.

He folded the envelope of letters shut again and stared up at the dark circle of starlit sky, enclosed by the bare branches of the surrounding trees, feeling his isolation intensely. The nearest house was easily fifteen miles away, but that wasn't the cause. For most of the last twenty-five years, he'd been more alone in Washington than he was here and now. Could his life have turned out differently if he had acted in some other way?

Well, what did it matter anyway. That book was closed, and if there had never been a wedding with someone named Clare, there would never have been a daughter named Marla, and he wouldn't surrender that gift to avoid a hundred failed romances. He stared at the fire and wondered whether it was time to place the envelope and his memories and dreams among the flames and let them perish together, once and for all?

An hour later, he was still staring at the embers of the fire, now turned to ash.

* * *

In the light of day on the long drive home, he tried to look at his past as dispassionately as possible. By the time he was back on the highway, he had decided that he finally had it figured out as well as he ever would. First loves, he reasoned, gave rise to a unique kind of fallacy. They left you with the lifelong, abiding conviction that both you and your first love still existed somewhere, just as you were, ready to reunite. Perhaps you both continued to exist in some parallel universe or maybe on some sort of psychic spaceship traveling at the speed of love, never changing while your corporeal self continued to age and emotionally fade decade after decade back here on Earth. If you and your *prima amore* could somehow meet your time-traveled selves again, you could miraculously merge back into them and pick up again just as you were, right where you had left off. Otherwise, what would be the point of continuing to feel the way he did?

But that was nonsense. He was a different person now than he had been then, and thank goodness, for that. And Clare certainly would have moved on as well. If only he could stop his rebellious thoughts from returning to his first romance.

Still, at least he had discovered one thing of value as a result of his uncomfortable hours with Clare's letters. He had always wondered why he had responded so furiously when she had left him; he doubted he had ever reacted to anything so violently before or since. He liked to think of himself as being introspective and logical, but he had been anything but that over the years that followed their separation. It was clear to him now that when she had decided for the third time that she no longer needed him, it had overwhelmed his emotions and everything else.

He emerged from the mountains and traded his deserted secondary road for the busy highway, transitioning back into the present and the complicated world he now inhabited. What had he been thinking when he decided to read those letters? Clare was now as alive as ever in his mind. He remembered that he used to enjoy watching her play the piano. He could see her now in his mind's eye, her head inclined downward and tilted slightly to one side, as if she was reading her music over the tops of invisible glasses. She concentrated so deeply as she played that she never noticed as he watched her large, brown eyes, set beneath perfectly curved eyebrows, follow the music, and absorbed the cadence of her hands as they rose eloquently high and fell confidently low onto the keys with smooth and steady grace. He wondered whether her balletic approach to the keyboard reflected the instruction of an early music teacher or was instead an unconscious manifestation of her intense involvement with the music. It had never occurred to him to ask her then, but now he was curious to know the answer.

And he heard once again the husky, deep-throated chuckle she often favored him with when they were together. That conspiratorial laugh seemed always to be lying just below the surface, waiting to escape.

When he reached the next town, he pulled over and Googled her name for the first time in years. He had always avoided asking Marla anything about her mother's activities, at first out of obstinacy, and later so she would not feel uncomfortable or caught in the middle between her parents. For her part, Marla had avoided mentioning her mother at all, all too aware of her father's obvious sensitivity.

The last time he had looked, Clare's web presence was minimal. Now he found many hits. And look at that—she was back at U Penn. He clicked on her faculty bio, finding a list of scientific publications that went on and on. Clare had obviously plugged away at her career, year after year, despite the challenges of being a single mother. He saw that she'd moved on quickly from the last post he'd been aware of, an assistant professorship at a small college. That was followed by an associate professor position at a well-regarded university, where in due course she was granted tenure. And two years ago, she'd achieved the ultimate—appointment to an endowed chair at an Ivy League school and head of her own lab to boot. How about that.

He set his laptop aside and resumed his drive, wondering what kind of person his first love had grown up to be.

* * *

It's Showtime!

P RESIDENT YAZZIE WAS seething as he approached the Situation Room, accompanied by his chief of staff. Here he was, nominally the most powerful man in the world, and yet only a few months after being elected, he'd been cornered and emasculated by the lesser powers that really ran Washington. He'd been particularly appalled when his cabinet voted unanimously not to reveal the Caliphate's attack, maintaining that the political cost would be too high—some even threatening to resign if decided to act otherwise. He'd been infuriated when the speaker of the house informed him in no uncertain terms that not a single administration bill would be passed by Congress for the duration of his time in office if word of the attack leaked to the press. His press secretary hadn't even tried to put any lipstick on that pig.

Now Yazzie wondered why he was bothering to go to the Situation Room to witness the events as they unfolded. Clearly, he was just a paper tiger—or perhaps a marionette—seemingly possessed of unparalleled power, but in fact only trotted out and manipulated for public consumption, powerless to control anything in fact.

This would stop. He did not at this point know how he would accomplish that, but stop it he would, and soon.

* * *

Tim barely spoke at all on the drive out to Langley, and when he did, it was in a monotone. Most of the time, he just sat still with his arms crossed, staring zombie-like into the blackness outside the car. Frank was worried but decided to keep his distance; Tim looked like he hadn't gotten a minute's sleep the night before, and given the argument he'd had with Marla, maybe that was the case. Or maybe it was just nerves. This was the big night they'd worked toward for weeks, and the stakes were about as high as you could get. Maybe Tim was worried that all the data he'd presented to the Agency might not hold up. That would make sense. After all, it wouldn't take much of a slip-up to result in disaster. Frank wondered whether maybe he should be worrying more himself.

When they reached the mission control room at CIA Headquarters, Frank saw that Tim wasn't the only one who looked haggard from lack of sleep. Each of the data teams had been working desperately over the preceding days to unearth as much as possible about the web of actors laboring behind the scenes to pull off the attack. An hour and a half from now, SEAL teams acting alone in the Atlantic and Pacific and in concert with their NATO counterparts in the Baltic, Irish, and Mediterranean Seas would spring into action. Simultaneously, CIA personnel and their coalition partners would burst into the offices of manufacturing plants, shipyards, and financial firms in multiple countries around the world and seize every piece of paper and computer that might contain a shred of data relating to the Caliphate's secret plan. Before the day was out, all evidence of the attack, as well as every individual outside the territory controlled by the Caliphate believed to be involved in planning, enabling, or executing it, would be under coalition control.

As the clock ticked down, a sense of tense aimlessness permeated the room. Despite the feverish activity of the past week, most of those assembled now had nothing to do for a while but watch the blips representing Caliphate ships inch forward on the huge display in the front of the room, hoping nothing had been left to chance.

A large screen on the side of the room winked to life, revealing a grim-faced President Yazzie sitting at the head of the meeting table in the Situation Room beneath the West Wing of the White House. Frank guessed that the half-dozen people surrounding him were the members of the National Security Council.

Captain James Lugar, the Joint Special Operations Command officer assigned to oversee the interceptions, stood up and faced that screen, and Frank realized everyone in the control room must be visible to the president.

"Greetings, Mr. President. Sorry to be keeping you up so late."

"Quite all right. What's the current status?"

"Excellent, Sir. All of the SEAL teams are in place on vessels on courses that will bring them within six miles of the Caliphate's ships while they are still approximately twenty-five miles off shore."

"Why so close to shore?"

"Unfortunately, Sir, we've had to take this right down to the wire. It was quite a challenge to get all of the units trained and in position, and then there's the constraint of intercepting the vessels at night in all locations. We weren't quite able to get all of our units in place to conduct the operation last night. Meanwhile, the Caliphate's ships have continued on course."

"I see. What chance is there that the target ships will realize they are being intercepted?"

"We believe the risk to be quite low. On a radar screen, the profiles and speeds of our vessels will resemble those of the fishing boats and other coastal traffic the Caliphate captains will be seeing on their radars. These are all pretty busy waters, so our forces shouldn't attract any particular notice from friend or foe."

"I thought you were going to use helicopters or Ospreys. Why boats?"

"You're correct, Sir, but not for the first phase of the operation. Helicopters are loud and relatively slow. We're afraid they might be spotted before they could attack. Ospreys would arrive over their targets very quickly, but we can't know for sure what kind of defensive capabilities the enemy ships may have. If they're keeping a sharp watch and are well armed, they could down one of our aircraft before its assault team could reach the deck."

"Don't boats make noise, too? And what about their radar?"

"Good points, Sir. We won't be approaching using the large craft the SEAL teams are currently on. When we give the word after the quarter moon sets on the west coast, each of our ships will deploy small stealth speedboats with muffled engines. They won't show up on radar and will be able to close on the Caliphate's ships within a short period of time. Using ropes and cushioned grapnels, the SEALs will be able to get on deck quickly and quietly under cover of darkness. If there are any lookouts, they'll take care of them before they can sound the alarm.

"After that, some team members will take control of the bridge while the rest lock down the crew quarters and take up positions where they can pick off anyone that might be able to come on deck from another location on board. Only after everything is secure will they call in the helicopters. Those aircraft will drop additional troops and specialists on board to help complete the operation. With twelve ships to seize stretching across a third of the northern hemisphere, this will be the largest number of SEALs that has ever been involved simultaneously in a single operation."

"Very good. How long should all this take?"

"We're figuring ten minutes for the speedboats to get alongside, and an hour for the SEAL teams to take control."

"That sounds like a long time."

"It is a long time, Sir. In point of fact, we don't expect any team will take longer than a half hour to assume control of its target vessel, and some may be in command in as little as fifteen. But we don't want to run the risk that someone on one of the ships gets a chance to alert the other ships that they're under attack. Otherwise, some ships might begin launching their drones before we can seize control. That's the reason that every team has been instructed to proceed cautiously and take as much time as they need. And of course we want to be sure that we've got total control of the bridges and the decks so we don't expose the helicopter-borne teams to hostile fire."

"I see." The president crossed his arms and leaned back in his chair.

His chief of staff took advantage of the pause. "And are you certain that this entire operation will go undetected by civilians?"

"We can't be totally sure, Sir. But our munitions people will be placing substantial charges below the waterline in multiple locations throughout the vessels. Once the helicopters have everyone off and we trigger the charges, the ships should go down in less than fifteen minutes."

"You said that those were busy waters. Won't there be a chance that another vessel in the area will see the ships go under?"

"We think we're in pretty good shape there, Sir. We lucked out with the phase of the moon and the time of year, and as it happens, the skies are overcast all across Europe; it should be pitch-dark in all locations. And we've been keeping an eye on the target ships at night by high altitude surveillance. For the last two nights, they've been operating without any deck lights, and, of course, all of our boats and helicopters will be blacked out. We'll be doing our best to time the attack so there aren't any other vessels too close, but we don't have too much flexibility there. Even though it's mid-winter, with ship locations spanning seven time zones, our launch window is only a few hours long."

"What happens if someone does notice?"

"If they do, the public story will be that Coast Guard helicopters rescued the crew after a vessel suffered a sudden emergency. Since no one is expecting any of these ships to land with a cargo and the crews are all Caliphate loyalists, there won't be anyone to ask any follow-up questions."

The president touched the arm of his chief of staff, and they held a muffled conversation before the president turned back and spoke.

"Very well then. I want to be informed immediately if anything unexpected happens, no matter when that might occur. How close are the ships to their destinations now?"

"If you look at the left side of the big screen in the Situation Room, Sir, you'll see all of the ships displayed on a map of the U.S. and Europe. Each white blip represents one of the Caliphate's ships. Now if you look to the right, you'll see inset maps of all of the twelve target areas. The red blips you see are our ships, and the white and red dotted lines indicate the courses of the various vessels."

The president had another side conversation.

"Very good. And the projected time until you begin the operation?"

The admiral looked to a technician sitting at a terminal at his elbow. "Approximately twelve minutes, Sir."

"Good. When the boats are almost alongside the ships, bring us back in."

"Of course, Sir."

"And one thing more."

"Yes, Sir?"

"Good luck."

"Yes, Sir. Thank you, Sir."

The side wall video screen went blank, and everyone in the room refocused their attention on their own monitors. With the counterattack now only minutes away, everyone had a task to perform. Everyone except Frank and Tim, who had only been included in case something unexpected arose that only one of them might be able to address.

Frank leaned back and looked at the maps on the big screen at the front of the room, trying to imagine what it might be like to be a SEAL getting ready to move out. He had a Hollywood-inspired mental picture of burly men in watch caps and blackened faces, using their thumbs to test the edges of brutal-looking knives worn at their hips, wondering how many throats they might need to slit before the night was over. But then a different thought occurred to him: Captain Lugar had referred to twelve ships when he was speaking to the president. Frank counted the white blips and confirmed there were only twelve. And he distinctly recalled the captain saying each white blip represented one Caliphate ship. Weren't there supposed to be thirteen?

He scanned the inset maps, and all of the presumed target locations were accounted for. Then he remembered—Tim and he had assumed it would take two ships to take out all of the data centers near Silicon Valley. And the inset map for San Francisco showed only one white blip heading for that location. He turned to Tim to get his reaction. But his chair was empty. *Crazy time to visit the john,* Frank thought.

He opened the latest action summary and found the list of targets and ships—

there were twelve in all. Was his memory just off? Or perhaps Tim and he had simply made a mistake? What else could he check to find out? He stared at the list and scanned it, looking for inspiration, and noticed that the names of the ships were included. None of them sounded familiar. But he was sure they had glimpsed the name of the ship in Myanmar. What was it? He couldn't remember. He looked at the list of ship names again, and still none of them sounded familiar.

Was he just off on a toot? Probably. Maybe. But he could at least go back to the drone video to check for that name.

He pulled the original drone video up on his laptop, remembering just in time to mute the sound. He tapped the fingers of both hands on his knees, hoping he rightly recalled that some part of the video had captured the name of the ship. No luck as the drone rose up the bow; the field of view wasn't wide enough. That was probably the end of it, but he might as well fast-forward through the rest of the video just in case. Then, as the drone pulled back, he saw the name of the ship and hit the pause button: *Ninotchka.* He toggled back to the list, and there it was: the ship was heading to San Francisco. So much for that. He hit the run button and watched as the drone returned to its owner. And then he hit the pause button again. Was that another ship with bow doors?

He rewound until the brief glimpse was on his screen again and then zoomed in. The bow doors were clear, but the name was hard to make out because the angle was oblique. His best guess was that it read *Dohna.* He went back to the ship list and saw no vessel with that name or even one that was close. Hmmm. Maybe the CIA had enhanced their copy of the video? He was sure they would have, looking for as much information as possible. He hunted up the official version on the CIA server and fast-forwarded it. But it ended just before the second ship came into view.

He shut his laptop and glanced to his right; Tim's seat was still empty. He took out his phone and texted him and waited, but he got no response. Could the idealistic young fool have done something truly stupid?

The room was starting to get busier; all of the chairs were now full, and the big screen showed twelve separate but similar images of blurred, eerily green-lit figures climbing down ladders into boats tossing about in a nasty chop. What if there was another ship no one knew about? And what could he do with so little time if there was? What was it Tim had said? Something about not being able to let this situation go?

He broke into a sweat and found himself trembling. Then he remembered the ship tracking software they had used when they first began theorizing about the Caliphate's true intentions. What was its name? Damn—he couldn't remember that, either. He pulled down his saved searches menu, found the site, and typed in

Dohna, hoping that he had read it right. And there it was. On a somewhat different course than the *Ninotchka* but scheduled to arrive at the same pier in Oakland at 9:00 AM the next day. He looked at his watch: it was already 1:15 AM.

On the big screen, the night-vision images now revealed the rapidly growing silhouettes of the Caliphate's ships bucking up and down as the SEAL team boats shot off the phosphorescing crests of waves. Captain Lugar was standing up, too, and now the side screen was winking into action, once again displaying the President and the National Security Council. What could he do?

He looked around the room, searching for George. Thank God, there he was, at the end of a line of seats a few rows ahead. Frank stood up and sidled to the end of his row, thinking feverishly. When he reached George, he leaned down and whispered in his ear. "Gotta talk—it's trouble."

George frowned but stood up slowly and followed him out the door in the back of the room. When they reached the hallway, he kept walking without allowing Frank to speak. Frank wondered where you went in CIA headquarters when you didn't want to be heard? The answer, apparently, was a men's room. After they went in, George entered one stall and nodded Frank toward the adjacent one. Okay, this was going to be weird. Frank wondered whether he was expected to drop his pants or whether he could just take a seat.

From George's example, the answer appeared to be that just sitting would be sufficient. He jumped when he saw a hand with a cellphone appear under the divider between the stalls. He took it and saw "What the hell is going on? Discard—don't save—this message."

Frank did as he was told and then tapped away as quickly as possible.

> *There's another ship, and Tim's gone. I think he wants to let one attack succeed so the government can't get away with keeping this secret.* He returned the phone.

Moments later, the phone came back: *Do you know what the target is?* Clearly, George was a cooler head than he was.

> *I think San Francisco. The ship is called the Dohna. I saw it on the original copy of the drone video on my laptop, but that part has been cut from the Agency's version. Tim must have deleted the ship from the other data, too, before he downloaded the video and the rest of our files from our laptops to the CIA system. What do we do?*

It was a full minute before there was any reaction from George. Then Frank heard the toilet paper dispenser in the adjacent stall make soft, unrolling sounds.

Finally, he heard the toilet flush. Frank followed suit and then followed George back to the meeting room.

Things were deathly still when they reentered the mission control room. The SEAL teams must be on the Caliphate ships now, creeping toward the bridges, because the split screens were showing twelve almost identical, spooky, aerial views of the ships. The CIA would, of course, have drones high overhead using infrared cameras. But the resolution was poor; all that could be seen on deck were the outlines of hatches and cranes and the long shadows of waves sweeping by on either side. The White House video screen showed seven intent faces staring toward the same images Frank was watching.

George walked up to Captain Lugar and spoke quietly in his ear. Frank could see the officer tense before nodding and turning to a lieutenant sitting to his right. After a few whispered words, the lieutenant stood up, and George followed him back to Frank's row. The lieutenant beckoned Frank to join them.

"Gentlemen, please wait for me in the back of the room."

George and Frank did as they were told. Moments later, the Lieutenant approached them, followed by Virgil Cooper. The lieutenant led them to a conference room down the hall.

"I understand we have a problem."

"That's right," George replied. "It appears that in all of the effort to staff this mission and accomplish it in a matter of days, one piece of key data fell through the cracks. Frank here thinks that there's one more ship we've got to intercept—headed towards San Francisco."

"How could that happen?"

"Let's figure that out later. Right now, we've got to stop that ship before it launches its V-1s. That could be any minute if any of the other ships gets a message off to the Caliphate before our men take over."

"Agreed. Give me everything you've got."

"It's called the *Dohna*," Frank replied. "It was taking on its aircraft around the same time as the *Ninotchka*, at the same facility. According to a commercial ship tracking site I just checked, it's approaching San Francisco right now. Can you send another team to take it out?"

The lieutenant turned to Cooper, who paused, frowning.

"Negative. We've already got more than half of all our SEAL teams involved in this operation. Given how far apart the ships are, we couldn't train a reserve team for every location, and since we're hitting every ship simultaneously, we couldn't centrally locate any pre-trained reserve teams, either—it would take them too long to arrive." He paused again. "Even assuming we could pull together enough qualified people near the Bay area, we'd have to pull them out of bed, equip them, and then brief them on the operation on the way to the ship." He looked at his watch. "And that just can't be done fast enough."

The lieutenant interrupted. "What about the Coast Guard? Or Army Special Forces?"

Cooper looked offended. "What about them, Sir?"

"Damn it, forget the inter-service rivalry bit. Do you know whether any other branch keeps any kind of qualified team at the ready?"

"I don't, Sir. But I don't know why they would, stateside. Maybe in the Gulf region, but that doesn't help us here." He paused again and then committed himself.

"Sir, I think our only option is to pull the advance SEAL team off the other ship off San Francisco the minute the Chinook lands to secure and sink the ship, and then do the same with the Chinook team when they're done. They already know the drill, and we can start briefing the team leaders as soon as they lift off from the first vessel. We should be able to scramble a Coast Guard cutter, too, in case we lose the advantage of surprise."

"Why don't you just disable the ship from the air, Lieutenant?" George interrupted. "If you put one missile into the bow, they wouldn't be able to launch anything."

"No. If we do that, the whole ship would blow; their flight deck will be full of jet fuel and warheads. You'd see the fireworks halfway to Sacramento, and our orders are to do this covertly."

A steady stream of CIA and military staff had been entering while they were speaking. The last to arrive was the Captain Lugar from the mission room.

"Brief me," he said to the lieutenant as he sat down.

"Sir, it looks like the new ship is heading towards San Francisco. I think our best option is to move the SEAL team from the other ship in the same area as soon as we possibly can. Anything else would take too long, running the risk that the ship starts launching before we act. And anything faster, from the air, risks blowing the ship up."

"There's no submarine nearby? A torpedo to her stern below the waterline should disable her without setting her off."

"But she might not sink quick enough, Sir. As soon as she was hit, she could start launching."

"Right. In that case, be sure that the redeployed SEAL platoon gets all the support it needs in taking on the second ship. Anything it needs, it gets. And direct immediately to that area any kind of backup we might possibly need in case we need to improvise. That includes air power. Not just drones, but the heavy stuff, too, just in case."

The captain frowned and paused before speaking again. "Mr. Adversego, thank you for this additional information. Better late than never, but sooner would have been a damn sight better. Lieutenant, I think that we've kept Mr. Adversego up late enough. Have someone escort him to the entrance."

* * *

"I'll follow you back in a minute," George said to Frank's escort when they reached the entrance.

"Should I read anything into being sent off home to bed?"

"Dunno. Right now, all the admiral knows is that he doesn't know everything he needs to. I expect he's being cautious. I would be, too—can you explain to me how this happened?"

"Yes, but there's something else you should know first. Have I mentioned to you that Tim and your godchild have been an item for quite a while now and that Marla's hoping they'll get married?"

George pursed his lips in a silent whistle. "No. No, you haven't. So that makes this more complicated."

"No kidding. Anyway, as you know, Tim's been livid ever since you told us you thought the government might try to keep this hushed up. I think he must have decided immediately that he might want to do something if that decision stuck. He was handling all of the data gathering and analysis relating to ships and shipyards. Since we weren't supposed to be moonlighting on my crazy theory, we kept all our data on our laptops until we finally convinced the Agency we were on to something, so Tim had time to delete all data relating to the *Dohna* from what he downloaded from our laptops to the CIA system. Frankly, he's been acting pretty crazy lately. I thought it was just strain and overwork, but clearly this was weighing on him a lot more than I realized."

"I see. So how are you going to explain your sudden revelation without exposing Tim?"

"I think this should work. Our analysis of the shipping records led us to guess that there were probably three different shipyards involved in converting the vessels, taking into account where the ships had been over the past six months and how long they stayed in each port. When I checked earlier tonight to find out where the *Dohna* is now and what was supposed to be her next port of call, I checked backwards, too. As it happens, the *Dohna* was the ship that was refitted at the only yard that worked on just one Caliphate ship. I'm sure that's why Tim picked it, since if he deleted the information relating to that shipyard, too, there would be a good chance the Agency would never find the *Dohna*. So I can just say that he and I missed the third shipyard."

"That could work to explain how you found it but not what made you look for it all of a sudden."

"This part is actually close to what happened. I'll say we didn't think one ship was enough for San Francisco, so when I noticed only one ship headed that way, I checked the records of any other ship due to dock in San Francisco the next day. I found one called the *Dohna* whose last port of call was the same one in Myanmar where the other ships picked up their V-1s."

George nodded. "I guess that all holds together. Anyway, it's not like they're going to want to publicly take you to court no matter what happens. Now what about Tim?"

"Yeah, Tim. I've been thinking about that, too. He's quite the fan of Edward Snowden. My guess is that Tim will be on a plane to somewhere this morning that doesn't have an extradition treaty with the U.S."

"Even if everything turns out okay, that's going to be hard to explain," George said. "Another ship suddenly pops up and the guy responsible for the data skips town."

"I know. Do you have access to the NSA database? Tim would have to book a plane ticket in his own name, so if I'm right, you could find out where he's taking off from and where he's headed."

"I do. Look for a text message with a telephone number in it. The flight number will be in the last four digits. You'll have to take it from there."

* * *

Frank walked to his rental car in the CIA parking lot, his mind spinning with conflicting thoughts and a hollow feeling in his gut. This was way too close to his own experience as a young teenager, when his father had—according to the false story given to him by his mother—abandoned the family without a word of explanation.

What, if anything, would Tim have said to Marla before leaving for the airport? Would he have left a note or just disappeared? Probably just disappear, since he expected the data centers to go up in flames any time now; anything he told Marla would either be a lie or might implicate her. Frank was furious at him for abandoning his daughter and risking innocent lives, but in the back of his mind, there was also a small voice expressing grudging admiration for the sacrifice the young man was making in order to be true to his convictions.

Or was he simply an arrogant fool? Snowden, at least, had his defenders; some people were even calling for him to be pardoned. Maybe someday he'd be able to come home. No chance of that happening for Tim if the SEALs didn't take control of the last ship before it got its V-1s away. No one would have any sympathy for someone who let a swarm of buzz bombs take out a few billion dollars' worth of corporate investment and incinerated the servers that supported the core of the technology industry. The data centers largely operated autonomously, but still, somebody might be killed by those V-1s, too.

He reached the car, unlocked the door, and then turned to look back at the looming bulk of CIA headquarters, floodlit in the night, looking as massive and impregnable as any medieval fortress. What could anyone ever hope to do to confront an organization like that, not to mention all the other secretive agencies and forces at the beck and call of the president? Likely enough, no one would ever learn what was happening tonight. If that proved to be the case, Frank was sure that no one would ever do anything about the vulnerability of the data centers.

He got in the car and drove slowly out of the parking lot and back toward Washington. What had he done about the administration's plan? Nothing. Just kicked the can down the road, always saying they would worry about it later. But whom was he kidding? He never would have done anything at all on his own. Would he even have backed up Tim, if Tim went public? He hoped he could at least head him off in time at the airport, so he and Marla could still have a future together.

Then he got another kick in the gut. If the SEALs did stop the attack, what would Tim think of him? Would he and Tim have to spend a lifetime pretending nothing had ever happened? Making nice for Marla's benefit even though Tim would secretly despise his father-in-law? And what about their future and his grandchildren's future? How long would it be before somebody really did take out the data centers—all of them? Even if he and Tim started telling everyone about the danger, would anyone listen to them? Should he have kept his mouth shut and just let Tim's plan take its course?

He looked for an answer in the glow of the sky over the nation's capital up ahead and then imagined everything suddenly going black—the spotlighted memorials to Washington and Lincoln and Jefferson; the rotunda of the Capitol; everything— plunging millions into confusion, with far worse to come. The blinking lights of a helicopter passed slowly through the glow, and in that image, he found his answer and a long-shot plan that just might work.

He gunned the car and sped off the highway at the next exit. Fifteen minutes later, he was fumbling in the glove box of his camper at the storage lot. Then he headed for the airport.

* * *

25

Please Proceed to the Gate Area; Your Flight is Now Boarding

TIM'S HARRIED EYES were riveted on the TV screen hanging from the ceiling. Passengers were beginning to queue up at his gate, waiting for boarding to begin, so he stood up as well. The news anchor was reporting that the Caliphate had just launched massive attacks against neighboring countries, but there was no mention of a data center being hit. Shouldn't someone have broken into the broadcast by now to report the attack?

"The fun should begin any minute now," a voice said softly, almost in his ear.

Tim whirled around.

"Why don't you sit down again? You wouldn't want to miss the show, after all the work you've done."

"Frank—what, I mean, ah, what do you mean?"

"Don't worry. But do sit down. Look—it's starting!"

Tim turned back to the TV monitor and didn't resist as Frank put a hand on his shoulder and gently pushed him back into his seat. Behind them, the passengers crowded around the gate began filing on board.

We've just received word from San Francisco that something unusual is happening just outside the Golden Gate. Let's go now to our local affiliate for live coverage. Ron Luton, can you tell us what's going on?

Hello, Doug. Not yet, but whatever it is, it's certainly something unusual. One of our helicopters was out getting ready to cover pre-rush hour traffic when the pilot spotted something he thought looked unusual offshore and decided to check it out. We don't yet know whether it's a rescue of a sinking ship or maybe a downed aircraft, but there's a lot of activity, and we aren't getting any answers from the Coast Guard. Let's go to the chopper and find out what they're seeing. Can you hear me, Steve?

The audio switched from the quiet clarity of the studio anchor to the sound of someone speaking loudly over engine noise. The video showed a face wearing a headset and a baseball cap floating like the nose of a dirigible against a black background, dimly lit by the glow emitted by the cockpit controls nearby.

Roger that, Steve. Okay, we're beginning to get close enough to see what's going on.

The feed went into split-screen mode, continuing to show the traffic reporter on one side, while on the other, the camera swung away into the darkness. Off in the distance, a bright light illuminated the deck of a ship, indicating the presence of a helicopter hovering above. Obviously, time had run out to take the last ship the same way as the others, forcing the Navy to make an outright assault on the ship instead of a stealthy approach.

What the heck's happening out there, Steve?

Dunno. I'm guessing it's probably a drug shipment being interdicted. I've got binoculars here, so let me get a closer look. Okay. Okay, I can see better now—it looks like there's a big SWAT team, or maybe a commando unit, advancing on deck towards the bridge in the stern of the vessel, supported by covering fire from a couple of Cobra helicopters. I'm going to see whether we can get a video close-up at such long range so you can see what I'm seeing.

He turned to the cameraman at his elbow and yelled in his ear.

The camera zoomed in, revealing the blurred images of dozens of men in military gear rushing toward the stern of the ship. Streaks of light were zooming in from the side, hammering into the bridge.

Holy cow! Will you look at that? That's got to be an AC-130 gunship pouring fire in! Look at those tracers! This is no drug bust! I wonder what they're after down there?

You better keep your distance, Steve. Whatever it is, we don't want you getting hurt.

Roger that.

The traffic reporter turned to speak to the pilot and then faced the camera again.

Ron, we're going to stay at this distance and keep the video going.

That sounds like a good move, Steve. I don't think we've ever seen anything like this before.

Me neither. Whoa!

They heard a roar, as the traffic reporter ducked and looked up through the Plexiglas bubble enclosing the cockpit.

Looks like we've got more company here.

Who's that?

I'm guessing a squadron of Super Hornets up from the Naval Air Station down near Barstow.

Really? What would they be there for?

More air support, obviously. But for what, I've no clue. They certainly aren't going to want to fire at the ship, now that we've got personnel on board. This is getting stranger by the minute.

The video was now focusing on the boarding party as it crouched behind a hatch cover that spanned most of the width of the ship. The heavy, spent uranium bullets the gunship was firing were now rapidly destroying the deck-level doors on either side of the superstructure in the stern of the ship. When the gunship abruptly ceased firing, the attacking party jumped up and dashed for the doors.

Wait a minute! Something really weird is starting to happen! The traffic reporter grabbed the shoulder of the cameraman and pointed to his right.

The video swung around to the bow of the ship, which now had what looked like an enormous, gleaming capital letter H tipped on its side spread across its bow. As they watched, the center grew brighter and brighter.

What the heck is that, Steve?

Giant doors, Doug! These humongous, big doors are opening up in the bow of the ship! This is starting to look like a James Bond movie—like a cross between Dr. No and Moonraker!

That's astonishing! What are the attackers doing about it?

I can't tell. I wonder whether the boarding party even knows? The helicopters are still overhead, and the gunship is circling around the stern of the ship right now, so none of them can see what we're seeing.

The video zoomed in for a closer look at the now fully open doors in the bow. Suddenly, the video washed out in a pulsating burst of light and fire and then began vibrating wildly, leaving the studio anchor alarmed.

What's going on? Steve! Are you all right?

There was no response until the video feed settled back into focus.

Wow—sorry. That was a close one. Some kind of jet or rocket came blasting right out of the bow of the ship and came almost right at us! Let's wheel around and see if we can get a look at it before it's out of sight!

The cameraman leaned to the side and captured the rapidly diminishing silhouette of some sort of aircraft. They were watching it fade into the brightening sky, heading toward San Francisco, when out of nowhere, it was intercepted by a streak of light that caused it to dissolve into a gigantic fireball.

Well, that explains the Super Hornets—whatever that was, they just took it out with an air-to-air missile. I wonder where it was headed?

The traffic reporter's face in the split screen turned to the side.

Uh-oh. Party's over. I'm being told by the pilot we'd better get out of here.

The video turned away from the sunrise and back toward the ship. One of the helicopters was now headed in their direction.

Looks like they finally noticed us hanging around over here, or I guess more likely they just didn't have time to do anything about it until now. We're being ordered to leave the area immediately.
All right. Fly safely. Thanks for that fantastic coverage.

The view returned to the studio.

Well, there you have it. For those of you just tuning in, you've been watching exclusive live video from one of our traffic helicopters, approximately four miles west of the Golden Gate Bridge. We may have lost our on-scene video for the time being, but we've got a boat with another camera crew on its way out to sea to keep an eye on things from whatever distance they're allowed to do so, so stay tuned for live coverage of this extraordinary event involving our military forces.

I've been joined now by telephone by local Silicon Valley technology reporter Roy Olsen to gain some early insight into what we've just been watching. Obviously, the military intervened just in time to protect the Homeland from an attack. But by whom? And what would the target have been? Roy, what's your guess?

Shocked, Tim recognized the reporter's name. He was the one trying to raise the alarm about data center vulnerability.

Well, I think the Caliphate has to be the first possibility to consider. Foobar has been promising a big attack against the West for months now, and his troops have been massing for days on the borders of Turkey and Egypt. An hour ago, they began pouring over those borders. I don't think that both of these things happening at the same time can be a coincidence.

But if so, what would this ship's mission have been?

There's only one target that makes sense to me.

What's that?

To take down our cyber infrastructure and keep it down.

How would they do that?

Simple. A ship that size could have been carrying dozens of drones, or whatever it was we just saw getting shot down. Let's say it had fifty of them. That might be enough to take out a big percentage of the data centers that support most of the public and private computing power for all of California and the Southwest. Were you able to get through to the Center for Infrastructure Studies?

Yes. On the line we also have Norman Belloque, the lead author of a startling new report commissioned by the Responsible Technology Foundation that will be released later today. Mr. Belloque, from what I understand, your report describes what the impact of an attack on our data centers would be like. I've only had a chance to read the executive summary so far, but based on what I read there, we should all be very, very grateful that our military forces were able to thwart this attack before it could succeed.

"Looks like you've missed your flight," Frank observed.

Tim jumped up. The waiting area was empty, and the door to the ramp was closed. He sat back down abruptly and stared straight ahead. "How did they find out about the last freighter?"

"I realized that we were only tracking one ship headed to San Francisco and there should have been two. Luckily, I was able to figure out the rest of the pieces just in time for the SEAL team to be able to mount back-to-back assaults on both ships."

Tim's face was a map of emotions wrestling with each other.

"I also realized something else. You want to know what?"

It appeared that Tim didn't trust himself to speak. Finally, he nodded.

"Here." Frank put a disposable phone in Tim's hand. He stared down at it for a moment and then back to Frank in obvious confusion.

"That's a disposable, and therefore non-traceable, phone I had leftover from the adventure I had eluding the FBI and the CIA. I used it to wake up that technology reporter who's been trying to blow the whistle on vulnerable data centers, and he was able to get through to a San Francisco radio station with traffic helicopters. He told them to send one of their choppers out to sea immediately and have the author of the RTF report standing by for the discussion he'd want to have within a couple of hours."

Tim's eyes widened and brightened. Then he frowned. "That's what you did—which is awesome. But you said you realized something. What was that?"

"Actually, several things. For starters, that averting big dangers can require big sacrifices, and also that if you're not willing to make them, you can't expect someone else to make them for you."

Tim nodded. "I'd say you got that right. Except you were a lot smarter in the way you went about doing something than I was." He handed the cell phone back to Frank. "You said 'several' things. Is that it?"

"The last one is that I'm pretty lucky that Marla met someone who could wise me up in time. Even if he can be an even bigger idiot sometimes than I am."

Tim was still frowning but no longer in a bad way.

Frank clapped him on the shoulder and stood up. "C'mon. I think we could both use a cup of coffee."

* * *

26

We Interrupt this Program...

IT HAD BEEN a day dominated by news and speculation. By midday, it was clear that the Caliphate forces were being destroyed on the ground by coalition forces. The press had piled on the news from San Francisco like jackals around a hamstrung wildebeest. There was no question now of scuttling the *Dohna* or sending it off to Guam, as a swarm of helicopters kept watch on the ship and the Coast Guard Cutter guarding it. Early in the afternoon, three tugboats and a pilot boat arrived on the scene. The pilot boat pulled alongside the *Dohna* and transferred what was presumably a new crew to the disabled ship. Soon, there was live footage of the *Dohna* being towed and nudged by the tugs into San Francisco Harbor, escorted by the cutter.

"Anybody home?"

"Yes, Marla. We're both here," Tim said.

"Great! How about we defrost a couple of pizzas and listen to the president's address? It's supposed to start in fifteen minutes."

"We're way ahead of you. We ordered the real thing a half hour ago."

"I knew there was a reason I liked you. Give me two minutes and I'll join you."

When she did, they had the pre-speech warm-up broadcast cued up and ready to go.

> *Good evening, and welcome to this special broadcast on today's extraordinary events, ending with a speech by the president that was announced just one hour ago. We begin our coverage with an update on the situation on the ground in the Middle East. Our chief foreign correspondent, Bill Henley, is broadcasting live from Ankara, Turkey. Bill, what can you tell us?*
>
> *Thanks, Bruce. "Extraordinary" only begins to describe what we've seen here today. The action began in the early afternoon when Mullah Mohammed Foobar launched a disastrous, all-fronts Kamikaze-style attack. When the final tally is taken, it's expected to show that the Caliphate suffered the largest one-day casualties of any force in any conflict since the Second World War.*

The video switched to a succession of aerial shots of battle scenes across the Middle East. Everywhere the camera turned, there were burned-out vehicles, abandoned artillery pieces, and endless numbers of bodies.

> *As you can see, wherever the forces of the Caliphate advanced, they were annihilated. Unlike prior attacks, Caliphate forces advanced in concentrated units, as if they expected to meet no resistance whatsoever. This made them exceptionally vulnerable to attack from the air, resulting in enormous casualties almost immediately. When Foobar's forces were confronted with overwhelming firepower, their discipline quickly broke, and they abandoned their weapons and scattered or surrendered.*
>
> *Bill, most of these troops were poorly trained, isn't that right?*
>
> *That's correct, Bruce. Most of the troops on the front lines were young men who had flocked to Foobar's banner when he announced himself as the Mahdi. That wasn't that long ago, and it doesn't look like they'd made very good use of what training time they had. Foobar seems to have spread all his experienced forces across the new battalions of raw troops, so to the extent that any of them have survived, they're now scattered across much of the Middle East.*
>
> *So where did things stand by nightfall?*
>
> *General Harvey Toffler told us at a briefing earlier this evening that Foobar's ability to wage war has been effectively destroyed and that coalition forces are expected to retake all Caliphate-controlled territory without meaningful opposition.*
>
> *Thank you, Bill. Stay safe.*

You're welcome, Bruce.

The video returned to the news studio.

But this was hardly the only extraordinary news we learned today. Stay tuned as we return to U.S. shores and report on a battle waged just off San Francisco, the true significance of which is only now just beginning to emerge after rampant speculation throughout the day.

Marla hit the pause button. "This all sounds too good to be true. Why would Foobar have thrown everything away like that?"

"From what I've heard, it's linked to the next story," Tim answered. "Let's listen."

Frank and Tim immediately recognized the footage and commentary playing now. They'd watched the same feed at the airport. After the anchor brought the story up to the minute, the camera angle widened to show that the network's military expert had joined him.

Here to help us understand what we've just been looking at is retired Army Colonel Alec Gainer, our regular commentator on terrorism, and on the line we've got Sara Ravitz, the founder and executive director of the Responsible Technology Foundation, which commissioned a just-released report by the Center for Infrastructure Studies on data center vulnerabilities.

Alec, help us set the stage here. What, if anything, do today's events in the Middle East and off San Francisco have to do with each other?

Well, Bruce, it could be everything or it could be nothing. A lot of people are saying that the targets of the ship that was seized off San Francisco today were the huge data centers that host most of the information and software for not just the high-tech companies in Silicon Valley but just about everything else as well—government, air traffic control, the San Francisco Stock Exchange, you name it. It's extraordinary to think about, but from what we can tell from the footage we just saw, drones looking very much like German World War Two buzz bombs— that's seventy-five-year-old technology—were about to shut down just about everything in the Southwest.

That's incredible, Alec, but what does that have to do with the collapse of the Caliphate?

Right, Bruce. That's where things start to get interesting. Ever since the San Francisco events hit the air, social media has exploded with accounts of unexplained events offshore of Seattle, Los Angeles, Savannah, and Boston. Things like fishermen seeing Chinook helicopters for the first time in their lives over their home waters or a private plane pilot reporting an oil slick and wreckage to the Coast Guard without any sort of response on their part. Similar stories have been coming out of Denmark, Ireland, and Italy.

So what do you make of all that?

Well, the most interesting theory is that the Caliphate had a whole fleet of ships capable of taking out most of the data centers in the U.S. and Europe, and allied forces were successful in destroying all of them. If that hadn't happened, our entire command and control capability would have been taken out, and Foobar's forces would have walked all over us.

That's quite a theory. What is the government saying about it?

No comment.

No, no, Alec. That's not something we say.

No, Bruce—no comment is what everyone is saying—the Navy, the Coast Guard, the president's spokesman, NATO, you name it. All we know at this point is that we're going to hear from the president tonight on the Middle East and "other topics."

Fascinating. Now let's hear from Sara Ravitz. Sara, I hear you had quite an interesting day on the Hill this afternoon on what may be a related story. Can you tell us about that first?

Of course, Bruce. As it happens, there was a hearing scheduled for this afternoon on exactly the same topic. The House Cybersecurity, Infrastructure Protection, and Security Technologies Subcommittee wanted to know more about data center vulnerability before the president signs the Cloud Computing Cybersecurity Act into law. Under that bill, data centers could become larger and larger with almost no physical protection at all.

And that's something you disagree with?

Absolutely, Bruce. In fact, my organization commissioned a detailed report from the Center for Infrastructure Studies detailing exactly what the consequences of the destruction of just one-third of our data centers would be. Suffice it to say that if Foobar had successfully launched such an attack today, eighty-five percent of our population would have been dead in one month from exposure and starvation.

That sounds hard to believe. Is that a well-accepted conclusion?

Not by everyone. As you can expect, there are some very large corporations that would like not to have to spend the kind of money it would take to make data centers safe from physical attack—and the only ways to do that are by burying them at least fifty feet underground or dividing them up into thousands of smaller data centers. Some of those opponents are willing to do almost anything to stop Congress from requiring that.

Such as?

Well, that's where today became interesting.

How so?

Originally, there were to be two other experts providing testimony at the hearing as well as myself. The others were Benno Patricoff, the executive director of the Data Center Alliance, and Sam Franklin, the chief security officer for WeBCloud, one of the largest cloud services providers. However, at the last minute, they decided not to testify.

Why was that?

The video feed switched to the hallway outside a hearing room in the Rayburn Building in Washington, D.C. Several uniformed men were intercepting two people in the hallway outside the door to a hearing room.

Because they were served with subpoenas on their way into the hearing room by U.S. Marshals acting under orders from the Security and Exchange Commission. Some time ago, I learned that someone had hacked into the computer system of my organization in an effort to sabotage our work. Just this week I was informed that totally false rumors had been planted on investor chat boards claiming that the only reason my organization commissioned our report was so that I could personally profit from driving down the stock price of cloud computing companies like Orinoco. Those rumors temporarily wiped out over 7.5 billion dollars in stockholder value.

They were now looking at the entrance to an opulent office building on K Street in Washington, D.C., where police officers were holding back a crowd as a startled-looking man wearing a business suit and handcuffs was "perp walked" to a squad car for the benefit of the camera crews on either side.

The SEC also arrested Paul Roach, a prominent Washington lobbyist. Based on an unnamed informer, it appears that he and his firm, Roach & Drye, had planted the rumor as part of a campaign they were waging against my organization on behalf of WeBCloud and the Data Center Security Alliance.

Fascinating! So what happened at your hearing?

On the advice of their legal counsels, Patricoff and Franklin asserted their Fifth Amendment rights and declined to testify. But their written testimony had already been submitted. I was able to demonstrate the specific ways in which their testimony had been informed by hacking our systems by pointing to specific inclusions relating to a decoy version of the actual report written by the Center for Infrastructure Studies.

Well, Sara. That's quite a story on a day filled with incredible stories. Thank you both for joining us this evening.

The news anchor paused and turned to face another camera, where another commentator joined him.

I'm joined now by Phillip Glasser, our chief political correspondent. Phil, I understand that the president will shortly be addressing the nation from the Oval Office, is that right?

That's right, Bruce. As you know, most presidential addresses are given from more informal locations, like the Rose Garden or a corridor in the White House. So clearly, the president wants to emphasize the gravity of what he has to say tonight.

And what do think that will be?

Well, Bruce, this is a very unusual situation, because normally the press gets a summary in advance of what he will say. This time, though, all we know is that it will be about the situation in the Middle East and "other matters."

Frank grinned when he heard that; he could imagine the arguments and debates that must have been raging all day about whether to talk about the skirmish that had been filmed off San Francisco, and if so, what to say about it. And most critically, whether or not to take a position on preparing for a similar attack in the future. Things must have gotten really interesting after the bombshell from Congressman Steele's Subcommittee hit mid-afternoon. He would have loved to have been a fly on the wall for those discussions.

So what's your guess on what those "other matters" might be, Phil?

Well, that's the question of the hour, isn't it? I've heard some people say that they think it will be related to the Middle East, like commitments from additional countries to help stamp out what's left of the Caliphate. Others think that it will have something to do with the military action that took place off the coast of California this morning. The administration still hasn't explained what that was all about.

Well, we won't have long to wait to find out. Let's go now to the Oval Office, where the president of the United States is making his first formal address in almost eleven months.

The video cut to a live stream of a very earnest-looking president seated in the Oval Office, his hands clasped on the desk in front of him. He began speaking immediately.

> *My fellow Americans, I've asked to speak to you this evening in order to announce that the United States, along with our NATO allies, has dealt a crushing blow to the Caliphate. Foolishly, Mullah Mohammed Foobar today launched major, almost suicidal, offensives against Egypt, Jordan, and Turkey. None of these advances was able to gain significant ground, and all of them were immediately met with overwhelming air, artillery, and cruise missile fire. Even as I speak, the remaining Caliphate forces are in full retreat on every front.*
>
> *I'm especially relieved to announce that while as many as eighteen thousand Caliphate infantry—more than half of all of Mullah Foobar's troops—have been killed or wounded, the United States forces suffered not a single fatality. Clearly, this bears testimony to the superb skill and dedication of our brave men and women in uniform, as well as those of our allies. We have also taken thousands of Foobar's troops prisoner. In some cases, entire brigades laid down their arms without resistance."*

I bet they did, Frank thought. Foobar would have promised them that U.S. and NATO forces would miraculously be denied the ability to communicate or fire their weapons and that the Caliphate army would overrun them with little or no opposition. He could just imagine Foobar's generals dashing forward on their splendid white Arabian stallions, scimitars brandished over their heads, only to be mowed down by allied forces. It must have been like the Charge of the Light Brigade, or more appropriately, the slaughter of the Mahdist forces by the British at the battle of Omdurman in 1885. Except that this time, no one at all would have made it back alive.

> *We believe that, in all, three-quarters of Foobar's troops have been killed, wounded, or captured. The balance is demoralized, disorganized, dispersed, and incapable of putting up effective resistance. Consequently, I have been informed by our military commanders that it is highly likely that all hostilities will have ceased by midnight tomorrow and that all territory previously seized by the Caliphate will be under the control of U.S. and allied forces. I am also pleased to report that al-Raqqa, the Caliphate's self-proclaimed capital, has already been retaken through the heroic actions of Army Special Forces, some of whom had secretly infiltrated the area over*

the preceding several days, and the 173rd Airborne Brigade, which launched its assault this morning.

That was all welcome news, but Frank and Tim were on the edges of their seats wondering whether the president would own up to the reason Foobar had been so over-confident.

While it is right to celebrate this momentous victory over a vicious foe committed to destroying our country, our people, and our way of life, we must not forget the thousands of citizens of America and our NATO allies, as well as the countless citizens of Middle Eastern nations, that fell victim to the Caliphate's atrocities before its destruction. Accordingly, we must dedicate this victory to their honor, and never forget their innocent sacrifice.

But there is another matter that I would like to speak to you about tonight as well. While related to the success we have just achieved, it represents an even greater existential threat to our existence than the Caliphate.

Frank and Tim exchanged glances—this must be it—he was going to take the plunge. The president's face now assumed an expression of determined satisfaction.

Many of you will have heard by now that U.S. forces seized a vessel off San Francisco just before dawn. What you will not have heard was that twelve other vessels, each one secretly purchased, refitted, and armed by the Caliphate, were also interdicted a few hours earlier, approximately ten miles off shore of Seattle, Los Angeles, Galveston, Savannah, Norfolk, Boston, and multiple European ports. The mission of each one of these ships was to launch primitive, but powerful, cruise missiles capable of destroying approximately sixty percent of the enormous computer data centers that today host the software and data of our increasingly cloud-based information technology infrastructure.

Had these attacks succeeded, a catastrophe that is difficult to imagine or describe would have been unleashed. Not only would our military command and control systems have been destroyed, resulting in the Caliphate's forces overrunning ours, rather than the opposite, but our power grid, transportation and financial systems, fuel delivery capabilities, and much, much more would have been incapacitated. This would have rendered it impossible to repair the damage to the data centers, and therefore impossible to restore the power grid and essential services. In the days and weeks to follow, untold millions in America and Europe would have died of hunger and exposure.

I will not dwell tonight on the details of what such a monumental calamity would be like or on how it was averted. What I will do is ask every American to take to heart the enormous vulnerability that we have unwittingly brought upon ourselves. Technology is a wondrous thing, and the scientists and engineers of America have led the world for decades in its advancement. But just as with the invention of the atomic bomb, technological advancement has the capacity to lead us to places where our innovative reach can exceed our grasp of the possible consequences.

We must take the right lesson away from the events of today, and not let the celebration of a well-deserved victory blind us to the vulnerability that this thwarted attack exposed, and which so nearly brought about our own downfall. That is why I am announcing tonight that, with the full support of the speaker of the house, I will not sign the Cloud Computing Cybersecurity Act, recently passed by both houses of Congress. Instead, I am declaring a national emergency and calling upon both the majority and minority leaders of the House of Representatives and Senate to immediately sit down together and agree upon a plan of action to draft and adopt a bipartisan bill within thirty days to accomplish the following:

First, mandate that no facility equipped with more than five hundred computer servers shall be built aboveground and that construction of any such larger facility currently in progress shall immediately cease.

Second, instruct the National Institute of Standards and Technology to take such steps, in cooperation with representatives of industry and the scientific community, to create effective standards for the construction and securing of belowground data facilities, with such standards to ensure that such a facility is capable of withstanding a direct nuclear strike.

Third, authorize a one hundred percent tax credit for the costs of relocating existing data centers underground, and, for the next ten years, for the incremental cost of building new facilities underground as compared to aboveground.

And finally, to create a fifty-billion-dollar fund to provide long-term, no-interest loans to owners of existing data centers to fund the relocation of their facilities pending cost recovery through the relocation cost tax credit just mentioned.

My fellow Americans, today we averted a disaster that so far exceeds any calamity this nation has ever faced that it is difficult to comprehend its full magnitude. We must pledge ourselves to work unceasingly to remove this vulnerability as speedily as humanly possible. I ask that you convey your unconditional support to your elected representatives for the initiative that I have just described so that not only we, but our children and grandchildren, will be able to live the safe and happy lives we all deserve as Americans.

Thank you for your attention this evening, and may God bless America.

Marla muted the sound before the news anchor could begin regurgitating everything the president had just said. "Wow, Dad—you must be on cloud nine, no pun intended!"

Frank's and Tim's eyes widened in shock. Had Marla somehow been on to them the whole time?

"I mean, you've been ranting about this for years! And now the president of the United States is, too!"

Frank relaxed with relief. "Uh, yeah. I guess I am. But how about that—it looks like we had a real near miss there, doesn't it?"

"We sure did. And I guess you won't even be able to say 'I told you so' because the people who figured out what Foobar was up to probably don't even know you exist."

* * *

Several days later, Frank visited the Cloud Data offices for his project exit interview. As he stepped off the elevator, he could see that George Marchand was already sitting in the conference room where Frank's latest adventure had begun. He weaved his way across the wide expanse of sprawling Whiz Kids to join him.

"Good to see you, Frank."

"And you as well. I guess Hermann and Tim will be joining us?"

"Any minute. By the way—how did things go with Tim at the airport?"

"Pretty well, except that I had to buy a two hundred and fifty dollar ticket to Pittsburgh I'll never use to get through security. I'm relieved to say that Tim is completely horrified now at what he almost pulled off. I guess he was under a lot more self-imposed pressure than I realized. Anyway, he's been bending over backwards assuring me he doesn't understand now how he could possibly have rationalized his actions to himself at the time. And he's decided that the CIA isn't the place for him."

"That's a relief to me as well. I don't think in good conscience I could have looked the other way if he wanted to stay at the Agency."

"Thanks, George—I appreciate it. How about with the Agency? Any lingering suspicions there?"

"No, and especially not after the president decided to come out against the cloud computing industry. As you'd expect, after the cover was blown on the naval operation, he's touting the defeat of the Caliphate's plan for all its worth. Without that video of the SEALs retaking the *Dohna* and blasting a V-1 out of the sky, the whole thing would be too abstract to capture the public's imagination. By the way, how do you suppose that came about?" George was suddenly looking at Frank very intently.

"Who knows? I guess it must have been just a good, clear night and somebody in the helicopter was looking in the right direction at the right time."

"And the reporter who hates data centers? He just happened to be up early, too?"

"Well, you know, the early bird gets the worm."

"What exactly does that mean?"

"Uh, as little as possible?"

George paused, frowning, before answering. "Yes, I suppose so." Then he shrugged. "Anyway, at this point, I expect the administration would just as soon know less rather than more about how that came about."

"Well, I have to say that's a relief."

There was a rap at the door, and Koontz walked in, followed by Tim.

Frank stood up to shake Koontz's hand. Then he took his Cloud Data ID badge off his shirt and handed it to him. "I guess I won't be needing this anymore."

"Oh, you never know. I think I won't send it to the shredder just yet."

"Anyway," George said, "I'm glad we could get together today to close things out. Frank, Hermann will need to collect the signatures of everyone, including you, whose work is summarized in his final report. You'll also need to return all materials you've received, if any, over the course of the project, and sign a certification that you've destroyed any notes that you may have taken outside this office. And finally, you'll need to sign this." George slid a document across the table. "All it says, in so many words, is that you understand and reaffirm the confidentiality requirements in the agreement you signed back in the beginning. So I guess you can't write a book about this one."

"Not much danger of that, unless I get another ghostwriter."

"I expect not. But anyway, other than that, you're a free man again. Any questions?"

"Just one—do you think we'll ever catch Foobar? It seems incredible he was able to get away, just like bin Laden and Mullah Omar."

"Yes, not being able to announce his capture is the one fly in the president's ointment, isn't it? As a matter of fact, though, it's a bit more complicated than that, because we did get him."

"Really? Then why isn't the president claiming the credit for that, too?"

"Because there was more behind Foobar than we had thought before. When we sifted through all of the records we seized on the day of the attack, we learned that most of Foobar's economic support wasn't coming from rich Saudis, Iraq, or any of the other sources we'd assumed must be backing him."

"Who was supporting him, then?"

"Believe it or not, the Chinese."

"The Chinese? You're kidding."

"Nope. And it makes more sense than it sounds like at first. You already know that relations between the West and China have been deteriorating for years now, what with China's military buildup and asserting control over the South China Sea. And you're also aware that China's been making economic alliances around the world with emerging nations, trying to lock up as many natural resources as possible for their own use. China doesn't have much by way of raw materials, and with more and more of its people entering the middle class, the government has an enormous problem coming up with the resources and energy it will take to keep them satisfied.

"They've also got their problems with the Uighurs and the other domestic Islamic populations they've been suppressing for years. Just as Russia does, which, of course, is right next door and also a long-term potential problem for the Chinese."

"Fine. But I don't see how connecting all those dots adds up to supporting the Caliphate?"

"It starts to make sense if you think what the world would have looked like if Foobar's attack had succeeded. The U.S. and Europe would be wiped out, leaving China free to do whatever it wants in Southeast Asia. And there'd be almost no competition for the rest of the world's resources. Most of the global market for commodities would have evaporated, so they'd all be available to China, and at much lower prices, too.

"That takes us to Russia. It hasn't moved into cloud computing yet, so the same approach wouldn't work to take Putin down. But Russia does have a big problem with the Muslim populations it's been oppressing for decades now. China promised Foobar that after he was in control of as much of Europe and North Africa as he wanted, it would support him in liberating Chechnya and the other Islamic parts of the Russian Federation. That would keep Russia preoccupied for years.

"In exchange, Foobar would reveal and acclaim China's support, which would make the Chinese government a hero in the eyes of many of its indigenous Muslim citizens."

"But still—supporting someone trying to kill a billion people? I can't imagine the government of any country, except maybe North Korea, taking a chance on a stunt like that."

"And you'd be right. But it might not stop some bigshots in the Chinese military willing to roll the dice. As you may know, the armed forces in China control all kinds of powerful businesses. A lot of generals are closer to being commercial oligarchs than military professionals. And they also control huge sums of money they can move around the world without worrying about the kinds of controls that would apply in most other countries. At any rate, a few of the top generals decided it would be a bright idea to back the Caliphate's scheme and then reap the global profits. Whether the party bosses were aware and just looked the other way is something we may never know."

"Wow. That's quite a story. How come we haven't gone public with it?"

"Let's just say that there are a lot of very high-level discussions going on behind the scenes between our diplomats and China's. Our military is still vastly superior to theirs, but neither side wants a shooting war. We and our NATO allies are pushing for a treaty that settles all kinds of issues, failing which the Western nations will cut off all trade with China. That will be tough for the West, but even tougher for China. It would totally tank their economy, and lead to all kinds of internal shortages. We'll have to wait and see how that comes out. Meanwhile, Mr. Foobar has been tucked away for safe keeping, and can be brought out at any time to bear witness where his funding and support were coming from."

"Amazing. It never occurred to me that there was more there than met the eye. What was readily visible was incredible enough."

"What about the cloud computing legislation?" Tim asked. "Do you think the administration will hold firm against the industry on that?"

"I expect so. In fact, the cloud computing vendors are pretty much at the mercy of the administration now, as the public is never going to tolerate big, aboveground data centers again. The administration was pretty smart to bait the hook with that loan fund and all the tax relief, so the big, diversified companies like Orinoco will come out just fine. Tough luck for WeBCloud, though. Apparently, they owned a lot of patents, but once the president killed the law that would have incorporated the DCSA, most of the value in those patents evaporated. With the whole cloud computing business on hold now, the financing round WeBCloud was relying on to survive collapsed, and so did the company. You probably saw they declared bankruptcy the day after the president's speech. The last I heard, the highest bid they're likely to get for the entire company will be less than pennies on the dollars they owe their creditors. So WeBCloud stock is totally worthless.

"So that's about it," George concluded. "Anything else? No? Then I guess I'll get back to my own office."

Frank accompanied George back to the street, musing to himself as he rode down the elevator that it had been less than three months ago that he had entered the building for the first time. So much had happened so quickly, and now he was right back where he was then.

He blinked twice when that thought struck him. Right back where he was then. As they walked across the lobby, he stopped and turned to George.

"Uh, George, you wouldn't happen to have anything else you need help with, would you?"

* * *

Epilogue

A FAMILIAR VOICE FROM long ago interrupted his thoughts. "Hello, Frank."

He turned around. "Hello, Clare." He'd already studied her from a distance earlier; she looked younger than he had expected. She still did now that they were face to face. He hoped he looked as good in his new suit as she did in her blue dress and that he had not been fidgeting when she noticed him and came his way.

"I thought you looked very handsome up there, next to Marla," Clare said. "It made me happy to see the two of you together that way."

"Did you cry?"

"Of course. Did you?"

"A little, yes."

"That's as it should be. No matter how good the groom, it's hard to give your only daughter to him."

"Especially…"

"I know. But I think they're going to do just fine. They're a lot more mature than you and I were, and older, too. You've been a fine father to her, Frank. I hope you know that. She thinks the world of you. Did you know you're her hero?"

He found himself unsuccessfully waging a war not to blush. "Ah, I haven't had a drink yet. Would you like one?"

"What a good idea."

They walked toward one of the bars set up on the broad lawn by the golf course clubhouse.

"Marla tells me you're married now. Is he here?"

"Of course, he is; what a question! He's over there, chatting up one of his big clients." She gestured toward a man in his mid-fifties, holding a drink in one hand and clapping someone on the back with the other. Frank frowned slightly, trying to form an impression of what type of person he might be.

"So I thought I'd hunt you up," Clare continued. "Marla tells me that you've been seeing an elegant professor from Paris."

"I'm afraid that didn't work out."

"I'm sorry. I also hear you're a cyber detective now. Is that interesting?"

"Sometimes." Time to try to change the conversation once again. He nodded toward another bar. "Look—don't they look great together?"

Marla and Tim were surrounded by friends, and he had his arm around her waist. Everyone was laughing at something he had just said. Frank felt his throat tightening and surprised himself with the next words out of his mouth.

"Do you think we were ever that happy together, Clare?"

She touched his arm. "Of course, we were. All the time for the first couple of years. Don't you remember?"

"I'm afraid I've never been as successful at remembering the good times as the bad."

"Well, you'll just have to believe me then." She paused. "You know, Frank, I only—"

"Did what you had to do for you and Marla." He was finding it even harder to talk now but pushed on. "I couldn't accept it at the time, but you were right. You and Marla deserved better."

"That's not the way I would ever phrase it, Frank. But I'm glad that you're able to understand it now. The important thing is that it looks like everything worked out for Marla."

"And for you?"

"I don't know. You know I didn't want to leave you. I just didn't think I had a choice."

He cleared his throat. "So do you think you've found the right person to spend the rest of your life with this time?"

"Yes, I really do."

"Then I'm very happy for you. Really."

"And you?"

"Not yet."

"I hope you do, Frank. Really."

Frank realized to his surprise that he was feeling nothing but happiness and pride as he stood there with Clare, watching Marla and Tim laughing with their friends. He felt a sudden sense of relief wash over him, and he felt as if a virtual version of himself had indeed somehow stepped off of a spaceship, merging back into him and wiping clean the slate of tortured emotions that had tormented him ever since he'd last seen Clare. He had passed the test.

He took a deep breath and recklessly took her hand as they watched their only daughter and their new son-in-law.

"Well, who knows about the future," he said at last. "That will just have to take care of itself. But I think I finally understand something now about the past. And for today, that's enough."

* * *

Did you enjoy **The Doodlebug War**? If so, please consider recommending it to others. Book promotion is a huge challenge for Indie authors, and I'd be very grateful for your help in reaching a wider audience.

You can read the first two chapters of the first Frank Adversego thriller in the pages that follow.

The Alexandria Project, a Tale of Treachery and Technology, and **The Lafayette Campaign, a Tale of Deception and Elections**, are available in paperback and eBook format at Amazon, and on order in paperback through your favorite local book store.

Follow the further adventures of Frank at Andrew-Updegrove.com *and on Twitter* @Adversego.

Sign up for the Friends of Frank Newsletter.
http://andrew-updegrove.com/newsletter

Acknowledgements

I'd like to express my gratitude to the many individuals who generously assisted me in completing this book.

First off, my thanks to Nora, may daughter and alpha reader. She provided many good suggestions to improve the plot, characters and flow of the book, as well as welcome encouragement along the way.

I'd also like to thank Sayeh Hassan, a Canadian attorney and human rights activist. Sayeh kindly agreed to review the book from a Middle Eastern cultural and religious perspective to ensure that I did not inadvertently give cause for offense to anyone through my own ignorance. Similarly, my thanks go to cybersecurity expert Ralph Rodriquez, who once again reviewed the text to confirm that everything I've written on the cybersecurity front is technically accurate and could indeed happen in the way I have written it. I'm also indebted to my brother-in-law, U.S. Navy Captain (ret.) Thomas Dee, who reviewed the book for military operational accuracy and made many helpful corrections and suggestions.

I am very grateful to the following faithful friends of Frank, each of whom volunteered to be a beta reader of my near-final draft: Sylva Fae, Eric Lahti,

William Lupton, Robert Minchin, Steve Oksala, Andrew Oliver, Frank Parker, Rob van Son, and my brother Steve. As always, they provided invaluable assistance by spotting the inconsistencies, improbabilities and other species of gremlins that an author becomes too blind to see in his own text after seven drafts.

On the production side, I am delighted to have made the acquaintance of Nelly Hartigan, who lent an eagle-eye and encyclopedic editing knowledge to the finalization of the text of this book. And once again, I've benefited from the excellent design skills and generous time and talent of Glendon Haddix, of Streetlight Graphics. As with my previous two books, his fantastic cover and clean interior designs make all the different. I would recommend both of these professionals without hesitation to other authors.

As I've noted elsewhere in the past, I'd never let Frank do anything truly stupid that I hadn't already done myself. Accordingly, my heartfelt thanks once again go to my long suffering bride, Kathy.

And finally, thanks to Frank, who bravely allowed me to share with you his difficult and very personal effort to reconcile himself with a dark period of his past.

THE ALEXANDRIA PROJECT

Prologue

L ATE IN THE afternoon of a gray day in December, a panel truck pulled up to the gate of a warehouse complex in a run-down section of Richmond, Virginia. Rolling down his window, Jack Davis punched a code into the control box, and the gate clanked slowly out of the way. Once inside, he wheeled the truck around and backed it up against a loading dock as the gate closed behind him.

After unlocking and raising the loading dock door, Davis threw a light switch, revealing long rows of pallets, each stacked eight feet high with boxes of paper plates, cups and towels. He closed and locked the door, and stamped on the brake release pedal of a hydraulic lifter parked against the wall. Counting to himself, he pushed the lifter along the wall of pallets. When he reached row nineteen, he turned the lifter and maneuvered its long tines under the pallet. Raising it a few inches, he backed up until he could swing the pallet through 180 degrees. Then he pulled it behind him until it was back exactly where it had been before.

Davis had plenty of room to work, because where the pallet in the second row should have been, there was only a large metal plate set in the floor. Near the edge was a small hinged panel, which he unlocked with a key to expose a biometric security pad.

When Davis pressed his thumb against it, he heard a familiar click. Stepping back, he watched as the plate swung slowly upwards, followed by the telescoping ends of a ladder extending up from a deep shaft barely illuminated in red light. Grasping the ladder firmly, Davis descended through twenty feet of reinforced concrete while the door overhead swung silently closed above him. At the bottom, he remembered to don a pair of sunglasses before opening an unlocked door.

As usual, even with this precaution the bright lights in the enormous room beyond nearly blinded him. But soon he could clearly see the endless rows of floor to ceiling metal racks crammed with identical gray boxes. Each box displayed a row of rhythmically blinking lights, and sprouted a bundle of brightly colored wires that ran down into conduits embedded in the floor.

The room hummed purposefully with the sound of thousands of cooling fans, one to a box. Davis felt more than heard the other vibrations that filled the room, generated by the pulse of the thousands of gallons of cooling water that every minute coursed through the collectors lining the walls of the room, absorbing the waste heat that the racks of computer servers threw off. No heat signature would give this facility away from above; once warm, the coolant was directed to the water intake of a nearby power plant, happy to take the pre-heated water from wherever it was that it came from, no questions asked.

Walking along the perimeter of the room, Davis could look down through the open metal grid of the floor at the first of many additional tiers of computer servers. But that always made him a little dizzy, so instead he looked out for the guard he was relieving. No surprise – there he was, heading Davis's way, more than happy to call it a day. When they met, the guard stopped to slip on the coveralls he carried over one arm. Like the semi-automatic pistol the guard wore in a shoulder holster, they were identical to those that Davis also wore.

"What's the weather like?"

"Sucks. Sleet and more of the same predicted till morning."

"Figures. Tomorrow's my day off."

With that, the other man was on his way. In a few minutes he would drive off in the truck Davis had parked outside.

Well, the weather won't be bothering me in here, Davis thought. The room was climate controlled to within a tenth of a degree of a chilly 54 degrees Fahrenheit, and well-insulated by the bomb-proof walls and roof installed above. It had taken two years for a fleet of delivery vans to carry all the dirt and rock away that had been excavated from beneath the warehouse. The same vans had returned with cement, steel, and, eventually, those thousands of servers, accompanied by technicians to set them up. The process had been tedious, yes, but not a single satellite picture had ever shown a trace of the ambitious construction project proceeding underground.

Of course, the effect worked in both directions. With no links to the outside world other than a voice line to his supervisor, the whole bloody world could come to an end and Davis would be none the wiser until after his shift was over.

Davis walked up a flight of steel stairs to the bullet proof, glass-walled security booth attached to the wall overlooking the room. His major challenge for the next twelve hours would be to stand watch in that booth without falling asleep. There'd be hell to pay if he did, because another guard, in another security room far away, would be watching him on a video screen.

The row of displays in front of Davis allowed him to see every inch of the outside of the warehouse complex. Racked on the wall behind him were a high powered rifle and a shotgun, but it wasn't likely he'd ever need to use them. One flip of the large red switch in front of Davis would flood the server room with enough Halon gas to not only put out a fire, but asphyxiate any intruder careless enough to leave a gas mask at home. Not for the first time, Davis wished that the house where he lived with his wife and their two small children could be as well protected.

But the government didn't put as high a priority on protecting suburban starter homes as it did on safeguarding its most critical computer network facilities. Some storage facilities, like those serving the needs of the Pentagon and the National Security Administration, were located not far away at Fort Meade. Others, like this one, were scattered far and wide, hidden in plain sight but highly secure nonetheless. No way was anyone going to crack this nut. He was dead certain of that.

If Davis had been able to electronically monitor what was happening on server A-VI/147 on Level Three, though, his confidence might have taken a hit. True, concrete and steel walls, surveillance cameras and Halon gas were more than adequate to protect the physical wellbeing of his facility against anything short of a direct hit by a "bunker busting" nuclear weapon. But the data on the facility's servers had to rely on virtual defenses – firewalls, security routines and intrusion scanners.

And those defenses hadn't been enough. Someone had gotten inside.

* * *

1

Meet Frank

T HE NEXT MORNING, a morbidly obese Corgi named Lily was sniffing a tree on 16th Street, in the Columbia Heights neighborhood of Washington, D.C. A cold, insistent drizzle fell on her, but Lily didn't care, because Lily was sniffing at her favorite tree. Indeed, the meager processing power of Lily's brain was wholly consumed by sampling the mysterious scents wafting up from the damp earth, for this was also the favorite tree of every other dog in the neighborhood.

Something was nagging at the edge of her senses, though.

"C'mon, Lily! Hurry up!"

Lily turned her head. The annoying distraction was coming from the person at the other end of her leash, someone with sockless feet jammed into worn, black loafers. Above bare ankles, a pair of pajama-clad legs disappeared into a rumpled raincoat. She saw there was an arm holding an umbrella, too, and under the umbrella, a stubbly, forty-something face topped by thinning black hair. Lily decided that the face did not look happy.

"Ah!" she thought. "That would be Frank." Relieved that the distraction could be ignored, Lily returned to the important work at hand.

"*C'mon*, Lily!" the voice said again.

The fact that Frank's face was unhappy was unremarkable. Even in pleasant weather, Frank tended to dwell pointlessly on the minor miseries of his life. Not long ago, those miseries had become much less minor when his mother Doreen entered a retirement home. After helping her move in, Frank took a deep breath and prepared to leave. No use dragging things out, he thought. Transitions are difficult and best dealt with quickly.

Still, it was sad. His mother was standing by the doorway of her new apartment, lower lip a-tremble and Lily held tightly in her arms. It was clear that she was rapidly nearing her emotional limits. Better hurry up.

"Well, Mom," he said, "I guess I'll be leaving now."

Then it happened. With a lunge, Doreen thrust Lily into Frank's arms. He stepped back with surprise into the hallway, too horrified to allow himself to grasp the obvious, while struggling to maintain his grip on the suddenly manic animal.

"The home doesn't allow pets," his mother blurted. "I could never have signed the lease if I hadn't known that Lily would be safe with you. Now don't you worry; I've made you her legal guardian, so it's all set. Now go! Get out of here, before I change my mind."

Frank desperately wanted her to change her mind. But his mother had already shut the door in his astonished face. He stared blankly at it as the enormity of his plight sank in. Now what? Lily was just three years old, and acknowledged his existence only by barking. He heard his mother sobbing piteously on the other side of the door. He felt like crying, too.

That had been two long, loud months ago. Only recently had he progressed from the denial stage to active mourning.

"*Come on!*" Frank hissed. At last, Lily turned away from her tree. She looked up at him reproachfully, and barked.

"Okay, okay," Frank said, fumbling in his pocket. He held a dog treat up for Lily to see. "*Okay?*"

Satisfied that her efforts would not go unrewarded, Lily began looking for just the right place to do what finally needed to be done. At last, she squatted, looking blankly ahead. Frank sighed with relief.

A blue plastic bag inverted over his free hand, Frank scooped up Lily's grudging gift. He handed over the treat, jerking back with his fingers barely intact.

Isn't that just the story of my life? he thought bleakly as Lily happily consumed her treat. Every day I give her a cookie, and every day she gives me a bag of shit.

Trudging home through the rain, Frank reflected that his day generally went downhill from here.

* * *

Lily shook herself mightily inside the foyer of Frank's dingy apartment house, wetting what little of Frank that was still dry. Satisfied, she planted her substantial hindquarters firmly on the floor, looked up at Frank, and barked. Frank sighed, picked up the still-wet dog, and labored his way up the stairs to his second floor flat.

As he climbed to the top, Frank's rising eyes met a pair of fuzzy pink slippers, a floral house dress, and then a pair of folded arms draped with a bath towel. Just above them, he knew, would be the perpetually hostile face of his across-the-hall neighbor. As that scowling visage hove into view, Frank once again noted the uncanny resemblance his neighbor bore to North Korean president Jong Kim-Lo. Only with hair curlers.

"Morning, Mrs. Foomjoy," Frank offered as Lily twisted wildly in his arms. He deposited the dog at her feet.

"Shame on you!" Mrs. Foomjoy barked as she knelt to massage Lily with the bath towel. "Poor, dear wet baby!" she crooned.

"It's raining, Mrs. Foomjoy," Frank observed. "Lily hasn't learned how to use the indoor facilities yet."

"Then why she not wear the lovely rain jacket I give her?" she snorted. "What is *wrong* with you? You don't deserve dog like this!"

Frank couldn't have agreed more. Lily groveled at Mrs. Foomjoy's feet, and then leaned to one side until gravity obligingly rolled her onto her back. The dog gazed up with adoring, goggle eyes as Mrs. Foomjoy rubbed her stomach.

His neighbor grabbed the leash from Frank's hand when she stood up. "I see to welfare of this dog!" she snapped, shutting her door loudly behind her. Frank stood suddenly alone in the poorly lit hallway, a warm, blue plastic pendulum swinging slowly from side to side in his hand. Relieved, he entered his own apartment and quietly shut the door.

Frank hung his dripping raincoat on a hook in the linoleum floored hallway inside. At one time, his apartment's décor might have charitably been described as "Late-Twentieth-Century Divorced Middle Aged Male." Now the most obvious theme was random clutter. He poured a cup of coffee and sat at the small table in the small kitchen. Before him the large screen of his laptop stared blankly back at him. With resignation, he turned the computer on.

Normally, the sound of a computer booting up would have struck him as cheerful; the imperceptibly soft whir of the cooling fan spinning up to speed; the blinking, blue light that assured him that the device was powering up; the screen phosphorescing into life with a pearly glow. After all, information technology – IT – was not only his profession, but the primary foundation of his existence.

Email was Frank's preferred link to the outside world, providing a social firewall between him and the random messiness of direct human contact. Frank was convinced that digital relations were far safer than their in-person analogue. Electronic communications brought him as close to his fellow man as he usually wished to be. Any more intimate than that, and things were apt to become at best unpredictable, and at worst, well, he'd been *there* all too often before. You never got enough time to think before things started spiraling out of control.

Which brought him back to the night before. Be honest, he mused ruefully. You got what you deserved. Or didn't get what you didn't deserve, to be more precise.

He stared at the keyboard. Should he check his email or shouldn't he? The rational side of his brain said, yes, what's there is there. Deal with it.

But the other side of his brain had a different opinion: "Go back to bed," it whispered urgently, "It's Sunday. You don't have to deal with anything today."

That was true. And who knows what might happen by Monday? There could be a typhoon tonight. Or maybe giant pterodactyls would erupt from a wormhole next to the Lincoln Memorial, scattering screaming tourists towards the safety of nearby Metro stations. That side of his brain was lobbying strongly to take two aspirin, pull the covers back over his head, and let reality take care of itself for another twenty-four hours.

He sighed and made up his mind. Might as well see sooner rather than later what people from his office had posted on line about the night before. A few clicks later and he was at the Facebook page of Mary, the sullen receptionist. Yes, there were pictures from the party. Lots of them. Later would do just fine after all, he decided. He snapped the laptop shut without turning it off.

The sad thing was, for once he had actually been looking forward to the Library of Congress IT Department Holiday party, even bringing his daughter Marla with him, a Georgetown University grad student. He appreciated the great impression she always made on his co-workers. Unlike her dad, Marla was self-assured and sociable. She worked the crowd like a pro, chatting and shaking hands, poised and laughing. How could he feel anything but proud? It was hard not to drink a bit more than usual as he watched her from the security of the bar in the rear of the function room.

More to the point, Frank had been looking forward to making Marla feel proud of her old man as well. Everyone knew that George Marchand, the Director of IT at the LoC, was going to announce his choice to head an important security initiative mandated by the Cybersecurity Subcommittee of the House Committee on Science and Technology. Frank figured he had the spot all sewn up. After all, he was – or at least at one time had been – a recognized cybersecurity innovator; a McArthur Foundation "Genius" Award recipient, no less, in recognition of his widely acclaimed creative work in the early days of computer networking.

So when George stood up and tapped on his glass, Frank sat up straighter. He listened impatiently as his boss welcomed the spouses, thanked the staff for their work that year, and told a joke at his own expense. At last, he began to make the announcement that Frank was waiting for.

And then it happened. One moment Frank was looking sideways to see the reaction on his daughter's face when his name was called, and the next he was hearing someone else's name ring out instead. And not just any name, but Rick Wellesley's – "only out for himself" Rick, a self-satisfied slug of a middle-manager who had never had a creative thought in his life. Someone who had even briefly reported to Frank when he first came to work at the LoC. *Rick Wellesley?* How could this be happening?

But it was. There was Rick, standing and basking in the applause, glancing briefly and triumphantly in Frank's direction. Frank was stunned, his face burning. And then he was angry. Without a word to his daughter, he stood up and marched to the bar, turning his back on the party as George finished his remarks. Knocking back another drink, Frank now felt foolish as well as angry. Everyone was probably looking at him, but he was afraid to turn around and find out. He sulked at the bar until Marla came looking for him.

Sitting now in his kitchen, Frank felt his face grow flush again. After all, everyone had expected the job to go to him. Then, with a wrenching feeling, he had a worse thought – what if no one had expected him to get the job? Maybe he was the only one in the whole damn department who hadn't seen it coming. Maybe everyone had been laughing up their sleeves as they watched him bask in his expected glory, just waiting for his jaw to drop when he realized that he had been skunked by Rick.

Of course that had been the case, he thought wretchedly. He was sure of it.

* * *

And why not? What had he really done in the last twenty years? Sure, he'd become a star at the Massachusetts Institute of Technology – "MIT" to anyone in the know. He'd enrolled at the age of sixteen after skipping two years of middle school. Not that skipping a few grades was unusual at MIT. As an undergraduate, he'd become part of Project Athena, an ambitious effort to create a distributed computing system for the whole university. Of course, the goal for the project's corporate sponsors was to use MIT as a testbed. Later, they hoped to productize the design and make a ton of money.

For some reason, Frank had intuitively locked onto the security challenges that such a system would present. He already had privileges to use MIT's gateway to the government-funded Advanced Research Projects Agency Network – the now-famous "ARPANET" that was the precursor to the Internet. Only select institutions had access to it then, but Frank immediately grasped where Project Athena and the ARPANET together could eventually lead. It hit him between the eyes that this was the start of something big. Linking terminals together around a campus was today's goal, but the next step would be to connect those networks together, using ARPANET technology.

That sounded awesome, but how would you restrict access to any particular data to one person, and not let it be seen by everyone else? MIT was already a hotbed of hackers. If students were going to great lengths now to break into restricted sections of university computers just for fun, what would criminals, or enemy countries, not do to break into classified computers, once someone had linked them all together? Frank tackled that issue with gusto, if not discipline. He was a big picture guy, and what a big and exciting picture it was! The idea of wide area networks was brand new, and big ideas were needed to make sense of it all; the details could come later. When Frank graduated, he stayed on at MIT, nominally in a PhD program, but for all practical purposes he lived at a terminal in the Project Athena lab, surviving on coffee and code like so many other young computer engineering students back in the day.

Luckily for Frank, he found a mentor – an engineer on loan from one of the sponsoring companies. Surprisingly, the two hit it off, and the older man reined in the younger one enough to keep Frank's ideas from flying off into too many directions at once. He also insisted that Frank get his best ideas recorded in some sort of coherent order. Often they talked until all hours, the older man channeling Frank's enthusiasm and helping him follow his insights down the most productive paths.

Frank never completed his doctorate, but he did finish his Masters thesis – and by anyone's account, it was brilliant. He anticipated just about every security challenge that would arise over the next twenty years as the Internet took off. He also suggested most of the solutions that were later refined and implemented to deal with a massively networked world. Even today, his thesis remained an obligatory foundational reference in just about every new network and Internet security paper that was written.

Frank's thesis also brought him to the notice of the mysterious keepers of the MacArthur Fellows Program – the unknown judges that every year contact a select group of exceptional individuals they have decided, "show exceptional merit and promise for continued and enhanced creative work."

Receiving a MacArthur Fellowship had been the high point of Frank's professional career. But as a practical matter, it also brought an end to it, because the payments of $25,000 every three months for five years gave him the freedom to do whatever he wanted to without ever having to acquire the discipline of making his way in the world. It also allowed him to get married.

It was not helpful that what Frank wanted to do usually changed every other week. It wasn't long before his work at Project Athena suffered. He no longer listened to his mentor, and his assigned tasks no longer got done. Instead, he plunged from one question that intrigued him to another, never getting very far along with any of them.

Like many people whose intellectual abilities matured before their social skills, Frank developed an abrupt and assertive manner that helped mask his discomfort around others. That was unfortunate, because his new–found fame encouraged him to become even more obnoxious than ever. Soon, the other guys in the lab were annoyed with his failure to meet his commitments, and also sick of hearing his latest revelations about security – or about any other topic on which he had decided he was now an expert.

Eventually, it was his mentor who took Frank aside and told him that if he didn't shape up, his days in the lab were numbered. Frank didn't take that well. What right did some middle aged, middle-management type with a degree from a state school in the Midwest have to tell a certified Genius anything about anything?

Quite a lot, Frank now reflected, gazing at his closed laptop. Like the immature idiot he was then, he had cleared his things out of the Project Athena lab the same day his mentor had called him out and never returned. Eventually, the MacArthur Fellowship money ran dry, and with a wife and young daughter, Frank had to get more serious about working. Or at least he should have. For a while, his thesis and MacArthur reputation carried him from job to job. But when the bottom fell out of the economy, employers received a flood of great résumés for every job they posted.

By then, of course, Frank's résumé was also getting pretty long in the tooth. He had no "continued and enhanced creative work" to show for his five years of subsidized, random behavior. He'd never published another paper, and it was others, and not Frank, who turned his thesis ideas into real protocols and products. As the jobs got scarce, reference checks counted a whole lot more, and the feedback about Frank always came back the same: brilliant, arrogant, unfocused, unreliable. That was more charitable than what his soon-to-be ex-wife had to say. But he hadn't listened to her, either.

Frank usually tried not to think much about the years that followed: the start-up that had signed him up as Chief Technical Officer and the VCs that fired him; the time spent without a job at all; the rut he fell into for years after his wife moved out with their daughter, when he said the hell with everything and everybody. That time was a blur of punching the clock in whatever high school, small business or municipal IT department would take him on until he got fired again, then waiting until his unemployment ran out before finding something else he could do in his sleep, until even that became too much to bother with.

Through all that time, though, industry insiders still sought Frank out, so he maintained a low-key consulting business on the side to make sure he could always cover his child support payments. Among the elite in the world of security, Frank still had the reputation of a wizard, able to come up with the kind of insights that would make the most impenetrable problems suddenly transparent. An emailed plea for help describing something dense and dark that had already defied all of the usual solutions would reliably generate a response from Frank an hour or two later, usually beginning, "It strikes me that..." and ending with, "I suggest you try...." Invariably, what Frank suggested worked. But requests for his ongoing assistance went unanswered.

It was his daughter Marla that finally set Frank back on his feet. One Friday when he was once again out of work, he picked her up for their weekend together. But something was wrong; his normally chatty preteen wasn't saying a word. As they walked, she looked down at her feet. Then she looked up as if to ask him a question, only to look down again. After a while, Frank got irritated. "Marla, if there's something you want to ask me, just ask it already!"

But Marla still paused. Finally she said, "Dad, you know I'm in a computer class now, don't you? It's something you have to take in seventh grade."

"Yes," he said, surprised. "So?"

"Well," she said, and stopped. He waited, now curious.

"Well," she started again, "today we went on a field trip to the computer department of a big company, and we all had to sign in and wear these name tag things. One of the people that worked there gave us a tour, and when she saw my name, she asked if I had a father named Frank, so of course I said yes."

"Uh huh," said Frank, not liking where this was going.

"Well..." Marla paused again, and then the words came rushing out. "She said that she went to school with you and you were the most brilliant person she had ever known and that you'd gotten a big award for being a genius and she wanted to know what you were doing now." Marla stopped abruptly for a long moment. "And I didn't know what to say."

Frank wished this could be all over, and quickly.

But, Marla, of course, needed an answer. "Dad, the guide said you used to be somebody really important."

Frank felt like he was dangling at the end of a rope, turning slowly in the breeze. He looked away, and tried to think what to say. What *could* he say? And then, with all of the disarming innocence of a child, Marla finished for him.

"Dad, she wasn't telling the truth, was she?"

Frank couldn't breathe. His daughter thought so little of him that she had to believe that the guide was thinking of someone else? Or was it that she would be too ashamed of what he had become to be able to deal with the truth? He felt sick.

By then, they were standing in front of the door of his cheap apartment building. The traffic rushed past the garbage cans and trash piled up on the curb, and Frank took it all in. The sights, the smells, his life — they all fit together perfectly, didn't they? Still, he couldn't think of a word to say.

Finally, Marla put her hand on his arm. "It's okay, Dad," she said softly. "Let's go upstairs."

That had been ten years ago. The following Monday he sucked it up and called his old mentor, George Marchand, and asked for a job. George was the head of the IT department at the Library of Congress now, and Frank called him out of the blue to ask if they could get together for coffee.

George had been as gracious as Frank had been uncomfortable. Frank had sent his résumé along by email, for what it was worth, and George cut straight to the chase after the opening pleasantries.

"You know I'll need to bring you in at the bottom, Frank. Can you deal with that?"

Frank was prepared. "Sure, sure, George. I'll be fine with that." George nodded, brows furrowed. Then he changed the topic.

"How's that cute goddaughter of mine these days? I can't even remember the last time I saw Marla."

"She's great," said Frank, suddenly determined; it helped to remember why he was sitting there. "Just great. We get together every weekend. She's in seventh grade now. She's smart as a whip and gets straight As."

They chatted about family for a few more minutes, and then George looked at his watch. They both stood up, and shook hands.

"I won't let you down," Frank said as he looked George in the eye for the first time.

"I know you won't," his new boss said. But Frank could tell he was only being polite.

* * *

Sitting in his kitchen, Frank reflected that he'd been as good as his word. But not much better, he made himself admit. Yes, he'd rarely missed a day of work, and no one could say he hadn't earned his paycheck. And yes, he'd earned every promotion he'd been given.

But the promotions had been few, and the last one had been awarded seven years ago. Frank still had tremendous insights into IT architecture, and he remained as interested as ever in new developments in security. His cubicle at the LoC was stacked high with articles covered in scribbled notes, and he read voraciously online as well. For anyone in the office with a thorny problem, Frank was the go-to guy who could always solve it, provided he was allowed to tackle it alone. Sitting at a keyboard, Frank was still The Man – the tougher the problem the better, just bring it on.

Three hours, eight hours or twenty hours later, he'd still be turning it over in his mind until suddenly an elegant and creative solution would spring to mind.

Management level work, though, was something else again. Every time George gave him a shot at a long term project with a couple of others to supervise, Frank could never pull it all together.

Half the time, he'd be up in the clouds thinking big thoughts that went beyond the task at hand, and the rest of the time he'd be down in the weeds, diving down rat holes to solve problems that could easily be ignored. The folks he was supposed to be supervising never knew what they would be doing from one day to the next, or what, if anything, Frank did with the work they submitted. Inevitably, George would have to take the project back. It didn't take long before the big projects stopped coming, and Frank settled into the solitary niche where he had stayed ever since.

He wasn't done beating himself up, though. Admit it, he demanded, you were relieved when the projects stopped coming. You've been marking time for years now, and that's all you'll ever do. What right did you have to think George would throw this project your way?

But this had been a *security* project, damn it. That (and the drinks he'd had last night) were what had led him to corner George later on in the cloakroom.

"I'm sorry, Frank," George had said, wrapping his scarf around his neck. "I thought about letting you know ahead of time, and then I didn't. I guess I should have."

"That's not the point, George! Rick can't find his own ass with both hands in a well-lit room. What were you thinking?"

George buttoned his overcoat, and reached for his hat. "Of course Rick can't hold a candle to you when it comes to security, Frank. There's nobody I've ever worked with who has the insight and ideas that you do. And everybody knows nobody covers his butt like Rick."

Frank let his breath out with a rush of exasperation as George settled his hat on his head. "So then why did you pick him?"

George squared off to Frank as he pulled on his gloves, looking him straight in the eye.

"Frank, you may know security, but when it comes to understanding people and how to manage them, you haven't got a clue. Yes, Rick is one hell of a weasel. But you can always rely on a weasel to watch out for himself. That means that if you give him a job to do and tell him his job is on the line, well, by hook or by crook, he'll get it done. And I can't say that about you."

Well, what could Frank say to that? He'd asked George for an explanation and now he'd have to listen to it.

"How many chances have I given you over the years, Frank? I can't remember, can you?" Frank looked away.

"You're twice as smart as I am," George continued. "You should have had my job by now! But that's never going to happen unless you grow up and learn how to perform. If you thought I'd stick my neck out for you with Chairman Steele grandstanding in the House, looking for the next poor bastard to eviscerate in front of the cameras during a public committee meeting, well, you're just delusional. Good night, Frank."

There hadn't been anything Frank could say to that, of course, so he was relieved when George turned and walked away. Furious at himself, Rick and George, in that order, he stalked back to the bar.

Frank decided that was as much of the night before as he was up to reliving; he'd leave the scene with Rick for his next exercise in psychological self-flagellation. It had all escalated so stereotypically anyway; Rick's approach and his smarmy condescension, Frank's insult in response. Okay, enough.

He felt the anger well up again, and with it, a sudden sense of purpose. Screw the jerk; just because Rick got the project didn't mean that Frank couldn't still show him up. After all, Frank had been so sure he had the spot in the bag that he'd already started writing up a proposal with his plan of attack outlined. No way was Rick going to be able to pull this job off; George would realize that soon enough, and then there'd be no one to turn to but Frank.

He snapped open his laptop and punched the keys with fury, rushing through the complicated log-in sequence that would take him into the heart of the LoC's system, where his proposal was archived. Highlighting the file name, he hit the Enter key, leaned back, and waited for the proposal to display.

Except it didn't. Frank leaned forward and poked the Enter key again. Still nothing. Perhaps his laptop was frozen. But no – he could still move his cursor.

Then Frank noticed that something on the screen was changing: the background color was warming up, turning reddish, orange and yellow, as if the sun was rising behind it. Now that was different! Frank watched with growing astonishment as the colors began to shimmer, and then coalesced into shapes that might be flames.

Yes, flames indeed – but not like a holiday screen-saver image of a log fire – this was a real barn-burner of a conflagration!

Frank wondered what kind of weird virus he'd picked up, and how. After all, he was an IT security specialist, and if any laptop was protected six ways to Sunday, it was his. So much for whatever he had planned for today; he'd have to wipe his disk and rebuild his system from the ground up.

He was about to shut the laptop down when he saw that the flames were dying away. Now what? An image seemed to be emerging from behind the flames as they subsided. Frank leaned forward; the image became a tall building – maybe some sort of lighthouse? Underneath, there was a line of text, but in characters he couldn't read. Truly, this was like no virus he'd ever seen or even heard of before. He reached for his cellphone and took a picture of the screen just before it suddenly went blank.

Frank was impressed. Whoever had come up with this hack certainly had a sense of style. A weird one, but hey, graphic art of any type wasn't the long suit of most hackers.

Frank got a pad of paper and a pen from his desk and punched up the file directory again, highlighted his proposal, and pressed the Enter key again. This time, he would watch more closely and take notes.

But all that displayed was a three word message: "File not found."

Frank tried again – no luck. He did a search of the entire directory using the title. Nothing. His proposal was gone.

Now he was alarmed. After all, the directory he was staring at was in the innermost sanctum of the Library of Congress computer system, and the LoC was the greatest library in the world. Within its vast holdings were books that could be found almost nowhere else on earth. Recently, the Library had begun digitizing materials, and then destroying the physical copies. If someone had been able to delete files in the most protected part of the Library's computer system, what else might be missing?

Frank raced through a random sampling of sensitive directories, and then let out a sigh of relief; it was hard to tell for sure, but everything seemed intact. He checked the server logs for the Library's indices, holdings and various other resources; everything appeared to be undisturbed, with no unusual reductions in the amount of data stored.

Frank drummed his fingers on the table in the cramped dinette. How to go about figuring this one out? Then he remembered his cellphone, and sent the picture of the screenshot to his laptop. The picture wasn't great, but once he enlarged it he could tell that the characters were Greek. He cropped the image until just the text remained, then ran it through a multi-script OCR program to turn the picture of the Greek characters into text. Finally, he pasted the text into a translator window. No luck – all he got was a "cannot translate" message.

Frank's fingers started drumming again. He reopened the drop down menu of languages in the translator screen and noticed that another language option was "Ancient Greek." He highlighted that choice and hit Enter. This time, the screen blinked.

Frank looked, and then he blinked, too. But the translation still read the same:

**THANK YOU FOR YOUR
CONTRIBUTION
TO THE ALEXANDRIA PROJECT**

* * *

Order **The Alexandria Project** at Amazon or at Andrew-Updegrove.com